A Christma

Helga Jensen is an award-winning British/Danish best selling author and journalist. Helga holds a BA Hons in English Literature and Creative Writing, along with a Creative Writing MA from Bath Spa University. She is currently working on a PhD.

Also by Helga Jensen

HELGA JENSEN

A Christmas in Prague

hera

First published in the United Kingdom in 2024 by

Hera Books
Unit 9 (Canelo), 5th Floor
Cargo Works, 1-2 Hatfields
London SE1 9PG
United Kingdom

A CIP catalogue record for this book is available from the British Library.

Print ISBN 978 1 80436 732 2
Ebook ISBN 978 1 80436 731 5

This book is a work of fiction. Names, characters, businesses, organizations, places and events are either the product of the author's imagination or are used fictitiously. Any resemblance to actual persons, living or dead, events or locales is entirely coincidental.

Look for more great books at www.herabooks.com

Printed and bound in Great Britain by Clays Ltd, Elcograf S.p.A.

1

To my wonderful readers and to Tracey, the original Mrs Claus.

Prologue

Christmas Eve in an old Welsh water mill

The fragrance from the bundles of cinnamon sticks tied to the wreath on the mantelpiece wafts through the air. I may have gone a teeny bit overboard at the wreath decorating event in the village hall, but who cares if the house is beginning to smell like a Christmas market? I love Christmas markets! I look at the wreath with its holly and pine cone cornucopia and admire it. Not bad work, if a bit OTT, I tell myself.

Going overboard at Christmas is something I have always done. After all, it is my favourite time of year. All that glitter and tinsel, parties and presents, there is nothing I don't love about it. I go by the adage that *more is definitely more* when it comes to Christmastime, and I enjoy spoiling everyone.

I get so excited about Christmas that I am one of those annoying people who start buying gifts in the January sales. Of course, it doesn't always make financial sense as very often I forget what I bought and where I stashed the stuff. But, as soon as January rolls around, I begin to look forward to the next festive celebrations.

I am pleased with myself that, as usual, I am super-organised and prepared for when Aunt Grace is due to arrive for Christmas dinner tomorrow. She isn't getting any younger, and I want to make the most of sitting down with her and listening to the stories she recalls from the past, which are mostly about family members.

So, by lunchtime, I have the vegetables peeled for the following day, the turkey is in the oven to pre-cook for tomorrow's lunch, and the brandy has been slowly seeping into the fruit-laden Christmas pudding over the past few months. Everything is exactly as it should be. All I have left to do is to wrap the last-minute presents that I picked up for Aunt Grace at the Christmas stalls that I came across at the wreath-making morning. Then, I can sit down with a mince pie and a sherry. I might even have two mince pies. Why not? It is only Christmas Eve once a year, after all.

Popping on some Christmas tunes, I sing along as I carefully wrap some Lily of the Valley smellies for Aunt Grace. The rest of her presents lay beside me in a pile. Looking at them all, I realise that it is not only the cinnamon sticks that I went overboard on. I don't care, though, as Grace is the only aunty I have left. She is the only one of four sisters to live to the age of eighty, which she jokingly credits to a daily avocado for its antioxidant properties and having slept in a separate bed to her late husband, my Uncle Harry. Some days, when Craig tries to pick a fight with me over nothing, I can see where she is coming from.

With Craig having some time off over Christmas, I can't quite decide if this will be a good thing or a very bad thing. Inevitably, it will either lead to arguments from nowhere, or time together to try and get our relationship back on track. It's not that I ever expected him to be an old romantic. Far from it. The signs were always there from the moment we met at a bowling alley when he had too much beer and couldn't remember my name the next day. Once I had repeated my name approximately five times, he remembered it, and I subsequently forgave him due to his dashing smile and naughty wink. I suppose it was meant to be, as next year we will celebrate thirty years of marriage.

I can't say our relationship has been the fairy tale that I dreamed of as a young girl. I always thought I would have children, a boy and a girl with ridiculously cute names, but it wasn't to be. Craig and I have always dealt with everything that has been thrown our way and are happy enough. Sometimes, it feels like we are a pair of comfy old socks. There are a few holes in them, but we can't bear to chuck them away just yet. Talking of which, fortunately for Craig, there are plenty of new socks all wrapped and waiting for him under the tree.

As I reach for the last of the Sellotape to wrap the final pressie, I mentally say my thanks to the universe for all that we have to be grateful for. Health, of course, is number one on my Christmas list of gratitude. Followed by the fact that we can afford a nice home, food on the table and modern-day comforts.

Craig's work as a mechanic in a neighbouring town keeps him busy, and my job as a bank teller helped us afford the mortgage on the beautiful eighteenth-century mill house that we live in. It sounds grander than it is, and when friends visit, they think we must be rich. However, the mill wasn't expensive since it was rather dilapidated when we first saw it, with its for-sale sign blowing in the wind outside. For once, Craig and I agreed on something, and we had to buy it; the moment we set eyes on this house we both fell in love with it at first sight.

I am hoping Craig will also fall in love with the special Christmas present I got him this year. I am rather pleased with the thoughtful, super-duper remote-control car that he is going to love whizzing around the grounds here. I can't wait to see his face when he opens it. He has wanted one for ages. He is such a big kid.

I lean at the foot of the Christmas tree that Craig chopped down from the garden and place the final gift carefully to the side. I feel a sense of satisfaction seeing everything in place for another year. I can't wait for Craig and Aunt Grace to open their presents.

With my Christmas preparations complete, I look out from the living room window to see if there is any sign of Craig yet. The River Towy that runs alongside our mill is starting to freeze over; I do hope Craig will be home soon. It is going to be a cold night, and I pray that the roads won't be too icy tomorrow when I drive over to pick Aunt Grace up from her home.

With the chilly blast outside, it is at times like this that I am grateful for the inglenook fireplace, which is burning bright and warms up the room. I love it when it is cosy like this with the Christmas tree lights twinkling beside the fireplace. I only hope the candy canes on the tree don't start to melt in all this heat.

Since everything is done for tomorrow, I pour myself the long-awaited Christmas sherry and take two mince pies out of the Tupperware container. I admire one of them and congratulate myself on the pastry coming out perfectly. Homemade pastry has never been a speciality of mine. But this could be the best Christmas ever if these mince pies are anything to go by.

I make myself comfortable whilst I wait for Craig to return from his last-minute shopping. I expected him to be back by now; he really must be struggling with gift ideas this year. I told him I wanted a new dishwasher, but I doubt he is going to manage to get one sorted this last minute. There was a time when he would buy me jewellery, or a nice dress, but I guess over the years, I have become appreciative of practical items that make life easier.

I finish munching my second mince pie when I feel a draught behind me as the door opens.

'Is that you, love?'

I turn around and see Craig standing there.

'Did you manage to get everything you needed?' I get up to my feet to kiss Craig's cheek, as I usually do when he walks in. He steps away from me as I get nearer.

'I'm not stopping, but I need you to sit down.'

'What do you mean?'

He appears anxious, and his cheeks are red from the cold. Maybe he didn't manage to finish his Christmas shopping after all. I refuse to sit down and wait for him to explain whatever it is that is wrong. He looks a bit dishevelled, and I fear something bad has happened while he was out. Has he had an accident on the treacherous icy roads and only just made it home safely?

'You'd better sit down, Olivia.'

'I don't want to sit down. What's up?'

'I'm leaving you.'

'You're leaving me to go where? It's Christmas Eve.'

'There's never a good time to tell someone their marriage is over. I'm sorry. I didn't want it to come out like this, but I've met someone else. It wasn't planned. It all just kinda happened.'

'*Kinda happened?*'

I stare at him in disgust.

'You don't *just happen* to meet someone else and throw away a twenty-nine-year marriage on Christmas Eve.'

'I... I am sorry. I never meant for any of this to happen. I didn't plan any of it. It all happened so fast, and the next thing I knew... Well, it doesn't matter.'

'It does matter to me. You can't just spring this on me. You *knew* what was happening. It's such a shock. I never suspected a thing.'

Craig stands there, like some spare part from his garage. He just stares at me blankly as though he wants me to understand and let him off the hook.

I feel like I am going to be sick, and it dawns on me that eating two mince pies was a big mistake. Had I known I was about to get the shock of my life, I certainly wouldn't have gone near them.

'Look, I'm sorry. I can't live a lie with you here. Someone brought her car to me at work, and it just went from there. To be truthful, I want to spend my Christmas with her.'

'Someone comes in for an MOT, and you decide to run off with her on Christmas Eve? Is that what you're trying to say?'

'It wasn't an MOT. It was a service, but anyway. I suppose it is, yes.' Craig looks at his feet as though gazing at them will guard him from my wrath.

'But what about the cruise we were going to book to celebrate our anniversary next year? I've even got the brochures from the cruise line.'

I don't know why I am concerned about the cruise, that is the least of my worries. But I don't know where to start with all the questions I have. I am in shock and can't think straight. The silliest of things seem so important right now.

'Well, that won't be happening, obviously. Although, you could get a single cabin, I suppose. If you still want to go.'

I stand and stare at him. I am pretty sure my mouth is open, but I have no control over it. I try to speak but no words will come out. I begin to realise that anything I say is not going to make this conversation any different. His mind is made up.

'I… but…'

'Look, I'm sorry. You can keep the mill. You got us that mortgage anyhow. I don't want anything, okay? It's just one of those things. Sometimes, you realise your marriage is over, and Josephine made me realise that.'

'Josephine,' I repeat.

'It doesn't matter who she is. I think we both know our marriage hasn't been plain sailing, and we're not getting any younger. I'll be fifty-two next month.'

'So, it's a mid-life crisis then. How old is this *Josephine*?'

'It really isn't relevant, Olivia.'

'Yes, it is. How old?'

'Twenty-five.' Craig looks down at his feet again.

'Twenty-five.' I repeat. If we had ever had children, Josephine could almost be our daughter's age.

'Wow.' I just stare at Craig, not knowing what to say or do. I can't even scream or cry. I just look at him in shock.

'Right, well, I've got to go. The roads are starting to freeze over. I'm sorry, Olivia. It's one of those things. We've run our course. But I have ordered you a new dishwasher. It should be here just after Boxing Day.'

Craig walks out, and the mill's front door slams shut. I watch the Merry Christmas sign I had excitedly placed above the arched doorway as it swings back and forth like a pendulum from the force of the door.

As I hear the engine of his car start up, I desperately want him to feel some pain too. In my temper, I pick up the biggest present from under the Christmas tree and, without warning, wrench open the door and hurl the thoughtfully chosen remote control car towards the rear window of his prized saloon. He doesn't stop. Instead, he puts his foot down faster as I stand there in a sorry state wearing my Christmas jumper as the ice bites at my shoeless feet.

I watch as Craig's car turns into a small dot as he leaves me all alone, distraught and utterly devastated.

'Merry bloody Christmas,' I bellow out at the car as I watch it travel further and further away from me.

Chapter One

Twenty-two months later

The sun reflects down on the river outside Willow River Mill as I lean against the wooden garden table with my hands curled around my mug of tea. I lift my face up towards the sunshine; I want to make the most of the rays that are shining down on me before the freezing temperatures start again. It is getting chillier now. The nights are drawing in, and I have already started hoarding wood for the log burner. Fortunately, there is plenty of timber in the two acres that belong to the mill, and I have become quite handy with an axe since Craig left. In fact, I find chopping logs quite therapeutic at times. It gets all my frustrations out as I picture his face.

I look around the garden and thank my lucky stars that we randomly drove past the mill when it was for sale all those years ago. If it wasn't for Craig making a wrong turn on the way to Llandovery and ending up accident-ally heading down a single-track road, we wouldn't have known about it. It is one of those places that you would never find unless you stumbled upon it, which is precisely what we did. There it was, all run down and uncared for, a bit like how I am feeling at the moment. It was as though it was meant to be, and we were its saviour. If only life were that easy. When we bought it and were so excited for our new start, I never expected that I would be living here alone all these years later, without Craig by my side. At least I am grateful that he had the decency not to fight over the house during the divorce. I suppose he wanted to get out of the marriage quickly when he knew all along that he wanted to marry Josephine and have babies with her. Number two is already on its way, and I suspect Josephine was pregnant with number one when he unceremoniously broke up with me.

I try not to think of either of them, and especially not the children they have that I couldn't conceive. What good would it do to torture myself like that? Instead, I have kept myself to myself since the moment Craig walked out. I don't need anyone. It is only at Christmas that it can get a little lonely, so that is why I have decided to no longer celebrate it.

Last Christmas, I mostly spent the day alone as Aunt Grace was in the hospital after a fall, and so, apart from my visit to her in the morning to give her some gifts, it was just me. My friends kindly asked me to have lunch with them, feeling sorry for me, but I pretended I had plans. I certainly wasn't going to be that sad person that friends feel obliged to invite over. So, the truth is that I have pretended I have other plans for anything I am invited to for almost two years now. The more excuses that I make, the more people leave me alone.

My best friend, Liz, who I grew up with, doesn't even check up on me any longer. She has given up. Of course, she isn't to blame. There are only so many unanswered calls that a friend can take. Liz would come all the way out here at first and drop cakes on the doorstep. When she knew I was home, but not answering the door, she would shout through the letterbox and tell me how she had made me a carrot cake and to get it quickly before a fox came along. In fairness, they were lovely carrot cakes. But I couldn't face seeing Liz because she has the perfect husband and three perfect children with cutesy names. I figured that she could never understand how I was feeling, and why should she?

The night that Craig walked out, my life immediately stopped. I no longer wanted to see anyone, not even my best friend, and only felt safe at home in Willow River Mill. It is as if my walls guard me from the harsh reality of the world. I don't have to explain to anyone that my husband left me for a younger model to have kids with, and I can sit around in a dressing gown or onesie all day without anyone judging me. I don't feel as if I need to be accepted into the world any longer. I am just me, with no make-up and greying hair that I choose not to colour. Some may say I have let myself go. I prefer the idea that I have decided not to conform to societal pressure.

I do make sure I get dressed properly some days, like when the supermarket delivery is due, or if I need my hair cut with the local mobile hairdresser. But, generally, I am mostly a hermit in a onesie. I grow vegetables in the garden, and I am pretty sure that this year my strawberries were better than any in the supermarkets. The blackberries this autumn were so juicy, and I made several tarts to store in the freezer. The idea is that I will eventually become completely self-sustainable. I don't want to depend on anyone.

I smile to myself as I take in the rays of this most glorious November day, and I am thankful for my safe haven. I look around to tell someone what a lovely day it is, but nobody, apart from the postman or the odd angler, come out this way.

If only Aunt Grace were here, I could have called her for a chat. We always had the best conversations. It has been two months since she went to bed one night and never woke up, which is exactly how she would have wanted it.

As her next of kin, her solicitor keeps asking me to go to the office to discuss her last will and testament, but I can't face going into town. It was a miracle that I managed to leave the house for her funeral, but I was determined not to let her down. It was incredibly hard for me, though, and I just wanted to run back home. It is far too *peoply* out there for me.

After staying out here for so long, I can't bear the hustle and bustle of towns with their crowds. The thought of meeting with the solicitor is just too much for me. So, I have told them, they will have to do it the old-fashioned way and write me a letter with whatever they want to tell me. I can't face speaking to them on the phone about it either. Aunt Grace always wrote people letters, so I am sure she would approve of that. She had penfriends all around the world at one point and always had the most beautiful stationery with matching envelopes on her bureau. She also sent charity Christmas cards. Nowadays, far too many people send e-greetings. When I enjoyed Christmas, I adored finding cards on my doormat. It doesn't feel quite the same to get a ping in your inbox.

Time flies, even when you're alone, and another Christmas is coming around so soon. My first without Aunt Grace. I will probably do the same as last year and have beans on toast and pretend it is another normal day in Olivia world where everyone has given up trying with me. I don't know how I would react if someone held a

Christmas cracker near me, but I'd imagine it wouldn't only be the cracker that fell apart.

I head inside to change from my nightgown and dressing gown to my daywear of a furry blue onesie when the ringing of the home phone takes me by surprise.

I pick it up, holding it as far away from me as possible as though it is a poisonous snake. Who on earth could it be?

I pull the receiver closer to me as I hear a female voice on the other end of the phone. It is Charlotte, the HR manager at the bank.

'Hey, Olivia, how are you doing?'

'I'm fine. Thanks.' Immediately I know the true purpose of her phone call. The bank was so supportive of me when I took sick leave and said that they would keep my job open for as long as it took for me to feel better. Thankfully, as Craig and I hadn't gone away together for ages, some holiday time has been added to my salary, along with a few weeks of unpaid leave. However, the truth is that I still don't feel any better, and the thought of sitting behind that glass panel all day handing out change and cashing people's cheques fills me with dread. I can already imagine the small-town gossips coming in, asking me questions about Craig and his new wife. I don't want to be the subject of this week's gossip. I hear them in my mind saying things about me. How I look, how I seem emotionally. I would have felt trapped in that little kiosk, but it was inevitable that I would have to return one day. They can't keep my position open forever. I try to calm down the panic in my voice before answering Charlotte about what my intentions are.

'Um, I don't know. I'll have to think about it. I still don't feel ready to come back in and face everyone, to be honest.'

'Okay, I understand. I don't want to push you, but we do need an answer. We can't keep the job open indefinitely, I'm afraid.'

'No, I get that. Can you give me a few more days to decide?'

'Sure. How about I call you at the end of the week?'

'That'll be fine. Thank you for your patience.'

Putting the phone down I realise the time to face reality has finally arrived. I can't sit around all day any longer. My money is starting to run out no matter how much I try to live sustainably. The thought of being back in the corporate world makes me feel terrified. I know I am lucky that they have been so supportive and paid me sick pay for so long, but the day has finally come when I must consider returning, and that is a highly scary proposition. Whatever will I do?

I take a blackberry tart out to defrost from the freezer. Comfort eating is a terrible habit of mine. Only lashings of cream and a piece of tart are going to make me feel better about the decision I have to make. I pop the kettle on for a cup of tea to soothe my throat, which has suddenly gone dry, when there is a knock on the door. My goodness, it is like Piccadilly Circus here today. A phone call *and* a knock on the door in one day is practically unheard of.

As I reach the front room, I can see the postie's van from the window.

'Hiya, lovely. You alright?' says Ken when I open the front door. He is always so jolly and my favourite of all the postmen. He never complains in the winter about the icy road up here, unlike some of the other posties.

'Yes, all good, thank you. What do you have for me today?'

'Ooh, not sure. But you'll have to sign for this one. Important, is it?'

'Hmm, looks like it.' It must be the letter I am expecting from the lawyer.

Even though Ken tries to chat with me, I don't reciprocate. I have a feeling that he thinks I have nobody to talk to all day and that he is the only person I will see, which is true – but that is the way I choose it to be.

'Ooh, you can feel the chill in the air. Not long until Christmas. It's come round fast, hasn't it?' he says.

'Yes, I suppose it has.' I will be fifty-three soon, another year passed by.

'What you doing for Christmas? Any plans yet?' asks Ken.

'No, nothing. Same old. Anyway, thank you for this. I'll be seeing you then.' I try to get away. I need to see what is inside the envelope, and besides, I am no longer the social person I was. I have nothing to say, but then, I suppose living like a hermit in a mill, I don't have many anecdotes to share.

I tear open the envelope to find a letter and another envelope inside with Aunt Grace's writing on it. She has written my name and I trace the letters on the envelope with my finger. It is so nice to see my Aunt Grace's carefully crafted cursive writing again and it leaves me emotional. Still, I look at the solicitor's letter first to see what he says.

> Dear Ms Edwards,
> As per your request, we are attaching the information regarding Mrs Grace Pugh's last will

and testament. We also enclose an envelope that she gave us to hand to you in the event of her death.

Please confirm that you have received and read this and how you wish to proceed.

Yours Sincerely,
Dewi Jones
Estate and Probate Solicitor

Before I look at the copy of the will, I pluck up the courage to open Aunt Grace's letter. I want to get it over with. My emotions are running everywhere, and as I see the first words, tears come tumbling down. Until now, I have had no tears. I didn't even cry when Craig left me or at Aunt Grace's funeral. I tried to keep up a brave face. But now the tears are flowing. Perhaps this is a good thing, or, like some over-saturated dam, I may have burst one day.

Dearest Olivia,

My darling, darling girl, where should I start? If you're reading this then I am afraid I am no longer with you. Please don't be sad though. I lived to a good age, which was longer than any of my sisters managed. I hope you will be thankful for this extra time we had together.

Darling girl, whilst I wanted to write you a letter to tell you not to be sad, I have something else that I must share with you. I have a secret, and I have thought long and hard about telling you this. I was going to take it to my grave, but I have changed my mind. You must wonder what I am going on about, my darling Olivia! But I need you to do a favour for me. You are the only person in the world I could trust with this.

16

Do you remember my friend Silvie? Well, many years ago, not long after your Uncle Harry died, we went to see a show in London. You know how I always loved musicals! We went to see Grease and it was glorious. We had the best day, and this sounds terrible, but I had never felt so free. You see, Harry could be a bit domineering at times. Nobody knows what goes on behind closed doors – but I will leave it at that.

Anyway, Silvie and I had just left the theatre when it started tipping down! The clouds had darkened whilst we were sat inside, and, as it was July, neither of us had thought to bring an umbrella. I'd only just had a perm, and we must have looked a right sight, running down a street in London, trying to protect our blow dries with our jackets over us! But then, this absolute gentleman came out of nowhere and put an umbrella over us. I turned to look at him and, well, I had never seen anyone as handsome! He had stunning dark hair and eyes that sparkled. Please don't think badly of me, but how I instantly wished I had met him years ago! I mean, I certainly wasn't looking for a man to replace Harry at this stage in my life. It was time for me to be free and go to movies and shows with Silvie.

But, seeing this man, he reminded me of one of those beautiful movie stars from the sixties. I must have looked a bit odd as I couldn't stop sneaking glances at him as we walked down the street with him carrying his umbrella and the three of us squashed under it.

Then, as we passed a coffee shop, Silvie suggested we buy him a coffee, to show our appreciation to him for saving our hairstyles. And that is how I met Marek from the Czech Republic, who I was to fall madly in love with. But then, I got scared. It was too soon after Harry's death for me to be with someone else. The family would never have forgiven me for moving on like that. I came to my senses and thought I should be practical. When he wanted to move over to be with me in the UK, Harry's mother, Elsie, was living with me, as she wasn't well by then, and I had to do the right thing, didn't I? Family must always come first.

So, I ended it so that I could care for Elsie, and he never wrote back or acknowledged anything. Along with this letter, that was the hardest thing I have ever had to write. I cried tears and smudged the ink so many times that I had to start over and over again. But I knew I had to be strong. Do you remember when Elsie died? It was practically a year to the day from when I sent that letter.

After Elsie's funeral and everything had settled down, I decided to write to Marek and tell him that I now had a chance to enjoy my life. But, like I say, it was a year after I'd ended things. What did I expect? He never bothered replying and so I had to move on. A handsome man like that was never going to wait around. But now, I have one dying wish.

I want you to tell him in person that I have died.

You are probably wondering why you can't just write him a letter, or find him online somewhere, like you do nowadays. But I would like you to visit him face to face in Prague. I never got to go, so my wish is for you to go and find out what Marek is like. Does he still have that thick head of hair? I have so many questions, and I know I will never have the answers, but I would like him to explain why he never replied. Even if he was hurt, he could have answered my letter when I asked for another chance – or at least told me to bugger off!

It feels like closure and then I will be at peace. I want you to tell him that he was the love of my life and I never forgot him. I am sorry if this comes as a shocking revelation, but Harry really wasn't the man everyone thought he was.

My solicitor has Marek's address. I have asked him to pay for the tickets and accommodation for your trip from my estate and, as I know how you procrastinate, I have told him that you must travel within one month of receiving this letter. I have left my estate to you, my gorgeous girl, apart from a little chunk to the donkey sanctuary. However, I have asked that any money is only released once you have completed this mission for me to Prague. I hope you understand.

I also leave you your favourite snow globe, which I have asked the solicitor to send you separately. It was given to me by Marek. You always loved that so much and now you know why I did too. Sometimes, receiving a gift is not about the gift itself but who has given it to you.

I love you my darling Olivia as if you were my own child. I hope that had I ever had a daughter she would have turned out just like you.

With all my eternal love,
Aunt Grace xxx

I spill tea down the front of my onesie and feel pretty sure that she wouldn't want a daughter who turned out like me right now. Then I place the letter back down in shock.

She had a secret lover in Prague! Her marriage wasn't as happy as I thought?

There is so much to take in right now. I mean, where do I start with this letter? Not only did she have a lover in Prague that nobody knew about, but also, how on earth did Aunt Grace expect me to go to Prague to find Marek? I can't even go into the nearest town without being overwhelmed. Well, there is no way I can do it, dying wish or not. Aunt Grace knows how hard it has been for me to leave the house. Why on earth would she ask me to do this? Unless she wanted to force me out of the house. I wouldn't put it past her.

Well, I won't be doing it. I shall write back to the solicitor and tell him. There is no way I shall be going to Prague and meeting a stranger that I know nothing about, and that is the end of it.

Chapter Two

Walking along the riverside in my onesie with a coat over me and my comfortable chunky walking boots, I think long and hard about Aunt Grace's letter. Why didn't she ever tell me about Marek before? At least I would have been a bit more prepared for her final request. Had I known about the two of them, perhaps I could have helped get them back together.

She could have told me there was trouble with Uncle Harry. What on earth did she mean about nobody knowing what goes on behind closed doors? Oh, Aunt Grace, what a mess. Why did you put Harry's family before your own needs? And how on earth am I going to sort this out with the solicitor?

I can't possibly go to Prague. In fact, I'm starting to panic about everything. I can feel my heart rate speeding up as I even think about it. If I can't face going back to work, or into town, how on earth does anyone expect me to leave the country? Aunt Grace's estate will have to go to someone else. Perhaps the whole thing can go to the donkey sanctuary.

I try to think if there is anyone else in the family who could perhaps visit Marek to carry out Aunt Grace's dying wish instead of me. I have a long-lost cousin of a cousin, but I don't think he got on with this side of the family particularly well. I wouldn't even know where to find him.

Then it hits me. What if I advertised for someone to have a free holiday to Prague if they go for me? There must be someone who would be up for it. I will suggest it to the solicitor. I run back into the house to plan my excuses and explain that I have come up with a solution.

I consider writing back to Mr Dewi Jones of Estate and Probate, until I realise it would mean going into town to the post office to get stamps. I couldn't possibly stand in that queue and hang around with all those people. So, I have no choice but to pick up the phone and call him. I can't have this hanging over me; I need to sort this out immediately.

Even though I don't particularly fancy this conversation, I dial the number that is stated at the top of the letter. I didn't expect to be able to get hold of him right away, so I am not prepared when the receptionist asks who is calling, tells me to hang on and then suddenly puts me through.

'Oh, hello, Ms Edwards, is it?' The voice isn't as I expected. He immediately sounds like a friendly Welshman you would chat to in the pub and not someone pompous that, for some reason, I had built up in my imagination. He sounds older, as though he should have probably retired by now but doesn't play golf or have anything better to do with his days. Perhaps I should have done this sooner and not assumed that he was some sort of scary young hot-shot lawyer. I start with my explanation.

'Yes, about this letter, I can't possibly go to Prague...'

'Sorry to butt in here, Ms Edwards. I know I should let you speak, but Mrs Pugh was very precise with her will. She also wrote me an individual letter saying the first thing you'd say is that you can't visit Prague and not to take no for an answer.'

His response takes me by surprise. I hadn't realised that people had seen through my excuses and been so vocal about them to others. I know that I thought she may have wanted me to make this trip to get me away from here on purpose but to tell someone that I would make excuses is another matter. I hope everyone else doesn't realise how I have been behaving. I try to comfort myself with the fact that Aunt Grace knew me better than most so perhaps that is why she realised. I persuade myself that friends and work colleagues think I am genuinely busy living my life.

'Yes, well, Mr Jones, I don't go out much. I'd rather stay at home, you see.'

'It's Dewi, please. Look, I'm going to level with you, right? Your aunt was a good client of ours and, well, we go back years. We might be solicitors, but we're also a family business. I don't want to embarrass you, but she was very worried about you. She said since your husband left, you have avoided going out. Please consider me a friend when I tell you this. I promised her I'd help you. You know, she hadn't been well for some time now. She didn't want you to worry. She told me on numerous occasions how she was more worried about you than herself.'

'She never complained about her health. I know she had that fall, but…'

I can't believe that Aunt Grace would confide in Dewi more than me. The news upsets me. 'Look, I'm sorry but you don't know anything about me, Mr Jones. I don't need help, thank you very much. I am fine by myself.'

'Yes, she also said you'd say that.'

'Look, I don't really want to talk to you about my private life. Now, about why I called. I have decided that I'll find someone else to go to Prague. I'll advertise for someone to go on my behalf. I most certainly won't be doing it, especially after my aunt has told you my business.'

'Please don't be like that. I don't want you to think me impertinent. We just want to see you out in the world again. I feel as though I have a duty of care towards you on behalf of your aunt. Did you know we go way back?'

Goodness, how old is he? He really should be retired by now. Maybe I should point it out to him in case he hasn't noticed.

'I'm not a charity case. I'm fine.'

'Are you though?'

'I told you, I'm not discussing my business with you. Now, I won't be going to Prague, so we need to find someone else. Unless you have any clever suggestions for that too?'

'I'm afraid that it is quite clear that it must be you who visits Prague. I suppose you could go to court and fight the will. But it would cost you...'

'If you don't have any other suggestions, then I don't have anything further to discuss. I'll leave the will, just give it all to the sanctuary. I won't take the money as I'm not going.'

'Look, I know it's all a bit of a shock now. You've only just received the letter and the copy of the will. I'm sure that it's also come as a shock that your aunt loved someone other than Harry. But why don't you take some time to think about it and not do anything rash, hey?'

Will this man stop telling me what to do? I never let a man tell me what to do, let alone a stranger.

'Well, I won't be going to Prague!'

'They do say it's beautiful at this time of year. My secretary went last year. There was carol singing, Christmas markets in the Old Town Square, she drank mulled wine. I was very jealous when I heard what a great time she'd had while I was stuck in the office.'

I remember when I loved all those things – but no longer.

'Yeah, well. As I say, I'd rather stay home.'

'As you wish. But there is quite a large estate at stake here, so I would urge you to consider your choices carefully. You are due a very substantial amount of money for one short trip to Prague. She's even thrown in spending money. What is there to think about?'

Eventually, I tell him that I will consider it. At least it gets me off the phone for now. That is what I always do when someone won't take no for an answer and pressurises me into something. Like when you bump into someone you haven't seen for years, for good reason, and they suggest a reunion.

He was also going on about the snow globe and how it should arrive this afternoon by special delivery. At least I can keep that bit of the estate.

I have only just put the phone down when it rings again. I have a good mind not to answer it as I presume Dewi has thought of another way to force me to leave Willow River Mill. However, I decide to pick it up to stop him from bothering me further. He is probably the type of person who will ring incessantly until he gets a response.

'What is it?' I answer.

'Olivia, have I rung at a bad time?'

'No, I'm so sorry, Charlotte. I thought it was someone else. A nuisance caller.'

'Oh dear, you know you can speak to your phone provider nowadays and see if you can field calls.'

'Yes, it's okay. It's nothing I can't handle. Anyway, sorry about that.'

'No problem at all, as long as you're okay. Anyway, the reason for my call is that we need to know whether you're coming back to work. I know I said I'd give you until the end of the week, but I've just been told that I have to be on a course on Thursday and Friday, so today's my last day for me to inform head office before the deadline. Have you had any more thoughts at all? Sorry to pressure you. I hate to do this.'

'Um, no. I haven't, to be honest. My aunt just died, and things are a bit up in the air. I can't think clearly at the moment.'

'Oh, Olivia. I'm so sorry to hear that. I know it doesn't sound like the best of times but if you could have a think. Is there any chance you could call me back by, say… four-thirty and give me the answer. Otherwise, we will need you back in on Monday morning.'

Monday! My heart starts racing and I feel that panicky feeling once again. I can't possibly face everyone next week. It's impossible. So, I make my mind up there and then.

'I'm sorry, I won't be coming back in. I don't want to mess you around, but right now, I can't face coming in.'

'Well, I'm very sorry to hear that, but I'm glad you've decided what to do. Perhaps you'll feel better once you know that this is a weight lifted off your shoulders.'

'Yeah, sure.'

'I'll arrange your P45 and get that in the post to you, okay? We'll also need your uniform back. Can you pop that in… or post it?'

'I'll arrange to send it, thanks.' I suppose I will have to face my fear of the post office unless Ken can arrange postage for me.

I put the phone down and make myself some tea and toast. There is nothing like tea and toast in a crisis. Although, I begin to realise that this isn't really a crisis. In fact, it is a good thing as I have made my mind up, finally! I told the truth and stopped making excuses. It feels liberating. Now all I have left to do is sort Dewi out before he comes back and gives me a hard time. But that's enough tough decision-making for one day. I crunch down on my toast with a sense of satisfaction. I made the right move.

I spend the rest of the afternoon pottering around the garden. I stop to admire the pink and purple cyclamen that have flowered in the corner near the pond. There are no fish in there, but sometimes, I spot tadpoles and frogs if I am lucky. There is so much wildlife here, which is another reason I love it so much. Badgers and hedgehogs, and all the other animals love the garden of Willow River Mill.

I check the bird feeders and realise I will have to add some bird food to the bi-weekly shop. One of my pleasures is looking out the window and watching the birds the garden attracts. I have seen kingfishers, owls, herons, buzzards, and doves who come in pairs. There is so much nature around here.

When I head inside, I go online to start my next supermarket delivery. I make sure I add all the bird food first and then carry on with my shop of frozen food. I enter my card Idetails and get an error message on the screen. I have still been getting payments from work until now, so I know there is money in my bank account. Still, I check to see if I can work out what the problem is. My eyes open wide as I see that, despite my humble and self-sustainable existence, the balance is very low. In fact, so low that it won't pay for the shop. No wonder my card has been refused! Fortunately, I have a small savings account that I can transfer money from, but as I look at the balance, I see that it won't take me long to get through that with all the birdseed I buy. Perhaps I shouldn't have been so hasty on the phone to Charlotte.

I put my head in my hands and wonder how I can continue living like this when there is a knock at the door. I was so distracted by my lack of bank balance that I hadn't even heard anyone coming up the lane.

It is a delivery guy that I haven't seen before.

'Alright, can you sign this for me?'

'Sure.'

Taking the little square box from his hands, I place it down carefully. It has 'fragile' stickers all over it.

I sign his hand-held computer gadget and pass it back to him, then I take the box inside.

I open it carefully in the kitchen, making sure that I don't damage anything as I know that what is inside is the most precious gift that Aunt Grace could ever have given me.

I release the two flaps of the box and pull gently at the contents.

The snow globe is released, and I place it in the palm of my hand. Then I shake it softly and watch as the snow falls steadily over a replica of Prague Castle. So now I know why Aunt Grace had a snow globe of Prague! All these years, I assumed it was a souvenir from someone who had been there on holiday. I finally know the truth.

'Oh, Aunt Grace, it is magical, and I will treasure it forever,' I say out loud.

Chapter Three

Looking at the snow globe almost makes me want to go to Prague. I sit down with it in my hands, gazing into it as if it is some kind of crystal ball and I am mesmerised by its magic. This snow globe is absolutely beguiling. I had quite fancied travelling to Prague with Craig whenever I saw a special offer come up at the travel agent. It always seemed like something out of a fairy tale with its big castles, flowing rivers and beautiful scenery. But I remind myself that I have a river right outside my door, and there is a castle not too far away that I could visit if I wanted to. In some ways, Prague might not be that different to Wales. So, you see, Aunt Grace, I don't need to leave my country.

I am admiring the details of the castle with its miniscule turrets when the phone rings. I have never had as many phone calls as in the past few days. I may end up unplugging it at this rate.

Nervously, I pick up the phone. Holding it like a lethal snake once again.

'Hello?'

I hope it isn't Charlotte asking for the uniform to be returned urgently by post. I haven't worked up the courage to go to the post office, or even ask Ken if he can help, yet.

'Ms Edwards, it's Dewi. Now, did you receive the snow globe okay?'

'Umm, yes.' I had to sign for it, so surely he knows I have received it. How much did Aunt Grace pay this man? I know he said that he knew her well, but Dewi must have over-charged her on the legal fees to be this attentive.

'And what did you think?'

'Well, I've loved it since I first saw it at my aunt's house. It isn't the first time I've seen it.'

'No, of course. But Prague. Isn't the castle beautiful, with the snow? Surely, you'd love to go and see it. For free, I mean… What an offer your aunt has given you.'

Surely, solicitors don't have time to persuade people to do something they don't want to. What is it with this man?

'We have castles in Wales,' I remind him.

'Oh, but imagine the smell of chestnuts in the air… I believe they roast chestnuts at all those lovely Christmas markets. You can't say it isn't perfect timing that this opportunity has come along?'

Of course, it sounds beautiful, and I could certainly do with some money in my dwindling bank account but, still, the thought of leaving Willow River Mill for a few days is just too much.

'I'm not really a Christmas person these days.'

'I don't understand that. Your lovely aunt was full of Christmas spirit. I always remember when the post office was open in Bethlehem, she used to go up especially for her Christmas cards to be franked with the Bethlehem stamp. That's how much Christmas meant to her.'

Bethlehem is a little farming village not far from here, and it always amused me the lengths Aunt Grace would go to for her Christmas cards. Emotions come flooding back as I remember the fond memory. The post office has now closed, and she was so disappointed the first year she couldn't post her cards from there.

'Yes, well, I do remember that.'

'A little Christmas cheer goes a long way. Things like that are what people remember.'

'Yes, indeed.'

'You know, I don't mean to speak out of turn—'

'But you will.' I interrupt. It's a good job I respect my elders, or I would probably put the phone down.

'Yes. I'm sorry, maybe it's the solicitor in me that can be a bit blunt. But your aunt was a lovely lady. A pillar of the community, shall we say. She did things for everyone else, putting herself last, and I just think you should do this one small thing for her.'

After reading her letter, I realise that she did more than most. Choosing to take in her sick mother-in-law and sacrificing her own happiness with the man she fell in love with is off the scale when it comes to putting other people first. Aunt Grace would do anything for anyone, and I am only too aware that I'm refusing to fulfil her dying wish.

'You don't understand my situation.'

'Try me.'

Can I reach out to a complete stranger, who can be annoying and persistent, and tell him that I have withdrawn from everyone and everything since Craig walked out that night? Should I tell him how the thought of receiving pitiful looks from people we knew as a couple would be too much to bear? How I am terrified of bumping into Craig and his new wife and how grateful I am for online shopping so that I can remain a recluse? Maybe it was the shock that turned me into the loner I have become. I don't know. I haven't told a soul how I truly feel. But at this moment, I consider that I can trust someone and tell the truth. Plus, he might then give this Prague business a rest if I am honest with him. If Aunt Grace trusted him, perhaps I can too. But I also know if I tell someone how I feel, they might think I am being silly. What will he think of me when he learns the real reason for my refusal to do anything?

'Come on. What's the problem with Prague?'

'I don't want to leave the house, okay.'

'So, you're saying that you're agoraphobic?'

'Well, not really, no. It's just that it's too peoply out there. I know that's not a word. I just find I would rather stay home and live a quiet life. I have a beautiful home, so why go out into all that hustle and bustle?'

'So, you don't work any longer?'

'No.'

'I know this is impertinent of me, but if you don't leave the house and don't work, how can you manage to keep your home?'

I think back to my latest bank statements. He does have a point.

'I'll be okay.'

'That's good to hear then. You wouldn't want to lose your home if you love it so much.'

Lose my home! This thought had never occurred to me. Now that, I couldn't bear. Until now, my payments from the bank have kept me afloat but I do realise that things will change before too long. Perhaps I can start selling my strawberries and other produce from home. Although, people would have to find the mill for that, and it would mean social interaction.

'It's just that obviously, if you had this inheritance, well, you wouldn't have to worry about anything like that.'

I can see he is trying to win me round, and I begin to wonder if he feels it is easier to persuade me to accept the clause in the will rather than deal with my refusal. Perhaps that is why he is making such an effort with me.

'I know, but it's not about the money. If I don't want to leave the house, then all the money in the world isn't going to make a difference.'

'It will make a difference if the bailiffs end up coming round. Look, would it help if you spoke to a doctor about your problem about going out? I know someone wonderful you can speak to if you like.'

'I don't need help; I just need to be left alone.' Why can't people understand I choose to live like this? I enjoy my own company and am perfectly fine.

'Maybe that's the problem. You've been left alone too long.'

'I don't want to talk about this any longer. You're supposed to be my aunt's solicitor, this conversation isn't appropriate. I shouldn't have said anything.'

'Look, it's just your aunt warned me I would have to be pushy. Just think about it all. Please say you'll do that, at least. Don't dismiss it. She gave you one month to do this. The deadline is 20 December. I could even book your travel for the latest possible day if you like so that you have time to psych yourself up for it. You could fly back on Boxing Day. It isn't like I'm asking you to go next week.'

'No, I can't do that date. It would be far too close to Christmas.'

'Oh, are you busy over Christmas then?'

I think about how it will be just me sitting here alone with my beans on toast.

'Yes, I might have plans.'

'Surely, there can't be anything better than spending Christmas in snowy Prague, sipping mulled wine, doing touristy excursions. Why don't you let me book this? You'll have plenty of time until you have to go and it means I can put this file down and get on with some of my other work.'

Pushed into a corner, I say something I know I will regret. What happened to me trying to be firm with people and wanting to stop making excuses?

'Okay, just book it then. But if something better comes along, then I will be cancelling.' I will work out what excuses I can come up with nearer the time.

'You drive a hard bargain, Ms Edwards. I shall book it right away. Your aunt chose a stunning hotel to put you up in; you won't regret it. I'll send over all the details.'

'It's not certain I'll go, you know,' I remind him.

I put the phone down, relieved that at least I have got Dewi out of my hair for today. But, as I look at the calendar on the kitchen wall, I realise the date will quickly arrive. I'll have to think of something soon.

After my conversation with Dewi, I need fresh air to clear my head, so I go back into the garden that I love so much. I sit down quietly as I notice a grey squirrel shooting up the old oak tree near the side of the river. I don't dare move as I watch him scuttling around the branches. I wish I was that nimble. I try to keep supple by doing the garden, but looking at this squirrel makes me feel stiff as a board.

I could sit watching the squirrel for hours, but then I notice something out of the corner of my eye. It is a little robin on the wooden decking. The robin beadily eyes me up and looks at me as if it wants to tell me something. It doesn't seem interested in the feeders, and I presume it is

35

searching for something juicier. The robin is so tame that I go inside to find some fruit and seeds so I can watch it eat beside me. I rush inside to find something, but by the time I come back out with a chopped piece of apple, the robin is gone. It is as though it was never there, and I begin to wonder if I imagined it. Did it fly off superfast, or was it some kind of sign? I once read that seeing a robin is meant to be a reminder from someone in heaven to have faith and trust in your future. Was it sent by my parents? But they died years ago, and I have never noticed anything special before, not even when I was in the depths of despair when Craig left. It must be Aunt Grace. What if she sent the little robin to give me a message?

Surely, Aunt Grace couldn't possibly have sent a robin to my garden out here in the middle of nowhere to tell me to have faith in my future to go on her mission to Prague. I roll my eyes and laugh at myself for being so ridiculous.

It is simply a little robin foraging for food on a cold day, with absolutely no surreptitious Christmas message.

Chapter Four

The problem with making excuses or agreeing to things that you hope will go away is that they come around before you know it. Already, it feels as though Prague is heading around the corner faster than one of those Japanese high-speed bullet trains.

For the first time in ages, I feel like picking up the phone to Liz and telling her about the shock of finding out that Aunt Grace had a secret lover from Prague and that I am expected to go and meet him. Liz and Aunt Grace always got on well, and she would love this little titbit of gossip. But now too much time has passed, and I have been the worst friend on earth. How can I possibly call Liz and tell her that I have been a lousy friend because I couldn't face meeting up since her life is so perfect? I didn't even invite her to Aunt Grace's funeral as I couldn't deal with her positive outlook on life. What will she think of me?

There was a time when we used to tell each other everything. I would confide in her as I failed to get pregnant one month after another. When she conceived and was overjoyed, I feared that our friendship would change. It did change as she got busier being pregnant and then bringing up her children. But I still wish I hadn't fallen out with her, and I could tell by the last text message she sent me that our friendship was coming to an end. I was in such a *sog* that I didn't really care. Perhaps it is a sign that I am getting stronger that I am even thinking about rekindling our friendship again.

There are many things that I need to face up to, including returning my uniform to Charlotte and thinking up a convincing story as to why I am too busy to go to Prague. I should never have agreed to this nonsense with Dewi. I am a grown woman who should simply be able to say no to things. So why is it that when I am put on the spot, I end up agreeing to stuff that I really do not want to do and then look for ways to back out nearer the time? This is why I hate being pressured into things. For many, this could be the trip of a lifetime, but for me, it's like that doctor's appointment you don't want to attend. As the date draws nearer, my nerves are getting worse. It doesn't help when Ken knocks on the door; I am a jittery mess.

'Hiya, bach. You alright?'

'Yes, fine.' My usual two words to anyone who asks me how I am. Although, I am acutely aware that I am anything but fine today.

'A recorded delivery for you,' says Ken, as he hands me an envelope with the address of Dewi's legal firm on the bottom corner.

'Probably just airline tickets and a hotel confirmation,' I mutter.

'Oh, lovely. You going somewhere nice?'

'Prague, but I'm not sure I'll actually be going…'

'What? You have to go. I've been five times now. Beautiful, especially this time of year. You'll love it.'

'So everyone keeps telling me.'

I try to smile but feel positively gloomy. Why would anyone want to go away alone as a single person not knowing anyone? Despite plenty of people doing this, for me, it feels like sheer torture. If I am going to be alone, I would rather it be in my own home. I drown out the voice in my head that tells me I'll sort of know Marek. But what if he no longer lives there? Anything could have happened, and there is a fair chance that I am not going to find him after all these years, no matter how much or how little effort I make. I may as well stay here.

'Oh right, okay. Anyway... Umm, listen... Did you know you have an injured bird on your windowsill?'

'Oh no, do I?'

'Yes, I think you'll need to take him somewhere, like a vet.'

Oh no. My stomach sinks. I can't possibly drive into town and take a bird to the vet, that would mean... *People!*

'Ah, that won't be possible for me today. I'm up to my eyes in it. Would you be able to pop the bird in your post van and take it? I'll pay the vet's bill.'

'Oh, I couldn't. I'm only just starting my rounds, and I can't leave the poor mite in the van the whole time. I think it needs to be seen by someone now. I tell you what, if I call the vet we use for the dog and make an appointment, you won't have to wait. You can dash in and out. It won't take long, I promise. They're very quick there.'

We walk towards the injured bird, and I try to think of every excuse I can. I'll say the car won't start.

When Ken takes me to the bird, I can see it is the robin. Oh no. The robin does look like something is wrong. As I crouch down to it, there is no movement, and it seems to stare into space. I wish it could tell me what the problem is. I wonder if it has hurt a wing? I suppose that would be the obvious reason for its behaviour. Oh, why does Ken have to know what a sucker I am for the birds around here and that I would never leave one suffer.

While I stand staring and panicking about how I can help it without leaving the house, Ken calls the vet and gets an appointment for thirty minutes' time. That means I will have to run upstairs to change and go immediately.

'Have you got a little box?' asks Ken.

'Huh?'

'A little box. We need a little box to put the robin in. I'll help you pop it in if you like.'

'Umm, no. I don't think I do.'

'Can you check? We really need to rush him to the vet in something.'

Oh no, this is just awful.

I rush into the house and look around. On the table, I spot the box that the snow globe came in. It is the only box I have. Aunt Grace loved birds, and I think she would probably approve of the emergency use of the box.

I make little holes in it and hand it to Ken.

'Oh, that's perfect. Big enough, but small enough that it should feel safe in there.'

As I change upstairs, Ken carefully arranges the robin in the box.

I quickly search in my wardrobe for 'going out' clothes. A onesie just won't cut it for a trip to the vet. I eventually find a thick woolly jumper and jeans, then grab a scarf and jacket from the peg on the wall in the hallway.

'Oh, how nice to see you dressed,' says Ken.

His cheeks suddenly look flushed, and he seems absolutely horrified.

'Oh, I didn't mean it funny, like. It's just, you know… I've only ever seen you in a onesie.' Since Ken is the most married of married men, his comment doesn't offend me.

His family and that golden retriever they have are his world.

'It's okay. I understand. Where's the bird?'

'Here.'

Ken picks up the box ever so carefully and hands it to me as I open the car door. The windscreen is frosted over. The last time I drove the car was for Aunt Grace's funeral. I am surprised that it starts the first time. I had hoped it wouldn't, and then I could have pleaded with good reason for Ken to take the bird.

I let the window defrost as Ken drives off and mentally prepare myself for driving into town. I am tempted to switch the ignition off, remove the robin from the box and set him free. But I realise that would be incredibly selfish of me. I could never do that. I have to help the bird and take it to the vet, no matter how hard it is for me. I look at the box to give me the strength to start driving.

I take my time heading through the country lanes. I have precious cargo and certainly don't want to hit black ice. I pop on some music to calm my nerves. The Christmas songs are already on the radio, but I suppose it is only a few weeks before Christmas. I start to sing along to an old Kim Wilde Christmas song when I stop myself. I almost forgot that I don't 'do' Christmas any more. As I remember the season of goodwill, my throat almost contracts. I swallow down as if there is a golf ball blocking my windpipe. I take a deep breath to calm down and rub at my chest as though it would help the pain. This is no indigestion though; this is what heartache feels like. I try to remember that it isn't the time of year that's the problem. It's what occurred then.

Thankfully, the roads are clear to the vet's surgery, and I am surprised that I manage to park okay. I couldn't bear the thought of driving around for ages trying to find a parking space with an injured bird in the car. In fact, the trip has been much less effort than I imagined.

I walk into a reception filled with tinsel and Christmas advent calendars for pets. It reminds me that it has been years since I had an advent calendar. Craig always bought me one, except for our last Christmas together. It was the only time he said he had forgotten to pick me one up. I used to love opening those compartments to find a nice milk chocolate behind them. Lucky pets to get one filled with Christmas treats. They never had these when I had my childhood hamster, or I'd have had to buy one for my beloved Roland.

A receptionist wearing an elf's hat greets me cheerily as I tell her about my appointment.

'Oh, you're the one with the injured bird, are you?'

'Yes, that's right. It's a little robin. I hope it's okay.'

'We have the best vets, I'm sure we can help,' she smiles.

Ken was right about the clinic being super-efficient.

A vet comes out in a white uniform wearing coordinating Crocs. I look closer to see if she is wearing socks in this cold weather. Surely, she must be with all those holes in them. Her feet would be freezing otherwise. I always believe in being warm and cosy.

'Hello, I'm Simone. Do you want to come with me?'

My palms start sweating, and I make an odd whimpering sound. I get this sudden sense of dread as I start to panic. I don't feel as though I can go into the room with the bird. What if the bird got worse, and the vet says something terrible? I honestly couldn't cope.

'Sorry, do you mind if you check it alone? I'm a bit emotional at the minute.'

'No, of course. Not at all.'

Simone takes the box with her and walks off to the examination room.

The receptionist smiles over to me.

'Would you like me to make you a hot chocolate to make you feel better? We have mini marshmallows. I got them in specially for Christmas for us all.'

My mouth feels parched after all the drama of the morning, so I gladly accept her offer.

Her name badge says Sally and she smiles at me kindly as she hands over the hot chocolate. It is frothy and filled to the brim with marshmallows.

'This looks lovely. I never realised I could get such a nice hot chocolate in a vet clinic,' I say after taking my first sip.

'I used to be a barista. It never left me,' says Sally.

I watch as the marshmallows plop further into the steamy hot chocolate, melting and frothing away as they sink.

'Goodness, that is nice. Better than anything I make at home, that's for sure.'

I have only taken a few sips when the vet returns with the box. I want to block my ears in case she says something terrible.

'It's good news. Little robin here is absolutely fine. Nothing wrong at all that I can see. A very healthy specimen, in fact.'

I look up at her in shock.

'But… It was just there on the windowsill looking sorry for itself and very poorly. How on earth can it be okay now?'

The vet lifts a flap of the box. The robin looks at me and sends out a little chirp and hops about as though nothing has happened. It is as though the vet swapped birds!

'What on earth?'

'It might be that the bird had a fright over something. They can be stunned sometimes and shocked if something tries to attack them. I suspect that might be what happened, but he is definitely perfectly fine now, and no damage has been done.'

'Oh, that is such a relief. Thank you.'

Poor robin, though. I hope nothing tried to attack him. Well, I will ensure nothing ever gets near him again on my watch.

I take a quick sip of hot chocolate and get up to pay the bill, but Simone stops me.

'No, there's no charge. It didn't take me two minutes to check over this little one, and we're trying to spread the Christmas cheer where we can. I mean, look at Sally here.'

Taking another look at Sally, I notice that she is also wearing a pair of elf ears that peek out from under her seasonal hat. Surely, she can't be comfortable wearing those!

'Thank you. You've both been so kind.'

I leave the vet with a smile as I carry the little robin towards the car. I want to get it home and back out into its habitat as quickly as I can. However, after all the Christmas cheer in the vets, I can't help but stop outside a newsagent that has a sale of left-over advent calendars in the window. I suppose most people will have theirs by now. Only 99 pence for a chocolate advent calendar? A bar would almost cost more than that! How can I resist? I rush in to buy one, but it is purely for the chocolate, and certainly not because I am getting excited about Christmas.

Back in the car with the little robin, I drive home slightly faster than on the way in. The roads have thawed, and the sun is shining right down on us, which makes me feel a bit safer and happier.

The radio plays another Christmas song. This time, it is Slade – which was previously one of my all-time favourite Christmas songs. I sing along to it even though I hate myself for it. But how can anyone not sing along to this one? It is physically impossible. So, I figure it is like some kind of reflex action, like when the doctor bangs your knee, and not because I am actually enjoying myself.

When I arrive home, I help the robin out of the box, and it hops away immediately. I feel such relief as I see it hurry across the grass in search of a mid-morning snack. I look at my watch and realise that it is only 11 a.m. and I have achieved so much. I think I deserve a mid-morning snack of my own, so I put the kettle on and start opening the windows of the advent calendar. I have five windows to open at once, and it feels as though it was both mine and the robin's lucky day. Goodness, it almost feels like… Christmas.

As I bite into the chocolate, I think what a nice morning I ended up having. It went from leaving home against my wishes to meeting nice people and getting a bargain on twenty-four pieces of chocolate! Not to mention the most delicious hot chocolate I ever had.

I settle down to read the latest book I had delivered, but I can't stop thinking about my morning. I went into town and nothing drastic happened.

What if the story about robins carrying messages is true? What if there could be the possibility of a hopeful future ahead of me, if I am prepared to leave the confines of Willow River Mill?

Chapter Five

When I was a child, Aunt Grace would sit with me and tell me stories. She was so much more patient than my mother, who was always rushing about and couldn't sit still. Mam was what people used to call a nervous wreck in those days. One of those women with a lot of nervous energy. I am sure she would have been given a different diagnosis today.

Aunt Grace was so different in that way. She was always a patient lady with a vivid imagination. She would tell me stories about unicorns in faraway lands and fairies at the bottom of the garden. She didn't need to read me a book to tell me a story; she would capture it all in her imagination and tell it to me as if recalling an actual event that she had witnessed first-hand. Sometimes I wonder if imagination is genetic. I mean, of course, a robin does not land in your garden to send you a message; it's hardly a carrier pigeon.

Still, the next day and the day after that, every time I go into the garden, there is the little robin, staring at me. In fact, as I am having breakfast, the robin lands on the windowsill and looks straight at me through the window as I eat my cornflakes. What on earth does it want with me? I have already saved it and fed it; hasn't it got little robin friends of its own? Or is it a loner too? Perhaps that is the common bond we have.

The robin stares at me so much that I decide enough is enough – I shall take my uniform back to Charlotte today and get it over with. That should prevent the robin from stalking me any further and will mean that one of my dreaded tasks is done. Since I can't face the Christmas queue at the post office, I decide I will quickly drop it at the front door of the bank and hope none of my former colleagues spot me.

Despite being under the watchful eye of the robin, it takes all day to find the courage to drive to the bank and face the outside world one more time. Since morning, I have done everything to procrastinate. I slowly opened my advent calendar and even chatted with Ken as he stood on the doorstep with today's post. He had his Christmas Santa hat on today and reminded me how many days were left until Christmas. Why does everyone have to be so cheery at this time of year?

By the time I eventually reach the bank, it is practically closing time.

I get to the big front door and throw the bag with the uniform into the side of the building where the security guard normally stands. I only hope they don't think it's a suspicious package and they open the worn old carrier bag I found under the sink before anyone panics and calls a bomb disposal expert out. I plan on messaging Charlotte to say where it is as soon as I get back in the car as I don't want to have to meet her with it. Hopefully, she can then send me my final settlement before Christmas with any luck, which will keep me going for a while longer. But then I hear a voice that sends all my careful plotting into disarray.

'Hey, Olivia. Is that you?'

I try to rush away, but it's too late.

'Olivia, hi.'

I am cornered like a frightened rabbit. My eyes stare wildly as I see Paul, one of the cashiers I used to work alongside. Oh, please, no. Even the queue in the post office would have been better than this. I thought they'd all be busy. I knew I should have got here earlier.

'Hello, I knew it was you. How's things?' he asks.

'Fine. All okay.'

'We've all been worried about you. We've tried calling, but your phone was off.'

I decide not to explain that I threw my mobile phone into the river after Craig left. What did I need it for? I certainly no longer required all those stupid social media apps. Who wants to post on Facebook that their husband has run off on Christmas Eve whilst everyone else is enjoying themselves with their families? And imagine if Josephine came up as a suggested contact and we had mutual friends. I don't think I could forgive them for betraying me. I have my laptop for my bank account, and quite frankly, it has been very peaceful without a mobile phone. Nowadays, though, you can't say that without sounding like some kind of oddball. But I'll bet any money that, in reality, there are a good few people who would love to throw their phone in the river and enjoy the freedom that it brings. To be on the safe side, though, I give Paul the highly shortened version of why nobody has been able to get hold of me on there.

'I lost my phone.'

'Aww, how inconvenient. I'd die without mine.'

'I'm sure you wouldn't die. You'd be surprised how well you can manage. We never had mobiles when I was growing up, and we just enjoyed the moment.'

'Right.' Paul looks at me as though I have two heads and I realise I probably should have kept that bit quiet to such a social media queen. Of all people, Paul would be the last to understand.

'Well, you're here now. What's your new number? We need to arrange a lunch,' he says.

'Oh, I didn't bother replacing it. Been busy, you know. Haven't had a chance to think about what type of new phone I want.'

'You must have been busy. I can't go anywhere without my mobile.'

That is because he is so popular. He never stops messaging people and people never stop messaging him.

'So, what's kept you so busy then?'

I think about how I can answer this innocuous question. I can't tell him that I sit about in my onesie all day. I consider telling him how I feed the wildlife out at the mill, but don't want to sound as though I am some kind of modern-day Snow White.

'A bit of this and that, you know.'

Paul waits in silence for me to give more away so I find myself anxiously babbling about the wildlife.

'If wildlife gets injured, I help them and things. You'd be surprised how busy I am taking care of the garden, and the vegetables too... In fact, I don't have a second to sit down.'

'Well, that's wonderful to hear. I'm sure, umm, gardening is very rewarding. But I hope you have some time off right now. We're all off for Christmas drinks. Can you join us? Please say yes.'

'Oh, no. I have to rush home.'

'Just one drink? Surely, you can manage that?'

'I've got the car.'

'Well, have a Coke or something.'

'No, sorry. I have to go.'

'Oh, come on. We can have a catch-up. I've got so much goss to tell you.'

Paul and I used to have so much fun. He always knew everything about everyone and would fill me in on all his weekend gossip on a Monday morning after a wild weekend. I don't know why I feel so strained talking to him now. But I suppose that was before, and now I have changed. I feel like some emotionless zombie. I would have jumped at the chance of work drinks a few years ago.

Suddenly, I feel someone grab my arm and take me by surprise. I look around to see Cheryl, who works in the back office.

'Hey, I didn't know you were coming with us for drinks, that's brill.'

'No, no. That's not why I'm here.'

This is just my luck. Why did I pick today of all days to drop my uniform back?

'Aww, it doesn't matter. You're here now. It'd be lovely to have a catch-up.'

'Yeah, that's what I was just saying,' interrupts Paul.

'Sorry, I can't. I've left someone at home who isn't very well. I've got to get back.' I use the little robin, who is now perfectly fine, as an excuse to escape. Immediately, I realise that I have once again made an excuse instead of saying the truth. I should have been stronger and just said no. But at least I am pleased with myself for not going along for drinks just to keep everyone else happy and doing something I really didn't want to.

'What a shame. Well, please don't be a stranger. Let's arrange a night out soon, yeah? Paul can tell you all about his latest dating escapade. I promise you'll die laughing.'

Paul giggles beside Cheryl. 'You will die. It could only happen to me.'

Even though I am very fond of them all, I smile and get away from them before they try to persuade me to name a date. They will have their own fun and certainly don't need me. Paul always did know how to spin a yarn in the pub when we went for after-work drinks once a month. I start to remember how much I truly enjoyed those evenings. But it's fine. I have the mill and that's where I want to be. My onesie is beckoning me.

When I get home thirty minutes later, I get changed into my lovely cosy onesie and think about the wonderful time all my ex-colleagues will be having right now and wonder why I was so scared of joining them. The fact is that there most certainly isn't anything waiting for me at home; even little robin seems to have gone wandering about, and I would quite welcome his stalking right now. I walk around the room, considering what I can do with myself and then see Aunt Grace's snow globe. I give it a little shake and watch as Prague Castle disappears under the flakes of snow.

As I think about heading out to the garden to check how frozen over the pond is, the house phone rings. It can only be Dewi as I have done everything Charlotte needed.

As usual, I answer the phone holding it far away from me, scared of what is on the other side.

'Ms Edwards, it's Dewi.'

'Hello, I thought it was you. You're the only one who rings me.'

'See, now that is exactly why you need to go to Prague.'

I ignore his remark.

'Now, I'm just checking you're all organised. Anything you need from me?'

'I still haven't made my mind up. I haven't confirmed I am going.' I feel pleased with myself for saying what I really think.

'If you don't go, I will personally hold your hand and take you myself. I might even be able to put it down as a business trip.' Dewi laughs down the phone while I stand there horrified. Does he really think I need someone to hold my hand? I am highly independent!

'Alright, I'll go. Anything to stop you going on at me.'

'Aww, don't be like that. It's for your own good. I promise. It's what your lovely aunt wanted for you. She was always right, don't you think?'

I think of Aunt Grace warmly. She was indeed always right and could work people out immediately. She seemed to have a knack for it. She never liked Craig; I could see it in her eyes, even if she wasn't particularly vocal to me about it.

'Now, can I arrange a taxi for you? I want to ensure this all goes smoothly, as per your aunt's request.'

'I suppose I will need a way to get to the airport.' Although, the thought of a taxi pulling up and taking me away from here is dreadful.

'Right, well, she has incredibly generously arranged the money for a car to take you directly to the airport to make sure you get there without any hassle. So, leave me sort all the arrangements; all you have to do is get in the car. I know you're struggling with this so I'm going to help you every step of the way.'

'Sure.'

'You know, you could try some enthusiasm, Ms Edwards. Most people going on an all-expenses-paid trip are ecstatic. Come on, time to drum up some excitement and get packing. It'll be cold this time of year, don't forget.'

Oh, what have I got myself into here?

As soon as I get off the phone, I return to my mission of checking on the pond and plan to look for the robin. I tell myself that if he is there then it is a sign that I must go to Prague. If he is not there then it is a sign that I should stay home for Christmas. I choose it this way around as I know full well that there has been no sign of it since I returned from town. So, I already know the answer. I'll make something up to Dewi. I obviously won't tell him the robin sighting was what contributed to my decision.

But, as I walk around the corner of the patio, there he is, staring straight up at me.

Tweet tweet. He looks up at me as if to say, 'Off you go. You're going to Prague.'

I roll my eyes and go back indoors. I can't leave my fate up to a robin; I will have to think of some excuse. I am so stressed about all of this that I am desperately in need of chocolate, so I reach for my advent calendar. I have now opened most of the little windows. There aren't many chocolates left. It seems the countdown has begun, not only for Christmas but also for my petrifying trip to Prague.

Chapter Six

Over the past two weeks, I have googled everything from 'how can I avoid going somewhere?' to 'how can I learn to say no to things?' and 'how do you tell someone firmly that you don't want to do something?' There was lots of well-meaning advice online but none of it will work with Dewi. He is not taking no for an answer. After all, he was warned I would try to wriggle my way out of this trip, and Aunt Grace was perfectly correct in her assumption.

When I open today's window on the advent calendar, it is a stark reminder that the day has arrived. It is finally Prague Day, and nothing I have said to Dewi has made any difference whatsoever. Although secretly, as much as I fought against this trip, I realise that nobody can force you to do something against your will, and there is the teeniest bit of me that is curious about what would happen if I went to Prague. Which is probably why I have only put up a half-hearted fight. Just why did December have to pass by so quickly?

I need all the chocolate I can get, so I open the four remaining windows and stuff every last chocolate from the advent calendar into my mouth.

Oh goodness, I really don't want to leave the mill for a few days, and I feel half resentful towards Aunt Grace and her annoyingly cheery solicitor. The skin around my nail starts to bleed, as I bite at it for the millionth time.

No matter how hard I try to stop, I can't. It is a nervous habit I have when stress becomes too much as my mind throws a barrage of worst-case scenarios at me. What if I can't cope being away? What if something happens to me? What if I can't find Marek's apartment? There are so many situations that could arise.

I would do anything to take my mind off the thought of travelling. So, I go and check on the birds and top up the bird feeders to make sure they have enough while I am away. Then I hear a car coming up the drive and see a flash of red from where I am standing. It must be Ken's post van. I wonder if he has some last-minute Christmas cards for me; I have only received a handful so far. Then again, I haven't sent any, which makes me realise that I must start making more of an effort with people. Another reason Aunt Grace felt I needed this mission.

I head round to the front door to say hello to Ken, who has his Santa hat on again today.

'Morning, isn't it today you go to Prague?'

'Yes, it is.'

'You're not still gloomy about this magnificent trip of yours, are you?'

'Well, you know...'

'What are you worried about? It's not like you can never come back. Do your trip, have a lovely time and make memories. I bet you'll even miss it there by the time you return.'

'Oh, I'm pretty sure I won't miss anything when I get back. But I'll certainly miss this place whilst I'm away.'

I look up at the deciduous wisteria. It may have lost its colour for the winter, but I still love the way it climbs towards the roof at the front of the mill and will even miss the way I admire it when I step outside.

Ken hands over the mail and I take it from him. I notice some bills on the top and am reminded that just because it is practically Christmas, they don't stop arriving. It is a reminder that I have no choice but to go to Prague and deliver my message if I am to remain living here.

'Looks like you have a Christmas present from someone,' says Ken, as he points at a parcel under all the bills.

'Goodness, I don't know who would send me a present.'

I look at the Christmas stamps with a donkey nativity scene. I notice the writing on the squishy parcel looks slightly familiar.

'Well, I wish you the most wonderful Christmas, and rest assured, I'll keep an eye on the mill if I come out here with any post. I'll even make sure the birds are okay, so you've nothing to worry about.'

'That means a lot, thank you. Merry Christmas, Ken.'

When I go back inside, I pop the parcel on the table beside the snow globe.

At first, I think I'll leave it for when I get back. But then I reconsider as I become more curious about that familiar writing. Why on earth do I recognise it?

I tear open the brown packaging to find a package inside that is wrapped in reindeer Christmas paper. It is tied up with a silver ribbon and matching bows that have been flattened by the post, but you can see a lot of care was involved in the wrapping of this. What could it be?

I look at the co-ordinating silver reindeer label. It says, '*Please open me before Christmas. You might need this in Prague.*'

There is no name, but the writing is that same familiar scrawl on the address label.

It seems a shame to tear open such pretty wrapping, but I carefully pull at the ribbon and peel away the paper at the ends.

As I pull out the gift, it feels soft, and I can see it is something red. I pull at it harder, and it stretches through the small opening I have made in the wrapping. It is clearly a jumper.

I place it out in front of me and see a smiling reindeer with a flashing red nose. A Christmas jumper. I used to love Christmas jumpers before that awful night. I never again wore the flashing Christmas tree bauble jumper that I was wearing when Craig left. I threw it in the bin that very evening.

Before then, I had loved that jumper, but this one is even prettier. The size even looks right too. How bizarre.

There are only two people who know about Prague. Ken and that pesky Dewi Jones, and I realise that, of course, that is whose writing it is. Did Aunt Grace give him the budget for a Christmas jumper as well? I throw the knitwear on top of the small suitcase that I am taking to Prague, which is ready by the front door as the taxi to the airport is due to arrive any moment. I suppose an extra jumper might come in handy. I don't think I even packed properly last night as I still thought I would come up with an excuse until the very last minute. I imagined that some miracle might happen, and I would end up spending the afternoon unpacking and relaxing on the sofa as my flight went without me, and I'd spend the week safely tucked up at home. Instead, I hear the taxi draw up outside. Then the horn honks. It is now or never. I take a deep breath as I realise that even for me – the master of excuses – it is too late to back out.

I make my way out through the door, passing the bills that came this morning. They are still unopened on the telephone table, a final reminder of why I have to do this. My palms sweat, and I close my eyes and take another deep breath. It takes every bit of strength inside me to leave Willow River Mill, but I somehow manage to close the door, checking it is locked at least three times before I jump in the taxi.

'All right?' says the taxi driver.

'Just about.'

'Oh, it's always a hassle getting everything packed for holidays. You sit back and relax now. You want a newspaper to read?'

I don't normally read in the car as it gives me a headache, but the driver passes a newspaper through the gap in the front seat. I take it from her and drop it down on the empty passenger seat beside me.

I look out the window and back at the mill as we drive away. The little robin is standing on the doorstep as if he is waving me away. How does he manage to spring up like this at the strangest times? I wave at the robin, hoping the taxi driver doesn't notice.

I sit back and try to relax. We pass some heavy frost on the bushes along the roadside, and I am glad to be in the warmth of the car. As we get stuck at some traffic lights, I notice an apple tree with the unmistakable pearlescent white berries of mistletoe growing along its branches. Ha! Mistletoe. Before, I always used to pick some from this very tree and hang it up on the heavy oak beam above the kitchen door each Christmas. I certainly don't need mistletoe any longer.

We start moving forward again as the traffic lights change, and I glance at the local newspaper on the seat next to me. I have to look twice at the headline on the front page. I blink and blink again, then pick it up to have a closer read.

> Local lawyer and businessman Dewi Jones makes
> Christmas dreams come true.

I look at it in disbelief. It has to be *him*. I unfold the newspaper and start reading the story. In the middle of the article is a photo of an old man with a grey beard – just like Santa!

> Lawyers aren't usually famed for giving out free-
> bies, but when it comes to local solicitor and busi-
> nessman Dewi Jones, he is certainly no Scrooge.
> Jones believes that everyone deserves a special
> Christmas no matter what their circumstances, young
> or old. All year round, donations flood in for his
> charity, 'Just Call Me Santa'.

No wonder he was so pushy about me going to Prague and sent me a Christmas jumper. He must think I am a charity case. I continue to read on.

> Jones explains, "Christmas can be a miserable time
> of year for many. We are surrounded by adverts
> of family Christmases where everyone is having a
> wonderful time and that simply is not always the
> truth. Many are facing a Christmas alone, or perhaps
> are poverty-stricken and can't afford food on the
> table, and so I am doing everything I can to help
> people have a wonderful Christmas regardless of
> their circumstances. From free turkeys and help with
> the costs of Christmas to cheering folk up, I try to put

a smile on everyone's faces at this time of year. That is why people locally started calling me Dewi 'Just Call Me Santa' Jones, and the name stuck."

Any annoyance I have for him thinking I am one of his charity cases evaporates as I look at the next photo of Dewi. He is dressed as Santa and leaning down to a child in a wheelchair. They are shaking hands after he donated a specially adapted wheelchair for the boy to use along the sand and enable him to get to the beach. The boy is looking up at Dewi and positively beaming.

Perhaps I should cut Dewi some slack after all. I ask the taxi driver if I can keep the front page to take this story with me. It can hopefully spur me on whenever my nerves get the better of me. Throughout this trip, I will try to remind myself that Prague is a gift from Aunt Grace and Dewi – 'Just Call Me Santa' – Jones.

As I fold the paper over, I notice another story. I read the headline and look at the picture of an old home with an overgrown garden. The article is about how an old lady lived there alone, and nobody realised she had died for two years. Where were her neighbours? It used to be that neighbours would look out for each other. Didn't anyone realise that something was wrong, as the post must have undoubtedly piled up? What if that happened to me? I would like to think that at least Ken would help raise the alarm, but I don't know that for sure. What if he was moved from his usual postal route?

I sit back and think about my life as we head towards the airport. I finally begin to understand that this journey is just as much for me as it is for Aunt Grace and tracking Marek down. If I am to have any kind of future, I need to do this. I must face my fears of travelling alone. The thought is terrifying, but what are the options? I can't stay fearful of every situation. I can no longer be afraid of the worst-case scenario. So what if the worst thing happened and my plane crashed? On the bright side, nobody would miss me, and if it doesn't crash, I get to explore a beautiful new country. I have got to stay positive, although I may pick up a new phone in duty-free in case anything goes terribly wrong and I need to speak to Dewi.

When I finally land in Prague and stand at the bus stop for the coach into the city centre, I am forced to face my mission. Still, I remain reluctant about the trip and would do anything to be safely sat at home watching one of my favourite home makeover programmes.

I look around at the signs at the bus stop, which are in a foreign language; they make me feel uneasy as they remind me how far away from home I am. All around me people are speaking a language I can't understand. There are so many chattering and excitable people that I could curl into a ball and hide. The fear starts to overcome me, and I begin to feel dizzy. Thoughts start racing through my mind. What if I get lost? Why did I even think I could do this mission? Aunt Grace may have believed I could, but I certainly don't have the same confidence. Quite frankly, I'd like to get right back on the plane I came on and, in fact, begin to wonder if I can.

Chapter Seven

The aeroplane takes off into the sky as it makes its way back to the UK. Its wings tip to the side as it tilts and turns over Prague, like an eagle creating a shadow over the city. I watch every movement it makes until only a tiny flashing light is visible.

I am too late; there is no turning back. The plane is heading home. I remind myself it is only six more days until I am back there too. Six more days! That feels like forever right now.

I console myself by thinking how Aunt Grace thought I could do this, and she was never wrong about anything. I remember that poor old lady in the newspaper again, and it reminds me how easily that could be me if I don't get a hold on my life. I steady myself by gripping my luggage and try to calm down. Somehow, I have to get through this, and I will. Although, first, I must put on my Christmas jumper. It's blooming freezing!

As I pull my head through the jumper, I notice a piece of paper flying out that must have got caught up inside. It is in Dewi's writing.

> *Welcome to Prague. Don't forget to have some fun.*
> *I've made an itinerary for you that I thought you'd*
> *enjoy. I hope you can get out and about once you've*
> *met with Marek. PTO.*

I look at the other side of the paper and see a list.

> *Day one, visit Marek. If time, Old Town Hall/Astronomical Clock. Must see this ASAP!*
>
> *Day two, Old Town Hall (in case you didn't make it on day one.) Even if you did, you must go up the tower there. Check out the views of the city! Then stop for a drink at the rooftop bar opposite the Town Hall. Cheers! Later, have dinner in the Old Town.*
>
> *Day three, don't forget to stop at the Christmas markets. By now you'll have walked among the Old Town marketplace, but make sure you go to the ones at Wenceslas Square and Charles Bridge too. Then head to Letná Park, there's a beer garden if you get thirsty after all the shopping.*

As I am about to read what I should be doing on day four, a bus arrives. I place the paper in my pocket and ask a lady who looks approachable if this is the correct bus into the town. Even though Dewi has drilled into me which bus I need, I still doubt myself and need to double-check.

'Yeah, sure. I'm going that way. You can follow me if you like.'

Her English is excellent, her smile is warm, and she makes me feel welcome in her country. It makes me think that we do need other people in life. After all, where would I be without this kind stranger and her help?

She sits beside me on the bus to make sure I don't get lost and puts her headphones on as I look out the window and watch the scenery for the next twenty minutes. We weave around roundabouts, and then the landscape turns to fields and trees as the bus makes its way to the final destination of the metro that will take us into town. As we pass all the greenery, it reminds me of home, which makes me feel a little more chilled. Although, despite starting to relax, I am still dreading the moment I reach Marek's, as I imagine a wife opening the door as I stand there blank and tongue-tied.

When we arrive near some apartment blocks, the lady tells me that we have to get off as this is the final stop. She kindly navigates me down some stairs and stays with me until we get to the platform for the metro, which will take me into the Old Town.

'Okay, it's five stops. It'll be about ten minutes,' she says as we board the metro together. Then she leaves me on my own and takes a seat further up the carriage.

As the metro moves along, I count each stop until I come to number five. Still, I doubt myself and start to worry that I miscounted. Fortunately, I see the lady further up ahead, who looks back to make sure I am getting off. She gives me a thumbs-up and rushes off.

As I reach the outside once again, I look up in awe at the old-style buildings that confront me. Renaissance, baroque and Gothic styles fuse together and reflect the city's historic past. The architecture is stunning here and no doubt every building has an important relevance.

My Google maps app informs me that the hotel is only a few minutes' walk from here, and I figure I will manage to find it since it is practically a straight line and then a turn or two. Surely, even I can manage that.

As I walk along, I notice again how much colder it is here. Between the cold air and the Christmas decorations that hang ubiquitously on the lamp posts and distinguished buildings, there is no disguising what time of year it is. I try not to think about it and hope that the clattering of my suitcase wheels hitting the cobbled street will eventually drown out the sound of Christmas carols that I can faintly hear coming from somewhere nearby.

A horse trots beside me at one point with a couple being towed behind in an ornately decorated pink carriage. I look at them enviously as they snuggle up together. Then the horse trots ahead of me as my wheel gets stuck in a cobble, and I fight with my case to get it released.

Finally, when I reach the hotel, I get quite a surprise. I hadn't expected anything quite this luxurious. It is the type of place where a man in an expensive-looking uniform opens the door for you. The hotel reception is so magnificent, with its stucco columns and old portraits of posh-looking people, that I walk straight into a statue in the middle of the lobby. I automatically apologise to it and scuttle away. Aunt Grace certainly gave Dewi the budget to book me into one of the best hotels. This is just the kind of place she would have loved. It is so glamorous and sparkly that I am not surprised she chose it.

I am so impressed that, for the first time since this whole trip was planned, I forget about not being at home. As I check-in, the receptionist hands me a glass of fizz, which also helps me forget where I am for a moment. It's as if the Olivia who enjoys gardening and staying at home has been transformed into some glamorous champagne-swigging socialite! Except that I don't give off the appearance of a socialite as Rudolph's nose on my jumper seems to be flashing particularly brightly under the hotel lighting. Even though I am warm, I button up my coat to try and hide the intermittent flashing light that beams out from the centre of my chest and seems far too incongruous in this place.

Once I am given my room key, which comes on a heavy brass ball, and I finish the lovely welcome drink, a helpful bellboy leads me to my room. We go up in a super ostentatious lift with gold leaf, befitting of the hotel, and then walk along the corridor to the room, which is as beautiful as everywhere else with its polished wooden doors and fancy blue wallpaper. The bellboy hands over my luggage and tells me that if I need anything at all I should not hesitate to contact him. I look at the huge comfy bed and luxurious room and begin to wonder how much room service is. I could snuggle right in here and have a bite to eat. Normally, I probably couldn't afford it, but with Dewi's holiday allowance and the imminent inheritance, I am tempted to push the boat out.

Before the bellboy leaves, I ask if he can arrange to send up another glass of that fabulous fizz I had at reception. This moment is deserving of a toast to Aunt Grace.

I can already see that it is going to be quite tempting to not leave the room for the next few days. No wonder Dewi gave me an itinerary. He probably guessed I wouldn't want to leave this luxury once I walked through the door. Perhaps he shouldn't have gone along with booking such a fabulous hotel then – this is partly his fault!

After walking around the room examining everything, including sniffing the gardenia toiletries in the bathroom, I think even Dewi could forgive me for staying put tonight.

With all the travelling, a lovely bubble bath would be perfect. So I skip the room service and decide that the roll-top bath is calling me the loudest right now. As I change into a lovely, soft, cosy, white dressing gown branded with the hotel's insignia that I found hanging on the bathroom door, a lady from room service knocks with my glass of fizz. What perfect timing.

I walk straight to the bathroom with my glass and pop it on a ledge beside the bath. I jump into the bubbles and soak right into them. This has to be the most perfect night in I've ever had. I can't remember when I last felt such pleasure. The water at the mill takes ages to heat up so I am normally too impatient by the time it gets to the right temperature to have a bath at home.

I sink deeper into the foam until I feel as though I could get lost. Amidst the bubbles I make the toast to Aunt Grace and remind myself why I've come to Prague.

—

After one of the best nights' sleep ever, I refuse to go anywhere the next morning until I have eaten the hotel breakfast, which has everything a hotel guest could wish for, from avocado and salmon to French toast with cara-melised bananas. There is, of course, no contest and I wolf down my French toast.

No matter how long I take at breakfast though, I can no longer delay the task ahead. I have to get on with the mission that I am here for. Every time I go into my handbag to get something, the piece of paper that has Marek's address on, given to me by Dewi, is a perpetual reminder.

I ask the helpful hotel staff where I can find a taxi, and five minutes later, I am on my way to the address that Dewi has given me. We start our drive, and I get to see some of the sights that I have been told to visit as we drive past them in the distance. The castle that is in the snow globe comes into sight, and I gasp out loud.

'Wow, that's beautiful.'

'Yes, it's our famous castle,' says the taxi driver.

If I remember right, the castle was on the itinerary for day four. Although, looking at it from here, I really think that I should go there today if I have time after visiting Marek. Dewi definitely got that bit wrong.

But I try not to let myself get distracted by the views. I have to do what I am here for, first and foremost. Then, I can relax and know that I am a day closer to heading back home. Right now, the thought of knocking on a stranger's door is making me a bag of nerves, let alone thinking about visiting any sights.

For the time it takes to get to the apartment block, I rehearse in my head what I will say when I arrive. When the taxi pulls up outside a *Vinohrady* apartment block I am still unsure where to start with this conversation. I hesitantly jump out with no idea what I am about to say to a total stranger. I attempt to stall time by looking up at the tall apartment building with its little white wooden sash windows. Like much of Prague, the building looks ancient but so elegant.

The taxi drives off, leaving me standing there at the door of an apartment block, where I realise that I will need to be buzzed in. None of this had occurred to me. How can I possibly explain over a buzzer who I am and why I am here? This puts me off my tracks a little, and I walk up and down the path a few times before I can think about how I am going to approach this. Unfortunately, Dewi didn't give me instructions for this part. This bit is all on me, and I need to think for myself.

Eventually, I decide that I have come all this way and that I can't let the fear of a door buzzer deter me from my plan. Bravely, I press it with determination. I wait for a voice, not sure who to expect on the other side. The thought of Marek's wife answering comes to mind once again. What will I say then? I rehearse the words I think I'll say over and over, but there is no reply.

I am about to turn away when someone comes out of the main door and holds it open for me. They smile, and I thank them. I am not sure if there is much point going to the second floor if there was no response from the buzzer, but I figure since I am inside, I may as well knock on the door.

The building is old and the staircase a little uneven. I almost tumble as I reach the top step of the second level. I begin to wonder if the prehistoric lift I passed on the way in would have been safer. Surely, Marek doesn't still live here? I guess he would be in his eighties by now, if not older. I assume he was around the same age as Aunt Grace, unless he was a toyboy. She didn't mention anything about that. But, even at my age, I can hardly manage to make my way around the apartment block. Perhaps he is in a retirement home, and a young couple who are out at work live here now. I realise how silly this idea is. Why on earth would Aunt Grace think he still lived at the same address?

I reach the flat I am looking for, number twenty-five. Outside the front door is a plain brown woven doormat. At least it shows someone is definitely living here.

I question myself again about whether I should knock. It is obvious nobody is home, or they would have answered the buzzer.

Then I decide, after battling with those steep stairs, it is surely worth one knock on the door. But even worse than nobody answering, I pray that a sweet little old lady doesn't answer and I will have to explain who I am. How are you supposed to tell an eighty-five-year-old that you're her husband's ex-girlfriend's niece fulfilling her dying wish?

I knock loudly and hear a noise inside immediately. Perhaps they have a cat I have disturbed. But then I hear footsteps coming closer to the door. They are almost shuffling. Someone is definitely coming to the door.

I clear my throat and nervously pull down the zip of my jacket. I can feel heat surging through my body and up to my face. I really wish Dewi could have come and done this instead of it having to be me, particularly given the fact that he is so enthusiastic about everything.

The door slowly opens, and an older man pokes his head around.

'*Ano?*' he says.

'Sorry, hello, English?'

'Yes.' The man looks at me confused, and I can't blame him. I am sure it isn't every day he has some British tourist turn up at his door.

'I'm looking for Marek.'

I try to say it as clearly as I can and hope he understands me.

The man steps back and looks shocked. It is as though he has seen a ghost.

He blinks a few times and then shakes his head. His voice begins to crack as he tries to speak, and he looks at me with suspicious eyes.

'Marek is dead.'

Then he closes the door in my face and it seems he has nothing more to say.

Chapter Eight

I stand outside the door of number twenty-five in shock. This definitely wasn't part of the plan. The problem is that I can't shake off the feeling that something isn't right. My imagination goes into overdrive, and I start to think that he may have been Marek and he has lied to get me to leave.

I have no idea what Marek looked like, but this man had very piercing dark eyes, and I imagine he was a handsome man once upon a time. What if he recognised Aunt Grace in me? Perhaps, unlike Aunt Grace, he wants to leave the past where it is, and that is why he never wrote back. This is such a silly idea. If he had wanted to then he would have got in touch with her. I really shouldn't have come here.

If Dewi were here, he would probably insist I knock on the door again and ask to find out more. But I am not that tenacious or nosy. I will just have to go home with the knowledge that I tried my best, but sadly, Marek has died. I am sure Dewi will understand. I have fulfilled my part of the bargain.

I turn on my heels when I spot a man walking my way. He looks as though he is about to walk straight through me.

'*Ahoj*,' says the man looking directly at me and nodding his fine specimen of a head. My heart does a flutter. I never expected to find such a hunk lurking around the stairs of an old building.

'Oh. I'm sorry, I don't speak Czech. Only English.' I try to move past him, but we have one of those awkward moments where we both move simultaneously in the same direction. I shuffle to the left, then he does. Then I move to the right, and so does he. Finally, we move in opposite directions. Just as I walk away, he turns back and smiles.

'This might seem strange, but do I know you?'

'No, I don't think so.'

'Oh, then you remind me of someone,' says the man.

'Oh, do I? Well, it can't be who you think. I'm Welsh, so you wouldn't know me...'

The man excitedly interrupts me. 'You even sound exactly like her. I studied in Cardiff. Maybe you're related.'

'Ha. Not all Welsh people are related. Besides, I don't think I've ever had family go to uni, but it's a small world.'

'It is indeed. Do you live here in Prague now?'

'Oh, gosh, no. I'm just looking for someone who lives here.'

'Who were you looking for? I know almost everyone in this block.'

'It's a long story. I was looking for someone who I thought lived over there.' I point to the door of number twenty-five.

'My uncle's place?'

I get a sudden tingle down the back of my neck. 'Your uncle lives there?'

'Yeah.'

Do I tell him why I am here or walk away before I say the wrong thing? What if Marek doesn't want to be found? What if this man doesn't know about Aunt Grace, and I make it awkward for everyone? Marek could have had an affair with Aunt Grace in the Nineties and never told her he was married. Stranger things have happened in life.

Oh, I wish Dewi was here now. He would know what I should do next.

'So, you were looking for my uncle?'

'No, not really. Well, I don't think he's the person I'm looking for. Ooh, I don't know.'

'Forgive me, but who exactly is it you're looking for?'

I bite at the edge of my nail nervously. I wish he would stop asking me questions.

'Do they live in the building? Perhaps I can help you find them?'

'I honestly don't know.'

'Okay. Why don't you try me?' He looks at me with his hazel eyes, and that is when I notice the resemblance to the man who opened the door. So, I blurt it out.

'I was looking for a man named Marek.'

Suddenly the man gives me an almost identical expression to the one his uncle gave me a few minutes ago. Then he shakes his head in exactly the same way.

'Marek?' he repeats.

'Yes, Marek.'

'Okay.'

I look at him as if to say, 'What's okay?' but my lips won't move. I look down at the floor, unsure of what to do or say.

'I'm sorry to tell you, but Marek died.'

'Yes, that's what your uncle said too and then he closed the door. I came here to meet him as I needed to give him a message.'

'A message?'

'Yeah, as I said, it's a long story. It involves my aunt who died.'

'Your aunt. Of course, the woman from Wales.'

The man clicks his fingers as if everything is falling into place. I am so confused.

'Umm, yes. You know her?'

The love story of Aunt Grace and Marek has come as a complete shock to me, so I can't believe that this stranger knows more than I do.

'Yeah. Well, I never met her, but I remember my dad – this would be Marek's other brother – telling me about her. He always told me that Marek died because of your aunt, in a way.'

I gulp, and instinctively, my hand flies up to my mouth. 'What?'

The door from the next apartment opens, and two women wrapped in scarves and big coats chat in Czech as they squeeze past us.

The man points towards the door of number twenty-five.

'Look, I think you'd better come in and meet my Uncle Albert.'

'But your uncle closed the door in my face. I don't think he wants to see me.'

'He will when we explain who you are. He must have had quite the shock, just as I did, upon hearing Marek's name after so many years.'

'So, he has been dead for a while?'

'Come on in and I'll explain everything. It's chilly out here in the corridor. Let's get inside. I'm Tomas, by the way.'

'Olivia.'

It is amazing how you can rehearse what you are going to say until you are blue in the face, but you can never know what will happen when you actually say what you need to. I certainly didn't expect to be told that Aunt Grace was the reason Marek was dead. What revelations will I find out next?

Tomas opens the door with a key he has for his uncle's flat and lets me in.

Inside, it is cosy but quite basic and I notice that Albert doesn't have a light shade in the living room. In the corner are a couple of small presents wrapped ready for Christmas, but there is no tree. Perhaps he is waiting for Tomas to help him put it up.

Albert looks shocked when he notices me following Tomas into the living room. Tomas starts speaking in Czech to his uncle, and I listen to what sounds like arguing. I hope my presence hasn't upset him. I don't know where to look as they chat and quite possibly bicker. It is difficult to know what is going on when I don't speak a word of the language they are conversing in.

Eventually, Tomas looks at me and offers me a *Becherovka*.

'I'm sorry, I don't know what that is?'

'It's Albert's favourite drink. He's had quite the shock today, and it's known for its herbal qualities. I think he needs one.'

I consider the hotel breakfast that I just had and the busy afternoon of sightseeing that Dewi has proposed for later on, so I pass on the offer.

'Oh, I'm fine. Thank you.' I realise that I could do with some caffeine to get through all of this though. He must have some sort of sixth sense as he offers me a coffee, which I politely accept.

75

'Please, sit down. I'll bring it to you.'

Tomas gestures towards a seat opposite Albert before heading into the kitchen. I am unable to sit still as Uncle Albert eyes me suspiciously. I cross my legs, uncross my legs, and then try to look out of the window in the hope that the view of other buildings will distract me from the fact he is staring straight at me.

You can hear a pin drop by the time Tomas finally returns with our drinks.

'So, I have asked my uncle to tell you a little about Marek.'

I look at Tomas. The lines on his face indicate that he must be in his forties perhaps. I wonder when he was at uni. I used to go to Cardiff on nights out when I was younger. We could have even crossed paths. Although I am sure had I ever seen a man like this, I would have looked twice with that olive skin and those bright, sparkly eyes.

Albert still hasn't spoken and simply observes me. It is hard to know what he must be thinking. He takes a big glug of his *Becherovka*.

He clears his throat and then starts speaking. 'I'm sorry, dear; it's a shock to open the door and hear Marek's name. I shouldn't have been so rude.' His voice is slow, and I notice he chooses his words carefully, as though he has to think before saying each word.

'That's okay. I understand. I'm sorry if I took you by surprise.'

'Tomas has explained who you are. For a long time, the family and I blamed your aunt. If only Marek had never met her, then maybe he wouldn't have died.'

76

'But, I don't understand. To be honest, it's all come as a shock. I'd never heard of Marek before I received a letter from my aunt recently.'

I take a sip of the coffee that is on the table beside me and explain why I am here.

'It was her dying wish that I come and meet with Marek to tell him that she had died. Apparently, until the day she died, she still loved him.'

Albert's eyes well up, and I realise I have made him cry.

'I am so sorry. Please, I never wanted to make you cry.'

'No, it's nothing you did. It's something I tried to put behind me. You see, Marek loved your aunt too much. When he came back from meeting her in London, he was so happy. I'd never seen him like that before. He also loved your aunt until the day he died.'

Now my eyes well up. How sad that Aunt Grace had put her mother-in-law Elsie before her own needs.

'You know, when he wasn't working, he was out fly-fishing down the river. He would do anything to try and make extra money. He had a bit put away; he was always good with money. He'd always wanted to travel, you see. But he thought he could earn extra to get him back to London sooner by selling trout. He knew it was going to be expensive to move to another country. He also needed bank statements for his visa, and every hour, he would try to make money so he could get back to her. He wanted to leave and make a life with her in Britain. When Marek wanted something, nothing could stop him. All he cared about was the money he'd get for the fish he caught. He took risks. He was getting closer to the amount he needed to get back to your aunt when...'

Albert's eyes fill up once again, and so do mine. Seeing an old man recall his late brother is making this so much more emotional than I could ever have imagined. Tomas gets up and returns with some tissues from the bathroom for us.

'He didn't come back. It was getting dark. His rod washed up ashore, but there was no sign of him. His body followed a few days later.'

'I'm so sorry. Now I understand why you must be upset about my aunt, even though she didn't have a hand in this. It's so tragic.'

'Over the years, I've come to understand that maybe this was his destiny.'

'Can I ask what year he died?'

'Yes, 1994.'

I think back to when I was in my early twenties. I remember going to Elsie's funeral around then.

'That's so sad.'

I reach for the tissues that are on the table and, in doing so, accidentally brush my arm against my chest, setting off Rudolph's nose. Why, oh, why did I wear the Christmas jumper again today?

Fortunately, it makes us all smile and Rudolph seems to ameliorate the atmosphere.

'So, you want another coffee... Or?'

'No, thank you. I guess I should be going. Thanks for clearing this up for me. I'll let my solicitor know.'

'Your solicitor?' says Tomas.

'Yes, Aunt Grace made a stipulation in her will that I had to come here, or I wouldn't get my inheritance.'

'Wow, so she really wanted you to come here, hey?'

'Yup. Exactly.'

'So, what will you do now? Will you fly back home?'

'I'm staying for another couple of days. I have an itinerary of places to visit. You know, all the tourist spots, like the castle and the Town Hall.'

'You should let Tomas take you around,' says Albert.

'Oh no, I'm fine. Honestly. My hotel is quite close to all the main places.'

I flash my hotel key card at Tomas as I can't pronounce the name. 'Yeah, it's very central,' I insist.

As nice as this family is, I don't want to be a burden and make Tomas take me around the city because he feels sorry for me.

'On that note, I'd best be off. I don't want to keep you any longer than I have already. Again, I am so sorry to spring up out of the blue like this. Thank you for your hospitality.'

Tomas starts speaking in Czech to Albert, and I get up to leave. They sound like they're arguing again.

I make my way towards the door and try to sneak away.

'Sorry, I was just discussing something with my uncle. Well, it was lovely to meet you, Olivia. You know where we are if you change your mind about having a local tourist guide.'

'Thank you. That's most kind. But I'll be fine.'

I wave goodbye to Albert and Tomas and close the door behind me.

There. Deed done. I look at my watch and see that it is only 12:30 p.m. Next on the itinerary is the Town Hall. Time to visit the Astronomical Clock so that I can start ticking off the sights before I go home. Only five more days to go.

Chapter Nine

The cold air outside hits my cheeks as soon as I leave the building. I pull my coat up around me to protect me from the elements. It feels as though the temperature has dropped further since I was in the cosy apartment. I look around for ways to get back into the main town. I notice that a metro station isn't far from the apartment building, but I don't feel brave enough to do it without that local lady's assistance. I don't want to risk getting lost on the underground. I am relieved when I manage to flag down a passing taxi. I jump in, still a little stunned about my meeting with Marek's family. Since this whole thing began, I was so worried about taking the trip that it hadn't even occurred to me that Marek could have already died. Although, with his advancing age, I should have realised that something could have possibly happened to him by now. I thought perhaps he may have moved from here and not left a forwarding address, but I never dreamed this would be the outcome of my visit.

I lean my head into the back seat. I feel stunned. I wish Aunt Grace could have known that Marek loved her as much as she loved him. Oh, Aunt Grace! Once again, I am annoyed that she never told me any of this when she was alive. It also makes me feel a little guilty. What if this had been on her mind all this time, and she felt she couldn't confide in me because she assumed that I was too busy with Craig and work? I have no idea what was going through her mind, but it is obvious that he was important to her, or I wouldn't be wandering around like a bewildered tourist in Prague right now.

As we get nearer the Old Town, the midday illumination of the Christmas lights make Prague look even more magical than ever. A warm glow radiates from an angel in the Town Square that towers above the crowds. The Christmas market is already bustling and packed with visitors. I get out of the taxi and jostle my way through the crowds. As I try to get from A to B, the last thing I am looking for is the Christmas magic that refuses to go away, but there is no avoiding it. It is like an annoying fly that won't buzz off.

The smell of local sausages sizzling on open-air grills combined with the sweetness of waffles and Czech *Trdelnik* (chimney cake) lingers in the air. Would I be giving in to a little festive spirit if I ate something Christmassy? I mean, we all need food, after all. Although a mulled wine is hardly an essential dietary requirement, I could certainly do with one to calm the nerves. Meeting Marek's family and introducing myself like this has shaken me up a little. I haven't spoken to my friends in yonks, let alone broken the ice with complete strangers.

For a couple of euros, I settle my nerves with a mulled wine from a nearby stall and look for a place to sit. It's a little too busy, though, so I walk away from the centre of the market to lean against the wall of a nearby building. As I sip on my mulled wine and look around, I realise that I have the perfect view of the Town Hall and see that the crowds are gathering to watch the clock as it is due to strike the hour. What perfect timing, and it means I can cross another thing off my to-do list. The thought occurs to me that I could catch an earlier flight home if I can continue to complete my itinerary in record time. Now, that's motivation to get moving.

I cup my hands around my drink as the Astronomical Clock strikes; it sounds like a little bell is ringing. Two windows above the dial slide open, and I spot the first of the Twelve Apostles, St Peter, holding a key. A little shiver runs through me as I remember from Sunday School as a child how St Peter was the patron saint of fishermen. It feels as though both Aunt Grace and Marek are watching over me. I hold my cup up to the clock and silently say cheers.

I turn back to watch the other apostles as they make their procession. What a mechanical wonder. They don't make things like this any more. After the figures finish their parade, there is the sound of a horn, like a little bugle, and then the windows close shut and the apostles move back inside. Dewi was right; this was not to be missed. I finish my mulled wine and return to the market stalls. I have a teeny smile to myself as I think how I would never have got to see this had I stayed at home. Still, though, it will be nice to be back in my own bed again soon.

During the afternoon, I walk through the rest of the market stalls with their traditional Christmas foods. There are snails, which I don't mind passing on, but then I see oysters and gorgeous local sausages. The smell of the sausages grabs my attention, and I can't resist them a moment longer. I bite down on a hot dog and look around at the crowds enjoying themselves and realise that I probably do need to get out more. Perhaps when I am settled again back home, I will call Paul and the girls at work and plan that drink. I do wonder if I should try reaching out to

Liz, but that might not be so easy after so much time has passed.

When I spot a stall selling homemade candles, I tell myself that I am here on a mission and not for splurging. Still, I fail to resist a vanilla-scented candle that I can use to light up at home in front of a lovely photo of Aunt Grace. She would have loved the idea of the candle coming from here and that persuades me to buy it.

Finally, I stop at a bar for the evening before heading back to the hotel. I am still in the Old Town, as instructed by Dewi, so that is another thing ticked off the list. I will be home in no time.

The bar is busy and crowded, but as someone leaves a table in the window, I grab the chance of a front-row seat to watch the people of Prague go by. Despite being someone who has recently shied away from people, I can be inquisitive. So, I enjoy watching everyone from the protection of the indoors as they walk by the window, all wrapped up for the chilly temperature outside, with bobble hats and thick coats.

As I am people-watching, a young lady comes up to the table and asks me if the other seat is taken. I smile and tell her no and she grabs the chair, whisking it away to a table full of friends. I sit at my table for two, now with only one chair, and it is a reminder that I am here in Prague alone. It hits me that perhaps that is why I don't like leaving the mill and would rather stay at home. Seeing people in couples and families is a constant reminder that it is just me.

When the waitress eventually gets to my table, I order a glass of *Becherovka*. I tell myself it is because I want to sample a local drink, but secretly, I want to feel closer to

Marek's family by trying it. This is what they drink, after all.

The little shot glass is put down in front of me, and I take a sip. As soon as it hits my oesophagus, I begin to think locals may drink this to warm themselves up. I don't drink much alcohol, and this is strong. Almost immediately I feel woozy. It gives me a warm and fuzzy sensation, like I am drifting on a cloud. I think one will be enough to send me off on a good night's sleep though. Thankfully, the hotel isn't too far away.

By the time I arrive back at the hotel, between the cold air and the *Becherovka*, I can almost feel my nose glowing as much as Rudolph's on my jumper. I rub my nose self-consciously when I hear a voice call after me as I rush through the reception area.

'Hello, Mrs Edwards.'

I stop and turn back to see the friendly bellboy looking at me.

'How was your day? Did you have a nice time?' he asks.

'Oh, yes, thank you. You live in a wonderful city.'

'Thank you. I hope you managed to visit our Christmas markets.'

'Oh, yes.' I hold up the little paper bag with my candle that I managed to keep safe despite stopping off at the bar.

'That's good. I'm glad you're enjoying your stay in Prague.'

I turn to walk towards my room when the bellboy stops me from leaving.

'Actually, the reason I stopped you was not to talk about the markets. This came for you.' He hands over an envelope.

'Oh, thank you.'

'You're welcome. Good night.'

I am bewildered, as the envelope has the hotel's name on it. Surely, they aren't giving me my bill already? I know I am keen to leave, but I do officially have a few more days to go before I have to settle it and check out. When I get into my room, I put my bag down, lie on the bed and tear open the envelope. I quickly realise that the letter isn't from the hotel at all.

> *Dear Olivia,*
>
> *It was our pleasure to meet you today.*
>
> *After you left, my uncle and I spoke at great length about you, Marek and your aunt. He told me something that I had never known before. It seems my uncle has been keeping his own secret. I would like to tell you about it. I suppose it won't change anything, now that Marek and your aunt are gone, but it might explain some things.*
>
> *Please forgive me for contacting you at your hotel. I noticed your hotel key, so it wasn't hard to find you. I do hope you don't think me forward in writing to you.*
>
> *I think we need to meet up to discuss this matter, so please call me.*
>
> *Yours,*
>
> *Tomas*

I look at the telephone number he has written down and store it in the new mobile phone I bought in duty-free.

I put the letter down and plump up the pillow behind my head. What could he possibly mean by Albert having kept a secret? What if it is some kind of earth-shattering secret? Do I even want to know? Don't they say to let sleeping dogs lie? Perhaps there is a reason they say that.

I get this feeling that I might be getting in over my head. I only came here to break the news that Aunt Grace had died, and now I may have landed in some kind of complicated family web of lies.

I don't plan on being here a moment longer than I have to. What if the secret means I have to extend my stay? I realise that I have a choice here. I can confront the truth and find out what it is that Albert has lied about, or I can walk away. But then I argue with myself. What if it is something I need to know about Aunt Grace? Something that is important? I am so confused.

I have done the bit I came here for; isn't that all that matters?

Chapter Ten

Just as I did yesterday, I tuck into my hearty hotel breakfast. Today, though, I opt for a creamy bowl of porridge to set myself up for the day. Then I go back up to the buffet again for some waffles. I tell myself that it will stop me wanting everything I see and smell at the markets, but I know that isn't really true. How can I resist? The food is far too nice here.

I check my itinerary for the day. Dewi suggests I go to the top of the Clock Tower to see the views of Prague. Hmm, but I saw the outside of the Clock Tower last night. I am desperate to see the castle. I debate whether I should stick with his itinerary or do my own thing. But the one thing I do know is that it is nice to wander around anonymously here and not have to worry about bumping into someone who knew me as Craig's wife or, worse still, coming face to face with Josephine and the kids.

I am deliberating what to do when the bellboy rushes up to my breakfast table.

'Mrs Edwards, there's a phone call for you. Can you come to the reception?'

Reluctantly, I leave the breakfast table. I hope it isn't Tomas, as I have made the decision that what is going on in that family is between them. While I am a teeny bit curious, it could involve Marek, and he can't speak up for himself, so it is not anyone else's business at this stage. As far as we know now, it was all a magical romance between them. Why should we shatter that illusion? I decide to tell Tomas that I have no interest in the family secret, but when I hear the voice, I immediately realise it isn't Tomas. Instead, it is Dewi, who has been waiting for me to update him.

'So, how's it going then?'

'Sorry, I know I haven't called you yet. I thought you'd be busy being Santa back home.'

'Ah, you read the story in the paper then.'

'I did.'

'Well, I thought I'd give you a quick call before I visit a care home later to spread some Christmas cheer. How's it going? Job done?'

'Yup, you'll be pleased to know I've been to the apartment.'

'That's brilliant. Well done. So, how was Marek? Was he shocked to see you?'

'It seems he died years ago. So, I just spoke to his family, and they told me that they knew about Aunt Grace. I was a bit surprised, given the fact that I never knew about Marek until the letter. It seems like a big secret for her to have kept from me when everyone else knew.'

'Well, I don't think anyone here knew apart from Silvie. Maybe Grace felt guilty about meeting someone after Harry and, in some ways, punished herself. I don't know why; he was such a bastard. Oh, I'm so sorry. That slipped out. Pardon my French. I shouldn't have said that.'

'What? That's harsh. He was a bit miserable, but is there something else you want to tell me?'

'Please forget I spoke. That was the most unprofessional thing I've ever said in my long career. Please forgive me.

He was a lot older and bullied me in school; we never got on. That's all. Sorry.'

'He was a bully?' I think back to how Aunt Grace said that Uncle Harry could be a bit domineering. What if he was a bully at home too?

'Yeah, but never mind. Look, it's Marek we're talking about now. Not Harry. I was hoping for a happier ending than him having died.'

'I know. Me too. But afterwards I had a strange letter sent to my hotel. It was from his nephew. He wrote, after I left the apartment, saying that there was some family secret he wants to tell me. But, to be honest, that's not what I came here for. I've done my bit, and that's enough.'

'What? Don't you want to find out what it is?'

'No, not really. That's between them.'

'Oh, but I bet your lovely aunt would have wanted you to find out.'

'No, I'm not nosy.'

'You don't have to be nosy to find out what he wants to tell you. Do it for me.'

'I've done enough.'

I think about how I do not want anything to extend this trip for a moment longer than I have to and regret confiding in Dewi. I also realise the receptionist is getting impatient and needs to use the phone.

'By the way, I finally got a mobile in duty-free. You can take my number if you like?'

'Sure, I'll contact you on that if I need to. Anyway, you having a nice time?'

'Not bad, considering. I'm off to do some of the sights in a sec, but I'd like to see the castle today. I don't think your itinerary is quite right. Plus, I was thinking, maybe I could get out of here early. Is there anything to say I can't change my flight? I mean, I've done what I had to do.'

'You can't leave early. You've seen nothing yet. Trust me. And I gave you the castle at the end so you can finish up with a bit of a finale. Everything on the itinerary was meticulously planned, you know.'

'Hmm. Look, I'm going to have to go,' I insist. I can't quite agree, as I am far too impatient for faffing about and taking my time.

'Alright, but promise me you'll speak to Marek's family and find out what they want to tell you. You should at least hear what they have to say.'

'I don't know. Can I just have a break now and start counting the days until I get home?'

'Oh, come on, find out what they want. You might learn something you never knew about your aunt, or Marek.'

I shake my head. Dewi is so insufferable sometimes.

'Merry Christmas, Dewi. I'll speak to you when I get back.'

As I put the receiver down, I can still hear him going on. I can just guess what he is saying. Sometimes, I think he is more invested in Aunt Grace and Marek's story than anyone else. I am saddened that Uncle Harry bullied him in school though. There is never an excuse for bullying. I try to remember how Aunt Grace was around my uncle, but I was probably too busy being a teenager to notice him being nasty to anyone. I mean, he died in the early Nineties. That was ages ago. Although now Dewi has said that, I do remember Uncle Harry berating her in front of all the family on a few occasions. We all just thought he had a bit of a temper and seemed to accept it.

I head back upstairs to get my coat before leaving the hotel for another day on the tourist trail and notice Tomas' letter on the bedside table. I read over it once again. His uncle has something he should have told me, hey? I can't begin to guess what it is. Is it some love child somewhere? What if Tomas is a secret relation of mine? No, that couldn't possibly be true. We can't be far off the same age, and Aunt Grace didn't meet Marek until after both of us were born.

Does it really matter if I never know what the secret is? I really don't care to know. This story is from the past. It is all history now. I grab my coat and ignore the letter as I walk out of the room.

As I follow Dewi's itinerary, I head to the Town Hall as instructed. This time I am not in front of the clock but at the back of the frame inside with all its workings.

The apostles spin around inside, and, once again, I am face to face with St Peter and his key. The patron saint of fisherman brings Marek to the forefront of my mind again. What if Marek deserves this truth to come out? Am I letting everyone down? Nobody could save Marek, but what if he has some sort of legacy I should know about? Or honour in some way? I look at my mobile phone with the number stored for Tomas. Then I put it back in my pocket. Anything could happen if I contact him. I could open the biggest can of worms.

My next stop is a cosy cafe near the Town Hall. I order a hot chocolate and then remove the phone from my pocket. As I sit here alone, the temptation to call Tomas starts to peak, and I find myself dialling his number. I want to stop myself and can't explain why I am doing such a thing. Boredom, I suppose. As soon as it rings, I want to put it down. What am I thinking? But before I can change my mind, I hear Tomas on the other end.

I stutter for a moment, unsure how to start the conversation; then I tell him that I received his letter.

'I was hoping you would call. Where are you now?' he asks.

'I'm in the Old Town, having a hot chocolate.'

'Can we meet?'

'Yes, sure. When?'

'Now? I can be in the Old Town in, say, twenty minutes. Do you know the name of the place you're at?'

I pick up a napkin with the name of the cafe and try my best to pronounce it.

'I know it. How about I meet you there and take you to my uncle's? I think you need to come to the apartment to hear what he has to say.'

'Okay, as you wish.'

I nervously finish my hot chocolate. Oh, what have I done now? Something tells me I should never have phoned Tomas. This is what happens when you don't keep yourself to yourself. You end up finding out things that you might not want to know.

It doesn't matter how lovely this place is, my nerves are on edge. I can't focus on anything apart from what Tomas and Albert might have to say.

By the time Tomas arrives, I am relieved to see him. I just want this over with so I can get on with sightseeing and the countdown to going home. Tomas leads me to his car, which is parked quite a bit away. As we walk through cobbled streets dotted with vintage gas lamps, Tomas tells me how difficult the parking is around town. Eventually, we jump in his car, which is pristine, unlike my car, which has all sorts of rubbish in the back. Although, I notice he has a book on the back seat that looks very familiar.

'Chekhov?' I ask.

'Um, yeah. I'm a big fan.'

'No way! I don't ever admit this to anyone, but he's one of my favourites. People would think I'm far too intellectual if I came clean.'

Tomas laughs, looks at me and winks.

'Ah. Yes, you don't want to appear too intellectual, hey? How funny. You might read Chekhov, but I bet you've gone drinking in the Angel in Cardiff.'

'I have! I mean, I'm not from Cardiff. I'm further away, but when I was younger, me and the girls used to sometimes go out drinking in the Angel.'

'You see, I knew it,' says Tomas.

When my all-time favourite song comes on the radio, I ask Tomas if I can turn it up.

'You like this song?' asks Tomas.

Will he tease me if I tell him how much I love this? What if he isn't a fan? I hesitate for a moment.

'Yeah. I do.'

'And me. Don't tell me Phil Collins is your favourite too?' says Tomas.

'Yeah, he's quite good.' I daren't tell him he is my absolute favourite and I have seen him in concert five times. At this rate, he'll think I am trying to imitate everything he loves, like some kind of love-bombing chameleon.

'So, do you live near here?' I ask. That is one thing we won't have in common.

'I live quite close to my uncle. It's easier to keep an eye on him. Generally, he's quite strong, but he's had a couple of falls.'

93

'Oh no. That must be difficult. Do you have any other family that can help?'

'No, I'm an only child. Albert is the last of the family. I've always been very close to him.'

'No way! I'm an only child and very close to my aunt. Well, I *was* close to her.' I can't believe that even a conversation about where he lives in Prague has shown us further similarities.

I see that he wears a ring, it's patterned with a design. It doesn't look like a wedding ring, although it makes me wonder if he has a wife who could help him out a bit. I don't mention it though. Perhaps he feels that it isn't her job to help with an ailing in-law.

'Yes, I'm very sorry about your aunt.'

'Thank you.'

Tomas appears to be thinking about something, and we fall into an awkward silence until we arrive at the apartment. I follow him through the main door that I remember from my last visit.

'Lift or stairs?' he asks.

I don't want to fall in front of him or be out of breath by the time we reach the top, so this time, I choose the prehistoric lift and hope for the best.

The lift is tiny, and as it slowly rises through the floors, I am almost pressed against Tomas and can smell the musky aftershave he is wearing. I am almost touching his dark stubble at this point, and I notice once again what a fine-looking man he is. I imagine it is those family genes. Perhaps that is what attracted Aunt Grace to Marek.

I can't help but stare at Tomas as the lift shudders and shifts, and I feel his breath practically on my face. Whilst it is a little uncomfortable, there is something nice about it too.

I concentrate on the buttons and the tiny screen on the lift as it lights up with the floor numbers. Tomas smiles at me as we reach the first floor. Why does he have to have such a cute smile? My cheeks start to burn, and I hope he can't see how red they are from his attention. I tell myself there is just one more floor to go. Thank goodness Albert doesn't live on a higher floor; I don't think I could bear much more of this. It is a bit too close for comfort. I haven't been this close to anyone since before Craig left, let alone a stranger in Prague. Although, the Christmas market was pretty packed. Perhaps I should get used to not having as much personal space as I am used to while I am here.

The lift finally dings and the doors open. Slowly. I almost leap out of them as soon as there is enough space for me to escape. It was getting quite hot and steamy in there.

Tomas opens the door of number twenty-five, and we walk in to be greeted by Albert, who is sitting on the sofa, just as he was the last time.

'Good afternoon,' says Albert.

'Good afternoon, Albert.' I smile at the old man, who has a kind face. He doesn't look like a liar with some terrible secret. Then again, what does a liar look like? Craig was lying to me for goodness knows how long in our marriage.

'Right, so I'll make you a coffee? Then Albert can tell you exactly what he told me,' says Tomas.

'Sure, okay.'

I hear some banging about, and the kettle whistles in the kitchen. Albert stares at me again, and I don't know where to look, so I keep smiling at him and then averting my eyes. Each time I look back at him, he is still staring at me, so I look towards the window once again and the view outside of someone walking a puppy. However, Tomas distracts me when he walks in with a big brown box and puts it down on the coffee table that separates Albert and me. There is no indication as to what the contents could be, apart from some writing in Czech on it that I don't understand.

Albert looks at the box and points to it.

'This,' he says.

'This?' I repeat.

'This is my secret.'

'Okay, so you keep a secret cardboard box. I don't quite follow, sorry.'

'It's what's inside,' smiles Tomas.

Dare I ask? Since I am here, I decide that I probably should.

'Right. So, what's inside?'

'Marek's post.'

Okay. I am still none the wiser here. What does his post have to do with me?

Tomas leans in between us to open up the box and pulls out a bunch of envelopes, all held together by an elastic band. As Tomas goes to remove the brittle band, it snaps in two between his fingers. Clearly, this post has been wrapped up for some time. He passes the bundle towards me, and I notice the envelopes have yellowed, despite being kept inside the box. As I flick through, there is no mistaking the writing on the collection of opened and unopened mail.

My heart rate quickens as I realise who the beautiful cursive writing belongs to. I slowly nod my head at Albert and Tomas.

'Ah, I get it. They're from Aunt Grace.'

'That's right. You see the Welsh postmark?' says Tomas. He points to an envelope with a stamp of Queen Elizabeth II underneath the Welsh franking.

'Goodness.'

I flick through the pile of pretty envelopes. There must be at least thirty letters. I can see Aunt Grace used her best stationery, which makes me smile. I can't stop looking at the writing on a neatly opened envelope, and I gently scroll my fingers over each of the letters. One by one, I trace the letters of Marek's name. Even though I wasn't privy to their love story, I can see that care has been taken to write his name perfectly. I imagine Aunt Grace taking her time as she swirled each letter around as she wrote. She was always such a perfectionist.

'So, what else is in the box? Are there more letters?'

Tomas tilts the box towards me and shuffles his hand inside, pulling out some brighter-coloured envelopes. Again, they are all carefully organised and held together with another elastic band.

'Bethlehem,' I say as I flick through the envelopes.

'Sorry?' says Tomas.

'The Christmas card. She took every one of her Christmas cards to a little place called Bethlehem in Wales so that she could have the stamp. There is no doubt my aunt sent this with a lot of love. She was always so thoughtful.'

I hold a bright red envelope in my hand and again feel the need to stroke it. The stamp is a nativity scene with Bethlehem stamped over it.

Albert has been incredibly quiet for a man who was supposed to explain everything, but now he finally speaks.

'She wrote to him after he died. I put the post that was sent here with the letters Marek kept in his bedside

97

drawer. I found them when we were clearing things out. Her address is on the back. I should have told her about his death. I'm sorry for that.'

I look at Tomas, unsure of what to say. If only Albert had written back, Aunt Grace could have known the reason she didn't get a response. It is too late now, but she would have been spared all the uncertainty she had about what had happened between them.

'It's okay. It's all in the past now.'

I play with one of my earrings, a simple stud I always wear, and twiddle it around. It is quite the shock to see proof of their love in front of me. Until now, apart from the confessional letter, there was no physical evidence of their relationship.

'I suppose at least she clung on to the hope that Marek was alive. It never occurred to her that he'd died, or she wouldn't have sent me here. It would have probably broken her heart, had she known,' I say, hoping this will ease his guilt.

'I know, but she sent you here now. Maybe if she knew then she could've died peacefully and not thinking about Marek.'

'It's done now. None of us can change anything. It's okay. But can I ask *why* you didn't want to tell her?'

'As I said when we met, I *hated* her for what happened to him for a long time. I resented her because Marek was working so hard to return to her. If he'd met someone here, maybe he'd still be alive. He wouldn't have gone out fishing, slipped and hit his head on a rock like he did. But now I realise that she never gave up on him, and for that, I'm sorry.'

'Well, it's not like her whole life was on hold. It's just that she put everyone else in front of her own needs, and she regretted it at the end.'

'It's quite romantic in a way though. I mean, they both thought about each other until they died,' says Tomas.

'It was a very big romance. Marek loved her very much and was desperate to get back to her,' says Albert.

'How was he after they split? She said she wrote and told him that it was over.'

'I don't know anything about that. He was happy when he died and excited to get back to her.'

'Well, I guess we'll never know what he was thinking. Although I suppose the letter could have got lost in the post, and he never knew.'

'Possibly,' says Albert.

'I still think it's odd she never confided in me. My one wish is that she'd told me about him.'

'I wonder what she wrote? I guess you can find out, since this is your property now,' says Tomas, pointing to the box.

'Oh, I only flew with a budget airline. I couldn't possibly carry a box of letters home. Besides, these letters are between Marek and Aunt Grace, and that's where they should stay,' I say.

'But what if they wanted their story to be told?' Tomas looks at me curiously. Albert stares at me, waiting for me to agree.

'No, absolutely not. Under no circumstances should we open the letters. That would be like going through someone's diary. In fact, maybe we should burn them and protect Aunt Grace's privacy.'

'That's terrible. Sacrilege! You can't burn a love story!' says Tomas.

I look at the Christmas card that is still on my lap. The postmark is dated from 1994. He was already dead when this was sent, and that's why it was never opened. Looking at the number of envelopes here, it seems she wrote for longer than she admitted. All these letters, just to lay in a box, never to be opened by their intended recipient. It is a waste, but that doesn't mean to say that we have any right to read them.

'I think the time might be right to open them,' says Albert.

'Definitely. What if there's something inside we need to know?' says Tomas.

'Like what?' I ask.

'He's right. You could be Marek's secret daughter, for all we know,' says Albert.

'I don't think so. I'm far too old. I was in the pubs by the time they met,' I laugh. I self-consciously feel for that one long grey eyebrow hair that always sneaks its way in. I must remember to pull it out when I get back to the hotel.

'No, you don't look old enough,' smiles Tomas.

I feel myself blush, as I tend to do, every time Tomas looks at me.

'But aren't you curious, Olivia? When someone passes, there's always so much we never knew. This is our chance to learn more about both of them.'

'I don't know. Besides, you're never supposed to open someone else's post. In fact, I think it might be illegal. I'm sure Ken told me that once.'

'Ken?' says Tomas.

'My postman.'

'Ah. I see. But if we don't open these letters, we will never know about their love. It would be a shame for their story to die with them.'

I look at the box, unsure how to persuade these two to stop. As much as part of me would love to learn more about Aunt Grace and Marek and this magical love story they are supposed to have had, going through their post seems far too intimate.

'Well, I don't agree. I'm certainly not their secret daughter, and I'm quite sure there's nothing we need to know about in that box. I'm sorry. I need to leave now.'

'Sure, I'll take you back into town, but will you please say you'll think about it?' says Tomas.

I would agree to anything to get some breathing space, so I nod and tell them both that I will consider it. But I decide that I will tell Dewi about the pressure they are putting on me, and he would never allow it from a legal perspective, so I am quite sure it is a hypothetical argument.

Chapter Eleven

Before I begin my search for somewhere nice to eat for dinner in 'Staré Mesto', as I heard Tomas call it, I decide to give Dewi a call. That way, if there is any more pressure from Tomas and Albert about the letters, I can quote the correct legal terminology. I ring his office and keep my fingers crossed that it is still open before they all slink off for the Christmas break. I am relieved when the receptionist answers and tells me that I have just caught him before he leaves for the care home. He comes on the phone with his usual chirpy tone. Does this man never have a bad moment?

'Hello. Nice surprise to hear from you again. What's the latest there?'

I explain about the letters that have been discovered and how I respect the law.

'I see what you're saying, and you are correct about the Postal Services Act 2000. It is an offence to open someone's mail, and you could be prosecuted.'

'Yes! That's exactly what I tried to tell them. Thank goodness I never—'

'Ah, but let me stop you there. What I was about to say is that there is a *but* coming... If you don't have consent to open the post, which you obviously don't, an acting executor of an estate can give you the authority. I give you full authority to open those letters. I mean, they're practically your belongings now, and besides, don't you want to know what Grace wrote to Marek?'

'No, I don't. It's between those two.'

'Oh, come on now, where's your sense of romance, Ms Edwards?'

'It left with my ex-husband!'

'Fair enough, but then if anyone needs some romance in their lives, surely it's you.'

'Pfft.'

'Well, I think you should spread their love and read the letters. You have to admit, this is all so romantic. Especially at this wonderful time of year.'

'But it wasn't a happy ending. My aunt chose to be a full-time carer over love, and Marek died, in case you've already forgotten.'

'No, I haven't forgotten, but they kept each other in their hearts forever. Now that is true love.'

Why does Dewi have to see the world with rose-tinted glasses all the time?

'Now, I've got to rush off because my sleigh is waiting for me outside. I'm off to a kids' Christmas party to give out presents after I've been to the care home.'

'Since when does a solicitor have a sleigh waiting outside for them?'

'Well, no. It's a Dacia estate covered in red velvet, but don't tell the kids.'

I laugh as I imagine him piling his Santa sack into the boot. He certainly is a character, no matter how annoying he can be at times. I can't believe a solicitor, who deals with wills, disputes and fights among people, can be so upbeat about everything.

After we bid each other goodbye and say another round of Merry Christmases, I remove the itinerary from my pocket. Dewi didn't give me the name of a restaurant to go to tonight; he left that decision to me. In fairness, I suppose he doesn't know what food I like. I quite fancy something traditional though. Thus, I juggle my way through the busy Christmas market and stroll around the side streets until I find something I like the look of. I am tempted by quite a few places but determined to try traditional food whilst I am here. A blue building with lanterns offers a pizzeria, but I feel sure there must be a Czech restaurant here somewhere.

It is bustling in the town, so I walk down the alleyways to find a quieter spot that might not be so geared towards tourists. A little further away, I spot a hidden alley. I eagerly rush down the narrow cobbled street, passing artisan shops with steamed-up windows due to the cold air outside. Then I come across an iron sign hanging from a building with decorative arches over the windows. The menu at the doorway is exactly what I have been looking for.

I am greeted with the loveliest of Czech welcomes, and the waitress sits me down in an alcove with a menu offering local dishes. She recommends the local beers and Moravian wines and I order a wine that she suggests. While I wait for my drink, I scan through the menu. There are so many intriguing dishes, like starters of spicy pickled sausage, or baked brie with cranberry sauce and even cabbage pancakes. Now I'm in trouble. I wasn't even planning on having a starter.

For my main course, I plump for beef and beer goulash, and when it arrives, I am pleased with my choice. The lovely red Moravian wine washes the goulash down delightfully. I am enjoying myself so much that, as I push my empty plate to one side, I realise I haven't given much thought to being at home in the mill. It is the first time I have properly relaxed. I do hope the little robin is doing well though. Hopefully, there will still be plenty of food for all the wild birds if the ground freezes over. I trust Ken will keep an eye on them.

I decide to order another glass of wine when I hear my mobile ringing. Surely, it can't be Dewi? He must be playing Santa by now.

I look at the phone and see that it is the number I saved for Tomas. Oh, what does the family want now? I hesitate before answering it but decide I may as well get whatever it is over with.

'Hello.'

'Hi, it's Tomas.'

'Oh, hi. How did you get my number?'

'It came up on my mobile when you called me.'

How silly of me; of course it would. That is why I was never keen on having a new mobile. Now anyone can get hold of me at any inconvenient time. Like when I'm enjoying a lovely smooth glass of red.

'What's up?' I ask.

'It's Albert. He's asked me to call you.'

'Oh. Is he okay?'

'Yes, he's fine, but he's going on about the letters.'

I take a sip of the red wine.

'I told him you're busy sightseeing. But he says he'd love for you to come over and talk about them. He enjoyed meeting you. It's been exciting for him.'

I consider bringing up what Dewi told me about the legality of the letters but then decide against it. I still feel they might be too personal to read, and I can't quite make my mind up.

'I don't know what to say, really.'

'I understand. Even though I'm strongly against it, I guess we could burn them all and never find out what's in them – if that's what you really want,' says Tomas.

'Oh, I don't know. My solicitor would probably be annoyed with me. Look, tell him I'll sleep on it. I'll have a think, okay?'

'That's great. I'll let him know. I hope you're enjoying your evening, by the way.'

'Yes, it's lovely. Thank you.'

I wonder what Tomas is doing tonight. It seems as though he is alone as there is no sound of anyone in the background.

I leave the restaurant thinking about Albert and Tomas. I have only just met them, but I suppose I should agree to open the letters. Family is important and you need to learn all you can while people are still around. Sadly, with Aunt Grace and Marek no longer here, this is the only way I can find out more about them.

–

By the next morning, I am ready to face opening the letters and I am even looking forward to seeing Albert and Tomas again. Well, particularly Tomas. I realise it's been nice to talk to someone who isn't my postman or lawyer.

Today, my itinerary says to go to the markets at Wenceslas Square and Charles Bridge. However, I can't think of anywhere I want to be more than at Albert's cosy apartment. I decide to phone Tomas to tell him that I have finally made a decision about the letters.

'Albert will be so pleased. Thank you,' says Tomas.

'I'm glad I can make him happy. Although he should have probably read them years ago.'

'I think it was all a bit fresh after Uncle Marek died. Then I don't think he gave them much thought over the years. The box was stacked up high on top of a wardrobe until you came along. Perhaps he feels it's finally the right time.'

'I guess so. When shall we open them? Should I head over there now?'

'He might be resting at this time, but we can go there later. Maybe early evening?'

'Yeah, that's fine.'

'Great, so what are your plans for the morning?' asks Tomas.

'Well, my itinerary says I need to go to the markets at Wenceslas Square and Charles Bridge.'

'Fantastic, how would you like some local knowledge? I mean, uh, to help you navigate the streets of Prague. I'm not a bad tourist guide, and I can tell you some things that you may not know. Like, I could take you to the lucky dog.'

'The lucky dog?'

'You see. You haven't heard of it, have you?'

'No, that's not on my itinerary.'

'Can you give me half an hour and I'll take you to it?'

'Do I have a choice?'

'No,' laughs Tomas.

'Okay. See you in half an hour then.'

I make my way to Charles Bridge and see Tomas rushing towards me as he crosses the Vltava River at the same time as I arrive. Even amongst all the crowds, he stands out. I think it's the way he walks so confidently and that smile as soon as he sees me.

As I go to shake Tomas' hand, he moves to kiss me on the cheek, which is all a bit unexpected. I giggle nervously as I return his kiss and then completely miss as he has moved away. Why am I so clumsy around him? Fortunately, Tomas laughs it off.

'I'm so glad I get to see you again. I was a bit worried you were upset with us after disagreeing about the letters.'

'No, it's okay. Anyway, even Aunt Grace's solicitor has authorised us to read them. He seems obsessed with their love story.'

'Well, from what my uncle tells me, they sounded good for each other. Not everyone finds the right person. It's just a shame they found each other but never got to be together,' says Tomas.

I smile up at Tomas who is looking at me with those big brown eyes. I turn away before I find myself blushing.

'Yes, indeed.'

Tomas is making me nervous. I am not used to such candid conversations about love, even if it is involving other people.

'So, where's this lucky dog?' I ask, to get him off the subject.

'Just over here.'

Tomas is excited as we rush towards a bronze plaque on Charles Bridge. The plaque is of a dog that is fixed to a baroque statue of St John Nepomuk. For some reason, the dog is shinier than the rest of the statue.

'Rub it,' he says.

'Rub what?' I ask.

'The dog. It's supposed to bring you luck.'

'Oh, the dog. Okay.'

I rub the dog and ask for luck. To be fair, this trip hasn't been particularly lacking in the luck department. I was lucky to bump into Tomas near the stairwell that day, I was lucky to find a gorgeous restaurant last night, and

I suppose that I am lucky to be standing here on Charles Bridge, the day before Christmas Eve, in the cold with a warm coat and a hat keeping my head toasty. In fact, I would say Prague is practically oozing luck for me right now. I am also lucky that I will be going home in a few days, and I have practically completed my mission.

Tomas touches the dog after me and then gives me a high-five.

'There, maybe luck will change for both of us now.' He smiles, and those beautiful brown eyes light up his face again. Then his phone rings and he looks at the number before answering it.

'Or maybe not. Sorry, I just have to take this.'

'Yes, of course.'

He speaks in Czech, and even though I don't understand anything they are saying, I overhear an angry-sounding female voice down the line.

I hope I haven't got him into trouble. What if one of my hairs fell out in his car and he has a wife who thinks he is having a torrid affair? As I watch Tomas frown and sound as though he is trying to reason with the woman, I begin to wonder if that dog is so lucky after all.

Chapter Twelve

I look at my watch and realise that Tomas has been on the phone arguing with this woman for ten minutes. I gesture to him that I am leaving. I can't stand around waiting any longer. He waves at me and indicates that he will catch me up.

The cold air bites at my nose and cheeks as I make my way alone to Wenceslas Square. I pull my scarf tighter around me to keep me cosy. Looking up towards the sky, it appears as if it may snow, but Aunt Grace always used to tell me as a child that in this sort of temperature, it is too cold to snow.

When I arrive at the Christmas market in Wenceslas Square, the smell of food hits me right away, just like the one at the Old Town. I am beginning to think that I could become an expert at sniffing out Christmas markets at this rate and decide on yet another creamy hot chocolate to warm me up. I feel like I could do with some comfort as I worry about Tomas. He is obviously in trouble with someone. Perhaps he is cut from the same cloth as Craig. After all, Tomas is pretty gorgeous. I am sure he could have any woman he wants and who knows if he takes full advantage of that. I clutch onto my hot chocolate for solace. But I soon put it down when I hear a funny tone come from my new mobile phone. When I take it out of my bag, I see that it is my factory-setting message tone.

My first text message has come through, and it is from
Tomas.

> Sorry about that. Where are you?

I decide to ignore the message and put my phone back in
my bag. I don't want the woman I heard during his call
stumbling upon a message from me if I respond, no matter
how innocently.

So, instead of replying, I look around the little wooden
cabins full of foodie treats and then come across some
charity stalls that sell local crafts. One of the stalls sells
cute puppets on a string and it reminds me of when Aunt
Grace gave me a ballet dancer puppet when I was small.
Just like her, it was so glamorous. I loved that little toy. She
also gave me my first hobby horse. I thought I was a jockey
on that thing and took it everywhere. Aunt Grace always
had the knack of knowing what to buy me. Seeing the
puppets cheers me up, and I remind myself I have done
the right thing for her by coming here. As Dewi said,
she would do anything for anyone. It makes me realise
that I should be more like her. Perhaps I will consider
helping the community when I get back home, just like
Dewi does, instead of only helping animals and staying
away from people.

I am about to make my way to Letná Park when my
phone bleeps again. I can see the message without having
to open it.

> Wait. I can see you.

I look around and see that Tomas is looking directly at me. He waves and then weaves his way through the stalls and the crowds of people, quickly getting closer towards me. I can't escape.

'Hi, you disappeared.'

'I thought I should leave you on the phone. You seemed to be having an issue with something… Or, well, someone.'

'Oh, it's nothing. No big deal.'

That's what they all say. It sounded like a pretty big deal to the woman on the phone.

'Right.'

'Anyway, where are you thinking of going next?' asks Tomas.

Typical! Men always change the subject. But I suppose his personal life is nothing to do with me.

'Letná Park.'

'Ah, can I take you somewhere before you go there?'

'Where?'

'It's a surprise. It'll be fun. I promise.'

I follow Tomas through the streets until we reach what looks like a shopping centre. I've not met many men who like shopping centres; perhaps he really is trying to be sweet.

'Why are we here?'

'Just wait and see.'

When we get inside, I see it is no ordinary shopping centre. Tomas leads me to a statue of a horse hanging upside down. The horse's tail hangs towards the floor.

'See that tail? Whenever I arrange to meet someone, I say I'll meet them under the horse's tail. Quite fun, isn't it?'

Then he rushes me over to a grand piano that is suspended from the ceiling. I'm beginning to feel like I have vertigo!

'But you've not seen the best bit...'

My life flashes before me as we go around a corner and I see a paternoster lift! Please tell me Tomas doesn't want me to go in that. The lift at the apartment block is bad enough.

'Come,' he says.

'No, I can't go in there.'

'Yes, you can.'

I watch in horror as the open lift quickly moves up.

'How am I supposed to jump into that?'

'Come on. I'll show you. I promise it's worth the ride.'

Tomas grabs hold of my hand, and we jump in the lift together. It reminds me of my panic trying to get on a chairlift once in Innsbruck. However, much to my surprise, I manage the lift much better than I did the chairlift.

Once I am safely on board, I laugh with Tomas as I watch the different floors go past in front of my eyes.

'That's bonkers,' I smile. I notice that Tomas is laughing at my reaction.

'You get used to it.'

The lift is much faster than the one at the apartment block, so I soon have to work a way to get out of it. Tomas acts like a gentleman and grabs my hand to help me.

'Well, I've certainly never done that before,' I say with relief once I am on the outside.

As I catch my breath, Tomas leads me outside onto a rooftop garden. In front of us is the most gorgeous 360-degree view over the city.

'Oh wow, this is something else.' I smile at Tomas, who is watching my expression.

'You see, I bet this wasn't even on your itinerary, was it?'

'No, I'll be having words with Dewi. I'd say his itinerary is lacking a few crucial things.'

'Fancy a drink while we're here? Or are you ready to go back down in the lift?'

'No, I think a drink sounds like a good idea before I go back in there.'

Tomas is grinning at me, and I notice his kind smile as we go to a pop-up rooftop bar that looks just perfect. That smile will get women everywhere falling at his feet, thinks the cynic in me.

'Now, are you going to try some local drinks while you're here?' Tomas asks.

'Oh, I don't know. Might be a bit strong if I have to time it right to jump back into that lift.' Besides, if I had something too strong, I might not be able to resist his charms.

Tomas orders a beer, and I choose a small glass of wine. I quickly begin to realise how nice it is to have company for a drink.

'So, what time shall we go over and read the letters?' I ask as we wait for our drinks. Although Tomas said it would be sometime this evening, I would still like to do Letná Park quickly if possible.

Tomas doesn't reply and appears to be thinking. Then I realise that he has a life and the woman on the phone that he probably needs to be with.

'I'm just thinking of somewhere I should be next. But, you know what, it's fine. I can change my plans.'

'Oh no, please don't do that on my account.'

'It's okay. I just have to go and buy a carp for Christmas, that's all.'

'Carp? Like the fish?'

'Yes, that's what my family eat for Christmas. We don't have turkey like you do.'

I picture Tomas sitting down with his angry partner and, I assume, children for a family Christmas meal with a huge carp. At least I won't be having beans on toast alone this year. Maybe I can get something at the hotel.

'But, no, it's fine. It can wait. Let's start on the letters as early as we can. I just need to do a few things first.'

When we have finished our drinks and I manage to get back down in the lift again, Tomas drops me off near Letná Park where I wander around until he is ready to collect me again. It overlooks the Vltava River, and the bridges of the city are clearly in view. I use my camera on the phone for the first time to take the most incredible shot of Prague. It is a lovely way to spend the remainder of the afternoon, but I am happy to have the company of Tomas again when he picks me up.

When we walk into Albert's apartment, it has been transformed since my last visit. Candles have been lit, and the smell of food is coming from the kitchen.

'What's all this?' I ask Tomas.

'I thought I'd make us all a meal, and we can relax a little before we start opening the letters. I got in a nice bottle of Moravian wine. I hope you like it.'

I think back to the wine I had in the local restaurant. I am sure it will be very nice, but it feels a little strange to have dinner with Tomas when he has upset the lady in his life. Surely, he should be wining and dining her?

I look over to Albert, who is smiling. He has a naughty grin, and I get the impression that there is much more to this man than it might seem. He is up to something, and I can't work out what.

Tomas opens the wine for me while I wait for him to plate everything up. I offer to help in the kitchen, but he insists I relax. It feels nice to be waited on, but I can't help thinking this should all be done for someone else.

'So, Albert… How are you doing?'

'Yes, very good, dear. Did you have a nice time with Tomas today?'

'Oh, he told you what we did today ?'

'Yes, I suggested it.'

'You suggested it?'

Albert looks a little flustered. 'You know, I just thought it would be nice for the two of you to get to know each other.'

'Get to know each other?'

'Yes, for you to see Prague.'

'Oh right, yes. I learnt a lot. Thanks.'

'Tomas is a very good guide.'

'He is indeed.' I smile.

'He's a very good man too,' says Albert.

I nod my head in agreement but don't quite know what else I am supposed to say. Thankfully, Tomas tells us that dinner is ready, and we get to move away from the topic of what a wonderful person his uncle thinks he is.

Tomas is clearly used to entertaining and brings out a delicious-looking Czech mushroom soup to start off. I wonder if he made this from scratch. We finish our bowls, and I am already feeling content when Tomas brings out the main course.

'What's this?'

'*Svíčková* with *Houskové knedlíky*.'

My face must give away the fact that I have no idea what he is talking about.

'It's like braised beef with bread dumplings.'

'Sounds delicious. I love a hearty meal.'

'I'm sure you'll enjoy it. More wine?'

Tomas tops up my wine glass. He is such a good host.

He has even added cranberries and whipped cream to the dish. It looks terrific.

'This is my favourite meal. Tomas is such a great cook, you know,' says Albert. I smile at how Albert is once again drilling into me how wonderful his nephew is.

'I can see that,' I agree.

When we finish the main course, Tomas offers us dessert, but I simply couldn't. I don't think I could stay in Prague too long or none of my clothes would fit. It is like comfort food heaven here.

I offer to help with the washing up, but Tomas is having none of it. He demands I sit down and enjoy the rest of my wine.

When Tomas finishes in the kitchen, he brings out the box of letters and puts it on the living room table, just like the first time I saw it.

'Are we ready to start?' he asks.

I take a sip of my drink and look at the box.

'I'm ready to hear all about this love story. I just hope this is the right thing to do,' I say.

Tomas and I pick out an envelope at the same time. It feels like a tug of war with a Christmas cracker as I hold one end and he holds the other.

'Sorry,' we both say simultaneously.

Finally, I take it, and my hands shake ever so slightly as I carefully peel at the corner of the floral-embellished envelope.

Chapter Thirteen

I quickly scan the letter before I start, just in case there is anything I shouldn't see. Imagine if Aunt Grace said something about her beloved Marek's appendage and I read it out loud in front of Albert! Oh, the shame! I don't see anything to do with them having hot, steamy sex in there, though, thankfully, so I clear my throat and begin to read the letter out loud.

> *'14 December 1993*
>
> *My dearest Marek,*
>   *Thank you for your lovely letter.*
>   *It was so nice to hear from you, although I am naturally disappointed that we won't be seeing each other soon. I would have loved to spend Christmas with you, and it was very kind of you to ask me to visit, but my mother-in-law isn't very well. She had a stroke, and I am all she has, so I can't really leave her at the moment. Hopefully, when she's a bit stronger, maybe next year, we can see each other again.*
>   *Anyway, for the time being, I can't stop listening to Elvis' 'Can't Help Falling in Love' and listening wistfully to the words. I know we only met five months ago, but those words were*

made for us. As you always remind me, we were meant to be.

Now that we've known each other a little longer, I have something to tell you. I need you to know that I am nervous about a new relationship. I haven't shared this with anyone, apart from Silvie, but my husband Harry was not a good man. I suppose it seems easier to tell you the truth as I know you're not going to tell anyone in my village. I was brought up to never wash your dirty laundry in public. I wonder if that's the same in your town?

Well, anyway, Harry was awful to me, so a new relationship seems scary. He used to speak to me terribly, so condescending. Then he would use all the housekeeping for betting on the horses and late nights at the pub with his friends. I had never felt so lonely in my life. He made me feel worthless by the end. I was so beaten down. Marrying a teddy boy with a big ego in the Sixties was the biggest mistake of my life. That's why when I told you I was a widow and you said you were sorry to hear that, well, I wanted to say that it was a relief, quite honestly. But I know how awful that sounds. So, I want you to know that it isn't that I am not falling head over heels for you, it's just that I'm scared. I'm still building myself back up and a bit fragile. You are gorgeous and nothing like him, I know. It's just sometimes these things leave you a little scarred. So, I suppose I want to ask you to be patient with me. I do truly love you, but I need time.

I've sent you a Christmas card, which hopefully you'll receive soon. I took ages picking out the best

card for you. I hope you like the verse — I mean
every word of it.

    With all my love, always,
    Gx'

That explains why Dewi, who is such a placid man, swore when he was talking about Uncle Harry. I had no idea what poor Aunt Grace went through with him. Was I too self-absorbed to notice? I am ashamed of myself for not being perceptive enough to suspect what she was going through.

'Oh dear, that's terrible about her husband. I hate men like that,' says Tomas.

'I honestly didn't know. I mean, he was a bit miserable, but I just thought it was his personality. I didn't know any of this. But you have to remember that I didn't even know she had a secret lover in Prague either. Aunt Grace kept a lot of things to herself, even her illness during her final days.'

'It's surprising how many secrets come out after someone has passed,' says Albert.

'So it seems,' I agree.

'That's nice that they both loved Elvis though,' says Tomas.

'Yes, I remember my aunt always wanted to visit Grace-land, but she had never been abroad. She felt the US was too long a flight for her.'

'You know, Elvis brings back a nice memory for me. Marek would sit in his room listening to his songs. He thought he looked like him, but then all us brothers did.' Albert smiles and then looks down at his hands, linked together on his lap.

I begin to wonder whether I should carry on or stop where we are. Does Albert really want to revisit the heartache of losing his brother?

'We can leave the rest of the letters. We probably shouldn't continue,' I say.

'No, please, don't stop. I want to hear more. It's been a long time since I thought about Marek. It's sad, but also nice to hear his name mentioned again as though he were alive.'

'Okay, if you're sure?'

'I'm sure.'

I grab the next letter that I come across, which has been opened and obviously read by Marek. I soon realise that this must have been the first letter she wrote to him after they met.

'21 July 1993

My dearest Marek,

I hope this letter arrives safely and that I have your address correct. Hopefully, this will arrive by the time you land back home.

How wonderful it was to meet you in London last week. To be honest, I haven't stopped thinking about it. I have never been so grateful for the rain! Who would have thought that an umbrella could bring us together. I hope you kept it safe and treasure the lucky umbrella!

It is hard to believe how much we have in common, considering we're from different parts of the world. I suppose our shared taste in music helps. I still can't believe Elvis is your favourite too!

Do you remember when we were sat at the tea shop? You told me stories of your family, and I told you about mine. Isn't it funny how you are all boys and I am one of all girls? I would love to meet your brothers one day. When we get together finally, maybe we can have a family celebration with them.

You were right that we had an immediate connection that was unexplainable. That is something we can definitely agree on!

I am so glad I got to spend time with you in London. Thank goodness Silvie and I had planned those few days away. She's a good friend. I felt terrible leaving her alone to have dinner with you that evening, but I think she could see that I looked the happiest in a long while. Well, approximately twenty-six years, I'd say!

I have kept and pressed that beautiful red rose you took from the vase on the table so that I can always remember our first meeting. It was rather naughty of you though! I do hope the cafe owners weren't too annoyed when they noticed it missing. Still, it makes me smile every time I look at it. That rose shall remind me of our special day forever. It makes me think of the term 'coup de foudre'. I heard that expression in a movie once. If you don't know what it means, look it up.

Anyway, I suppose this is a test letter to make sure you receive it. Once again, it was so wonderful to meet you.

With much love,
Gx'

I place the letter on the table and gulp down some wine. She sounds so happy. We all go silent and sit around staring at the cardboard box on the table.

Eventually, Tomas speaks. 'Life's so short. We have to grab every moment. When do you leave Prague, Olivia?'

'Another few days.'

'Okay, let's make sure we get through the other letters before you leave. But first we have Christmas and you're here alone, right?'

I nod my head and try not to look too pitiful.

'Will you please join us for our Christmas dinner? We have it on Christmas Eve. Tomorrow.'

'Oh, I don't know. I don't want to intrude.' I think of that woman on the phone again. I don't think that sounds like a good idea at all. Surely, she won't want me around.

'Tomas is a good cook, as you'll have noticed tonight. You'll enjoy his Christmas dinner,' says Albert.

'Yes, please join us. You're definitely not intruding,' says Tomas.

Both of them stare at me, and I don't know what to say. I want to be here for Albert, but I really don't want to cause any trouble for Tomas or a possible partner.

'Oh, I really don't know. I think the hotel will do something.'

'Nonsense. You can't stay in a hotel all alone. That's terrible. What sort of family would we be if we didn't welcome you into our home? You must come, and I won't take no for an answer,' says Albert.

'Okay then. I'll look forward to it. It'll make a change to the beans on toast I had last year,' I say.

'You eat beans on toast for Christmas? Is this what British people do?' asks Albert.

I laugh at the idea.

'No, it's just me because I was on my own last year. Other people have turkey and all the trimmings.'

'I know which I'd prefer,' says Albert.

Yup, so would I, but we don't always have a choice in the matter.

'Then maybe you need a dog for company, nobody is an island,' says Tomas.

It's okay for him to say that with his cosy little family around the fire, or whatever he does at home. Anyway, I guess I will get to meet them tomorrow, and hopefully, I can prove to this woman that she has nothing to worry about.

I look at Tomas with a frown. Is he so perfect? He seems to be hanging around a lot on his own too and quite possibly neglecting a wife.

'I'm quite fine as an island, thank you. At least I get to choose who comes on shore.'

Tomas and Albert look at me, baffled. I thought that was quite good, personally.

'Anyway, let's get back to the letters.'

Tomas picks up the box and gently tips the contents out onto the floor. There are envelopes in piles held in elastic bands everywhere. It appears as though a highly organised Santa has dropped his sack of letters with present requests from all the children in the neighbourhood. Aunt Grace must have written a few times a month by the looks of it.

However, something else falls out too. It is a little purple velvety box. I move from the sofa to sit on the floor with the envelopes and the box. I can't resist picking it up and examining it in my hand. Tomas sits on the floor beside me and huddles in close to see the box.

'It was the ring he'd bought your aunt,' says Albert.

Marek bought Aunt Grace a ring and she never knew? That's terrible.

'You should have sent this to her, Uncle. She should have known,' says Tomas.

'I know. I've made many mistakes in my life, and I regret that. I try to do things to protect people, but sometimes, I get that wrong. Plus, I blamed her for Marek's death.'

'But that sounds spiteful,' says Tomas.

'I know. I was stupid. We all make mistakes. Like you and Milena.'

Tomas looks annoyed and makes a cross face at Albert.

'Old people. Why do they always have to say what they think?' says Tomas, looking at me.

I shrug my shoulders, unsure what to say. I don't want to come between Tomas and his uncle. I can't help wondering who Milena is though. It sounds like a name that has clearly hit a nerve and I suspect it is the woman who was talking to Tomas on the phone.

'Have you ever known someone who always lets you down?' Albert asks me.

I think about Craig and the promise he made that we would go on a cruise for our anniversary when he probably knew all along that he was leaving me.

'Oh yes, indeed.'

'Well, that's Milena. He gives her too much time. He's far too nice, my boy is.'

Tomas starts to fidget, and I notice his ears have gone red. I am not sure if he is annoyed or embarrassed. But it seems that there is more to the story than I first thought. Perhaps Tomas isn't the type of person to play around after all.

'Anyway, let's see what's in the jewellery box, hey?' says Tomas.

I press open the box, and inside is the most beautiful diamond solitaire ring.

'Is that an engagement ring?' says Tomas.

'It is. He'd planned on proposing. He was so happy the day he bought it. He got it from a small place in the market with the money he worked hard for. I'll always remember,' says Albert.

'Wow. He had good taste. I wish Aunt Grace could have seen this. I just know it's exactly what she'd have chosen.'

'Try it on,' says Tomas.

'I can't try on someone else's ring.'

'Yes, you can. Nobody has ever tried it. Someone may as well,' says Albert.

I remove it from the box and place it on my ring finger. It only goes halfway down my knuckle. Aunt Grace was much daintier than I am. Marek must have even worked out the right size for her.

'It's beautiful.'

I pop it carefully into the jewellery box and then place it back inside the cardboard box, even though it is a terrible waste for it not to be worn.

'Right, are we ready for the next letter then?' I ask.

I check through the bundles and see some yellowing envelopes. The postal date on the first envelope in the bundle says April 1994.

'Okay. I'll start with this.'

I pull the letter out from the open envelope and scan over it. I start reading the words out loud.

'10 April 1994

My dearest Marek,

It's been nine months since we were last together, and I'm counting down the days until we are reunited. Since you left, there hasn't been much excitement to report back to you. My darling, Marek, the truth is that it's so hard living without you. I can't wait for your next letter. I treasure every word you say. I can't wait to feel your arms around me again and to kiss you. I don't want to kiss anyone else in my lifetime, nobody compares to you.'

I look up at Albert, slightly mortified. At least it is only kissing she is talking about. I clear my throat and start again.

'Sometimes, you don't need to spend a long time with someone to know you should be together. In case I haven't made myself clear enough, I can't wait to see you again. I love you, I love you, I love you!

Love always and forever,

Gx'

Tomas sighs as I finish reading the letter. 'That's beautiful,' he says.

'I know. They were so lucky to have met each other. I've no doubt it would have worked out eventually had the accident not happened. Isn't it awful? Some people are destined for each other, but then something like this happens.'

'It's all quite emotional. Should we have a day off the letters tomorrow?' says Tomas.

'That sounds good. Anyway, since it's Christmas Eve, I'm sure you'll be too busy with all the preparations.'

'No, it's fine. In fact, I was going to ask you if you wanted to visit Prague Castle in the morning. I could take you around.'

I consider whatever is going on with any woman in his life. I don't want to make her mad, and feel I should refuse. However, Albert interrupts before I can decline.

'You have to let Tomas take you to the castle. You'll love it,' says Albert.

'Oh, I don't want to put anyone out. I can go alone, it's okay.'

'No, I'll not have that. You have to let Tomas take you. He can tell you things about it. He wants you to go with him. It's no problem at all, is it Tomas?'

'No, please. I'd very much like to take you there.'

I look at the both of them smiling at me.

'Well, if you're sure it won't upset anyone or not be a problem, then I'd love to go. You have no idea how much I have desperately wanted to visit the castle! You see, my aunt gave me a snow globe of Prague Castle. It is the most precious thing and—'

'Hang on a minute,' says Albert. He gets up slowly and goes into his bedroom. When he comes out, he is holding a snow globe in the palm of his hand.

'That's exactly like the one I have!' I say.

'I thought it might be. Marek bought them on a school trip to the castle when he was young. He bought one for our parents and one for me. But the one he bought my parents went missing. Not long after he met your aunt.'

'Ah, that's so cute.'

'Finally, the mystery of where it went is solved,' laughs Albert.

'Well, it's very beautiful, and my aunt treasured it for the rest of her life. It's safe at my home if you want it returned.'

'No, it's yours now. Think of it as a Christmas present. Anyway, I have this one to remember Marek by,' says Albert.

'That's most kind. Thank you.'

I look at Albert and across to Tomas, who is smiling at me. I feel warm and fuzzy, as though I have found a new family.

What better Christmas present could there possibly be than receiving the magical snow globe and getting accepted into this wonderful home?

Chapter Fourteen

I wake up to the sound of church bells ringing out from somewhere in the distance and realise how Christmassy I feel. I never believed it would happen, but Prague has awoken my Christmas spirit, something I thought had been lost forever. I feel like a child waiting for Santa as I know that today I will finally visit the real-life castle from my snow globe. It seems Dewi was right, as usual, and that the best things are worth waiting for, even if I have been impatient.

Tomas meets me immediately after breakfast to take me to the castle. He has already made me aware that he has to be home in the afternoon to prepare the Christmas feast for this evening, so it seems I will have to spend the afternoon sightseeing alone. I am getting quite used to his company now and can't help but feel slightly disappointed that I'll be alone. But the sight of the castle soon makes me forget about any disappointment as it comes into full view when we walk through the sixteenth-century gardens and then further along to what Tomas calls 'Powder Bridge', which he says has something to do with it being where they kept the gunpowder. It is so handy having someone with me who knows everything. My own personal tour guide.

Two guards stand to attention as we head into the courtyard.

'Wow, they look like wooden Christmas nutcracker figures,' I say.

'Oh, that reminds me. I have something for you,' says Tomas. He goes into his pocket and pulls something out. He hands me a ticket.

'What's this?'

'Well, I'll be busy this afternoon, so I thought you may like it.'

I read the ticket and see that it is for a ballet at the Broadway Theatre. They are performing *The Nutcracker*! Well, that certainly wasn't on Dewi's itinerary.

'No way? A ballet on Christmas Eve?'

'I hope you like ballet?'

'Oh, Tomas, my aunt always took me to see a ballet at Christmas when I was young. It's like you knew. This is such a precious gift.'

I hold the ticket tightly in my hand, terrified that it will blow away. It feels as cherished as a Golden Ticket to Willy Wonka's Chocolate Factory.

Instinctively, I lean over to hug him and give him a kiss on his cheek. He leans in, and I feel something in my heart that I never thought I would again. I realise that I am becoming a little too fond of Tomas. This mustn't happen, so I quickly step back, look away and try to return to being more formal with him.

'Wow, this is an amazing gift. Thank you very much.'

Looking up to the sky, I can see the clouds have turned darker, and the air seems to have warmed up a little. I think of Aunt Grace's words about it not snowing when it is too cold. Then, a wet blob lands on my cheek, followed by another as I look up. When I look at Tomas, he has something on his eyelash. I lift my hand to brush it away. It is a little snowflake!

'It's snowing!'

'Wonderful, isn't it,' says Tomas.

In the castle courtyard, I dance around with my head facing up towards the sky, waiting for the snowflakes to land on my face. It feels as though the snow globe has come alive!

'So, do you want to do the tour or shall we dance in the snow?' asks Tomas.

I look around and notice that people are trying to get to the next part of the castle grounds as I dance about, oblivious to everything surrounding me.

'Ooh, sorry. I got a bit carried away then. I've always been a sucker for snow.'

Inside the Old Royal Palace, Tomas tells me it is one of the oldest places in Prague. I look up at the Gothic vaulted ceiling in the hall in amazement. I use my imagination to picture the lavish banquets that must have been held in here.

As we move along, we arrive at the cathedral within the grounds. With all the excitement of today, I find myself struggling to concentrate as Tomas tells me a snippet of information about the carving on the front of the building, honouring some bankers who financed the completion of the cathedral. Perhaps I should have offered something like that as a conciliatory gesture back at the mill to pacify the electrical supplier if things were to get worse. Then Tomas points out a magnificent stained-glass window with the bank's emblem. Somehow, I don't think my local branch would take that instead of collateral. We then walk up the almost 300 steps to the cathedral's tower and look across at snow-tipped spires across the city. The view is worth the workout on my thighs, and I vow to never complain about the steps to Albert's again.

The snow has stopped by the time we get back down and walk a little further where we come across cute little houses that soldiers used to live in. They are pink and blue and such pretty colours that they remind me of a main street near where I live, in a place called Llandeilo. It once again occurs to me that I haven't thought half as much about home as I thought I would. There are only forty-eight hours until I am due to fly home, and as I look across to Tomas, I realise I am no longer in any hurry to leave. Before I can think further about how fond I have grown of him, Tomas looks at his watch and says we must leave right away.

'Yes, of course,' I smile, even though I am slightly disappointed that we have to rush off.

'Come, we have to get to the main gate quickly.'

I rush behind Tomas, realising that he has to get home and try to keep up with his power walk.

When we get to the main gate, he stops amidst crowds of people standing around.

'What's everyone waiting for?' I ask.

'Twelve o'clock,' smiles Tomas.

I hear the sound of a trumpet and pomp and ceremony as the changing of the guards takes place. The guards, with their rifles tucked into their shoulders, march and walk to their little guard boxes and change places with the next person on duty. They are like little tin soldiers.

'What timing!'

'Yes, sorry, I had to rush you, but I wanted you to see that. Anyway, I'd better head off. You have your ballet, and I have lots of cooking and preparations to do for tonight.'

As Tomas puts his hand on my arm to say goodbye, I feel a tingle down my spine. Perhaps it is for the best that I am heading back home soon. I remind myself that I don't know all the facts about Milena, and so this can't possibly happen.

Before Tomas leaves, he asks me if I want him to drive me to the theatre, but I insist I am fine as I need the fresh air. I will find my own way there.

As the temperature warms up, I realise that so too have my feelings towards Tomas and that is not good for anyone.

'See you later,' I smile.

I walk away from the castle, looking back at it, and see that same view from my snow globe. I always knew that the little snow globe was magical, and the castle is just as special in real life.

I make my way to the theatre for my afternoon of ballet and try to stop any thoughts of Tomas from entering my head.

As the show begins, I focus on the ballet dancers, the music, the scenery of *The Nutcracker* and everything else, but no matter how hard I try, Tomas' smile keeps flashing back into my head. I remind myself of the ring he wears. Perhaps Milena gave it to him. Someone like that was never going to be single.

The ballet enchants me as a male performer takes a female into his arms and spins her around in the air. Watching them gives me a flashback to a pink jewellery box that Aunt Grace bought me one Christmas. It was the most precious thing, with its mini wind-up ballerina that would spin around as I opened the box. I start smiling to myself, and once again, I feel as though Aunt Grace is somehow here with me, watching me and making sure I am okay. Subconsciously, I stroke the arm of my theatre seat and almost scream out loud as I realise that I have just touched the hairy hand of the man sitting next to me. I give him apologetic gestures as he glares at me. Fortunately, the show is coming towards its finale, so I don't have to face this hairy stranger for much longer.

I dash for a taxi before the lights go up fully and notice that I don't have that much time to get ready. I tell the taxi driver I am in a hurry. I have to pick up a Christmas gift for Tomas and Albert from the market before I get dressed up for tonight.

I want to look my best. After all, in two hours' time, I will see Tomas again, and maybe even get to meet Milena.

Chapter Fifteen

I only have one pretty top in my whole wardrobe. Not that my wardrobe is that extensive. I don't know why I even threw this top in my small suitcase, but now I am super thankful that I did. For tonight's Christmas celebration, I decide I'll wear my favourite comfy black trousers as I figure there might be lots of food on offer. Then I throw over the black and gold sparkly top.

As I look in the mirror, I am surprised to find my hair isn't looking too haywire after using the hotel hairdryer, but then again, the hotel is quite posh, and it isn't one of those usual bendy hairdryers that are stuck on the bathroom wall. I don't look too shabby for someone who hasn't taken any care of themselves for the past two years. With a little make-up, I can even see Aunt Grace's legendary cheekbones under there somewhere.

When I get downstairs to reception, happy families are entering the hotel to celebrate Christmas Eve. They laugh and chat amongst themselves, completely oblivious to me walking out through the revolving doors alone. I feel like some kind of invisible ghost.

It makes me grateful to Tomas and Albert for being so hospitable. They could easily have left me on my own over Christmas. Until now, I didn't think I wanted company at this time of year, but having been given this opportunity, I find myself relieved to be celebrating with somebody.

It was so incredibly generous of them to include me in their plans, and I keep their Christmas gifts close to me as I jump into the taxi.

I bought a little glass robin that can hang from a Christmas tree for Tomas at the Christmas market. It reminded me of the robin from home. As soon as I saw it, I had to buy it for him. I will tell him that it means he should have faith in the future, even though he probably doesn't need to be told this since he seems quite confident. But I thought it would be something to remind him of the strange Welsh woman who turned up unannounced one Christmas.

For Albert, I have bought some local honey. I thought he might enjoy it on his toast in the morning. I didn't know what else to buy a man in his eighties who rarely leaves home. I do hope they will both like their gifts.

When the taxi pulls up outside the apartment block, I begin to feel nervous again. I tell myself not to be so silly. I have been here before. I just can't help but think that if I see Thomas with Milena, I may feel awkward. I remind myself that he invited me, and if he didn't want me there, surely he wouldn't have just done it merely to seem polite. Perhaps he has explained to Milena who I am and that I am absolutely no threat.

I listen to the sound of Christmas carols as I knock on the door. I hope they can hear me over the music in there. Then I hear a woman's voice near the door saying something in Czech. I brace myself to smile and be pleasant to her. I can smell the scent of her floral perfume clashing with the smell of cooking as the door swings open. I plaster a big smile on my face. She is every bit as sophisticated as I imagined in my head, but much older than Tomas.

I hold my hand out to greet her.

'Hi,' I smile. She returns my smile and calls for Tomas, who shoots out from the kitchen. I look around for other family members. I thought that Tomas might have children who might be here, but it is only Albert and, I assume, Milena.

'Hi, so glad you could make it. I hope you enjoyed the ballet?' says Tomas.

'It was fantastic, thank you.' I decide to keep the escapade with the hairy hand to myself.

The woman moves away from us and sits with Albert. She chats to him in Czech. They seem to get on well, considering what he has said about her.

Tomas points over to her. 'I'm afraid she doesn't speak much English. Only Czech.'

'Oh, no problem. A smile is universal.'

'So, I'll get you a drink, and why don't you take a seat while I finish off the Christmas tree?'

It surprises me that the tree is left until Christmas Eve, as I always used to have mine up by the end of November. But, as Tomas prepares a drink, he tells me this is their family tradition and that of many other Czech families. No wonder there hasn't been a tree up before now.

'Well, I'm quite happy to help you. I can't sit here and watch you do it. In fact, one of my specialities is decorating Christmas trees.'

'That's a speciality?' Tomas laughs.

'Yup, it is.' At least I used to be good at decorating our Christmas tree. I hope that I still have that magic touch.

I take a seat on the floor beside Tomas and pick out some ornaments from a box beside us that are wrapped in paper. I start to unwrap one of the baubles and think how they must have been passed down from Albert's parents as they are beautiful antique-looking glass-blown snowdrops and birds. The robin will fit right in. I lean over to the bag I brought with me and pass Tomas' gift to him.

'Here, I think you should have this now. Do you want to open it with your partner?' I look towards the lady I assume is Milena, but she is busy laughing with Albert.

'My partner?' Tomas laughs and says something in Czech, and then Albert and the woman laugh too. I am left out of the private joke, and my cheeks flush.

'That's not my partner. This is Zuzana, she lives next door. I'm sorry, I didn't introduce you properly. How rude of me.'

'Oh, okay. Sorry.' In that case, Milena must be joining us later.

'Nothing to be sorry for. She's very close to Albert. You do know she is in her seventies?'

I thought she was older than Tomas, but I would never have thought that she was more Albert's age than his. It must be all the good food in this country.

'Wow, she looks amazing.'

'So, you want me to open this now?' says Tomas, looking back at the present.

'Of course.' I watch his expression carefully as he opens it up.

'No way? Olivia, this is my favourite bird!'

I think about telling him about the robin back home but then decide I will probably start nervous rambling, so I stop myself and say no more.

He takes the robin and hangs it at the top of the tree in a prominent spot right at the front.

'I will treasure it,' says Tomas. His smile is so genuine that I believe him.

'I'd better give this to Albert,' I say, remembering his honey.

Albert seems pleased and clasps his hands together to thank me.

Zuzana says something in Czech to Tomas, and he blushes. My gosh, what did she say to the man? Then she looks at me and smiles. I have no idea what is going on here. That is the problem with language barriers. I wish I spoke Czech right now, but I ignore everything and carry on decorating the tree.

'Zuzana said you're a very pretty lady,' says Tomas, as I hang a bauble up on a branch.

Zuzana grins at me, looking pleased, and nods her head.

'Thank you.' I can't ever recall being called a pretty lady. Let alone since I turned fifty. That is so sweet of her. Aunt Grace used to call me pretty, but she was a relative, so she couldn't exactly say anything derogatory. Relatives never count when it comes to compliments. The best Craig could manage was calling me a 'fit bird' when he'd had too many cherry brandies at Christmas. Maybe Zuzana is just a nice lady and being polite.

Tomas says something back to Zuzana, and then I notice he blushes. I am intrigued. Did he just agree with her? I feel another of those little tingles down my spine at the thought.

Tomas looks back at the Christmas tree.

'Anyway, we're all done. Thanks for your help, Olivia. It looks like the best tree we ever had here. You're right. It's your speciality.'

'Oh, I'm sure I only put a couple of baubles on, it was all your own work,' I say.

Tomas touches my arm as he walks away, and that tingle happens again. I try to focus. This must not happen.

'Right, so who wants more drinks?' says Tomas.

I agree to have another glass of wine but tell myself that under no circumstances can I get carried away. The next thing I will be telling him how lovely he is, and we can't be having that when he has the mystical Milena.

Tomas gives us all refills and we clink our glasses together.

'Merry Christmas,' says Tomas.

'Merry Christmas, everyone,' I say. The image of that Christmas sign swinging back and forth as Craig slammed the door as he left flashes back into my mind. That was the last time I decorated. Now, this is a proper Merry Christmas, unlike back then.

When we finish our drinks, Tomas goes into the kitchen to serve up the food.

Then I hear his mobile ringing. He answers it, speaking in Czech. However, I can only understand the part where he uses the name Milena. As he cuts off the call, he throws his phone down on the worktop. His mood seems to have changed. Albert shouts something in Czech, also throwing in the name Milena.

'I've told him, he needs to stop her,' says Albert looking at me. It is as though he assumes I know what is going on. Does he think that Tomas has confided something to me? Because I certainly don't know anything about her, except that I have heard her shouting down the phone.

I shrug my shoulders.

Tomas starts laying the table with the feast that he has prepared. I can see that he is trying to keep a brave face, but he looks upset.

'Please, let me help you with the plates,' I say.

'No, it's fine. You're my guest. Please, you relax.'

I feel guilty sitting like a queen while Tomas does all the work. But I figure that perhaps he needs some space in the kitchen. I feel a bit awkward being a stranger brought into this. I hope nobody mentions the Milena word at dinner.

When Tomas puts down the final plate with a huge carp laid out on it, his mood has improved.

'This looks amazing, Tomas, thank you,' I say. I try to cheer him up as it looks like both of us have had a problem with someone of the opposite sex on Christmas Eve, although he is probably handling it much better than I did. At least he hasn't thrown a remote-control car at anyone.

'You're welcome. I hope you enjoy your first Czech Christmas Eve and I promise you will have a special day tomorrow too. Cheers,' says Tomas.

'Na zdrav!' says Albert.

Zuzana lifts her glass towards me and also chimes in with Na zdrav.

I lift my glass and attempt to say it, but it comes out nothing like the way they pronounced it. Instead, I stutter over the word. Thankfully, everyone smiles at my ridiculous attempt, and I get that warm feeling of being welcomed into the family yet again. Despite any language barriers, we laugh together all night, and, for the rest of the evening, the name Milena is not mentioned again.

Chapter Sixteen

On Christmas morning, my bed is so snuggly and warm that if I wasn't looking forward to a day with Tomas and Albert, I probably wouldn't want to get up.

I stretch my feet across to the other side of the bed and throw my arm onto the pillow beside me. I try to stop thinking about how I wish Tomas, with his dark curls, was lying on that pillow. I don't even know where the thought comes from. Perhaps my subconscious is trying to tell me something. It appears that all the desires I didn't allow myself to think about seem to be escaping. I desperately try to shake the image of Tomas before I force myself to get up. I need to get myself ready and suitably wrapped up for a river cruise along the Vltava that Tomas has organised for this morning.

Meanwhile, at the hotel breakfast, the staff are cheerful, and everyone is wishing each other a Merry Christmas. Tinsel is wrapped around a giant ice sculpture of a reindeer on the breakfast buffet, and I treat myself to the ubiquitous Danish pastries and chocolate muffins that are laid out beside it. There is no way I am going for the avocado on wholemeal toast on Christmas Day.

I am still tucking into the feast when Tomas turns up looking for me. We had agreed to meet in reception, but I have been so busy getting carried away with the buffet that I didn't notice the time.

I offer him a muffin, but he declines. I figure he eats healthier than I do. After all, you don't get a body with a washboard stomach like he has by eating muffins and pastries for breakfast.

'How did you sleep?' asks Tomas politely.

'Great. Like a log after all that fabulous food I ate last night. Albert is right. You're such a great cook.'

'Ah, thank you. I used to be a chef.'

'Oh, you never told me that before.'

'I studied food science at uni in Cardiff, but I enjoyed being hands-on in the kitchen. I like making people happy with good, nutritious food.'

I do hope he isn't too disgusted by my plateful of muffins. After all the time we have spent together, I didn't even know what his job was. We haven't spoken much about his personal life. Not even the story of Milena, which is getting more confusing by the minute. He certainly can't be serious with her or surely he would be with her on Christmas morning? Maybe this is my chance to learn more about him.

'So, you're not a chef any more?'

'It's a bit of a long story. With the cost of food at the moment, it's been difficult. But I'm opening my own bar soon. Time for a bit of a change.'

'That's amazing. I'm sure it'll be a wonderful success.'

For someone who is about to open a new business, he doesn't look too thrilled when he talks about it. He quickly finishes the coffee I ordered him and downs it in one go.

'Anyway, we'd better go. We don't want to miss the cruise.' For some reason, I get the feeling the bar business could be a sore subject, just like the name Milena.

'Oh, of course. Sorry, I've been enjoying breakfast a bit too much this morning.'

I try to resist throwing one of the gorgeous Christmas pastries in my bag for later as we pass the buffet table on the way out. I can't say I will have as much restraint when Tomas isn't with me though. But then I realise that I fly home early tomorrow and there won't be time for another breakfast here. That makes me feel incredibly sad. Never in a million years would I ever have thought that I wouldn't want to leave Prague, and if I am honest with myself, I don't especially want to leave Tomas either. I try to put it out of my mind and instead focus on enjoying what is left of my stay.

I take out my bright pink bobbly hat and pull it down over my ears as we walk towards the river. The temperature feels like it has dropped again. Maybe we won't have snow on Christmas Day as I had hoped we would. So far, there has only been a sprinkling while we were at the castle, although the clouds in the sky hint that there might be something on the horizon.

Arriving at the pontoon, I think at first that we might be in the wrong place. There are big boats, which appear to be ferries transporting people around, but the boat at our mooring is much smaller and more intimate. The captain greets us in a sailor suit and tells us that we are the only ones onboard today so we can set sail immediately.

'This is perfect,' I say to Tomas.

'Just wait,' he smiles.

As we set sail, a hostess comes up to us with a glass of champagne.

'Sorry, but I haven't ordered any,' I say.

'It was pre-ordered by your friend here,' she explains. Tomas smiles and then clinks his glass to mine, saying

Happy Christmas once again. I take a sip of the delicious, chilled bubbles as a swan swims alongside our boat. Then we head under a little bridge decorated with a Christmas garland, glass of fizz in hand. What an experience Tomas has introduced me to. I could get used to this.

Tomas' eyes light up as he looks at me and smiles with that beautiful grin. Then, he points out an empty building.

'You see that there?'

I look up to see a place that used to be a restaurant, with the menu stuck on the door and chairs on top of disused tables. Even though it is looking a little neglected, it is in a beautiful spot with its riverside location.

'This is where I'm opening my new bar next year.'

'Oh, it's going to be beautiful.'

'I hope so. A new beginning.' When he says that, I see the same look in his eyes that he has whenever Milena is mentioned. I wonder if the closure of his restaurant is to do with her. I have a feeling that something is definitely linking them both.

'It's good to have a new beginning sometimes,' I say, clinking my glass to his.

'For sure. Here's to new beginnings, Olivia.'

I could listen to him say my name all day with that bewitching Czech accent he has when he speaks his perfect English.

I may not know much about Tomas' background, and he doesn't know much about mine, but sometimes perhaps it is better that way. Who needs baggage?

As we weave our way along the river and through tight tunnels, the air gets chillier. The hostess brings blankets over to us, and we huddle under them with our chilled champagne. What a way to celebrate Christmas. This is heaps better than slaving over a turkey and then realising you forgot to put the spuds on, which is what I once did, despite insisting I was organised.

I look up towards the castle, the cathedral, and all the sights I have enjoyed on my trip, and that gloomy thought that I have to leave tomorrow reoccurs.

'I can't believe I'm going home tomorrow. We haven't even got through all the letters yet.'

'There are so many. Do you have to go home? I was thinking we could start them again this evening, and tomorrow perhaps. Is there any chance you can delay your flight back?'

'Oh, gosh. I hadn't thought of that. I'd have to check.'

'You know, I have a good friend at the airport. Which airline are you flying with? Let me see if he can arrange something for you. Lucky for you, airlines don't close on Christmas Day.'

'Really? You can do that?'

'Leave it to me. How about you stay until the New Year? We have a party every year on New Year's Eve. You're invited... Unless, of course, you already have plans back home?'

I pretend to think about it for a moment. I am usually in bed by 9:30 p.m. on New Year's Eve with a cocoa that I forget about that eventually gets cold.

'What about the hotel? It's not cheap, and it might be full.'

'Let me make a few phone calls. I'll let you into a secret. I used to be the head chef at your hotel before I started my business. I know the right people, and I still get discounts.' Tomas winks at me, and I wonder if any man on earth could be more gorgeous.

'You never cease to amaze me,' I laugh.

'So, if you can leave me to arrange everything, will you stay?'

'You know what? We do have quite a few letters to go through. Give your friends a call and see what they say. Why not?'

I feel excited at the thought of doing something so unexpected. This is so different for me. I never thought I would extend my stay. It means I still have to leave in a few more days, but at least I have a reprieve for now. Who knows, it might give Tomas and me the chance to get to know each other better?

As Tomas speaks on the phone to his friends at the airline and then the hotel, I drain my champagne glass.

'Would you like another?' asks the hostess. I would normally say no, but it's Christmas and a whole day intended for indulgence and sheer gluttony.

'Ooh, why not?' I smile.

By the time the hostess has finished pouring my fizz, Tomas has put the phone down.

'All sorted. I'm so pleased you can join us for our party.'

'Me too.'

As if by magic, the sky opens up, and flakes of snow drop down upon our boat. It feels like my every wish is coming true – snow on Christmas Day!

'Oh, Tomas. Thank you for arranging everything so that I can stay. And for this today. I've had the time of my life.'

Tomas smiles shyly. I notice how he always gets uncomfortable when someone hands him a compliment. He does the same shy smile when Albert compliments his culinary skills.

As the snow collects on the bow of the boat, I sit back and enjoy myself. The birds will still have plenty of seed left in their feeders, and nobody is going to miss me back home. I am confident that I made the right decision by extending my stay.

In fact, looking at Tomas as he gazes out at the river, I *know* I have made the right decision. I snuggle deeper into my blanket with the biggest smile on my face, even as I try to deny my feelings towards Tomas.

What I don't realise is that Tomas has arranged a further treat for us after our boat trip. I assumed we would visit Albert right away to wish him a Merry Christmas, but Tomas insists that he doesn't get up until late at this time of year. Not even the thought of opening more of the letters can get him out of bed on Christmas morning.

So, after we leave the riverside, we head back towards the Old Town where two beautiful white horses and a carriage are standing. It is just like the carriage I saw when I first arrived here.

'Your carriage awaits, madame,' says Tomas.

'We're going in this?' I am flabbergasted. This was not what I expected.

'It has to be done. You're not a tourist if you haven't done a horse and carriage ride around *Staré Město pražské*.'

I can't hide my excitement and clamber in, almost diving into the pink velvet seat for two. It isn't the most gracious entrance, and I dread to think what Tomas must have thought of me. But then, I haven't had much practise at climbing into a carriage.

As soon as we are seated properly, the horses start clip-clopping along the cobbled street. I feel like a princess in a horse-drawn carriage as people move out of the way to let us go ahead and tourists admire the scene. My cheeks start to hurt with all the grinning I am doing.

'Are you enjoying this, by any chance?' asks Tomas.

'It's amazing.'

We clippity-clop near the Astronomical Clock, the market stalls and the Christmas trees on the square. Since it is higher up in here than by foot, I notice pretty, decorated windows and Gothic arcaded houses that I missed when walking around. What a way to spend Christmas Day!

As we turn a corner, the wind catches me, and I try not to show Tomas that I am shivering. But I can't seem to hide anything from him. He is one of those people who notices everything.

'Are you cold?' asks Tomas.

'I am a bit.'

Tomas leans forward to the two empty seats in front of us and grabs a blanket.

'Here, put this over you.'

'What about you?' I notice there is only one blanket on board.

'I'm fine.'

'No, you're not. It's really cold.'

'Excuse me, driver, do you have any more blankets?' I ask.

'No, they got wet earlier with the snow.'

Tomas pulls the collar of his coat up towards his chin, and I feel terrible. It is such a lovely ride that I can't have him cold like this. I shift closer to him and spread the blanket over both of us.

'You'll just have to share this,' I say.

As we sit tight under the blanket, with the sound of the horse's hooves hitting the cobbles, more snow starts to fall.

'It's snowing again!'

'I love how enthusiastic you are about the snow,' laughs Tomas.

'Well, it's just the icing on the cake, isn't it? I mean, could this day be any better?'

Tomas looks at me seriously and puts his arm around my shoulder.

'No, it doesn't get much better than this.'

'I agree. This has to be one of the best Christmases ever.'

'For me too,' grins Tomas. 'For me too.'

Chapter Seventeen

At home, Boxing Day with Craig was normally spent in a food coma, trying to muster up the energy to clear up all the mess left from the day before. Then Craig and I would try to polish off more of the food that we had overestimated we would need. It is dreadful the amount of wastage that Christmas brings with it. But, here in Prague, we have none of that. Everything has been simpler and much more intimate.

Back at Albert's flat, the Christmas tree continues to light up the corner of the room, and I think how it is just the right size. It is simple but perfect and, I suspect, much easier to clear away than the seven-foot tree we used to get from our garden. At least there are no shed pine needles to discover for months afterwards when you have a small fake tree.

The three of us sit around talking about what a wonderful Christmas it has been before we begin the box of letters. Last night we stayed up late reading through the correspondence from Aunt Grace telling Marek what she had been up to and general news about our family. Now it is time to begin the next round of letter-opening. Tomas hands me a coffee and then passes over the box so that I can start going through them again.

'I'm looking forward to the next letter,' says Albert.

This one is dated two days before Marek had his accident. I tear at the unopened envelope and feel a mixture of emotions when I scan over the words. I am relieved that he never opened this one.

'*20 September 1994*

Dearest Marek,

I've tried to write this letter so many times, but all I ended up with was a piece of paper with splashes of mascara. When you finish reading this, you may understand why.

I am so incredibly sad that I find myself writing this, but I know that it is the right thing to do.

The past year we have had together has been truly incredible, even though we haven't managed to see much of each other.

I've looked forward to every letter you've sent me and every phone call we've had. To hear your voice and to see your writing fills me with joy. You are the most charming man I have ever known and to be with you seems too good to be true. Which, quite frankly, it is. I could dream about our relationship all day and think how things could be and how we could make things work, but I realise I am being foolish holding onto such hopes. The longer I leave our relationship to run along, the more painful it is going to be when we have to face the truth. At the end of the day, my life is here with my family and, in particular, my mother-in-law, Elsie.

I've given it so much thought, but I realise that she has nobody and since she had another catastrophic stroke a few weeks ago, I can't leave her for a sneaky London trip. That just feels sordid and incredibly irresponsible at my age. Don't get me wrong, you make me feel wonderful, but I want our relationship to be out in the open, in the sunshine, not hidden away, and that is something I don't feel I can do right now.

I have to do my duty and be a good daughter-in-law. It's how I was raised – to always help others and do the right thing. To be a good girl and all that. So, I am going to do the right thing, although it breaks my heart, and put a stop to our relationship.

You are one amazing man, Marek. I will always keep you in my heart, and I hope you will remember me with fondness as much as I will you. Having met you and the glorious way you made me feel is a gift I will treasure forever.

I'm sure you will very easily meet another love and have a very happy life. I would die with jealousy to see you with another, but I want you to find happiness with someone. That woman can sadly not be me.

My love always,
Gx'

I look up at Tomas, whose chin is trembling. Albert is looking for tissues in the box in front of him and I am finding it hard to stay composed. This is just tragic. She should never have had to sacrifice everything like this, but that is Aunt Grace for you.

'That's heartbreaking,' says Tomas.

'Yup,' I agree.

'Well, I'm glad he never read this. It would have broken his heart. Although I doubt he'd have given up without a fight. It was a bit late for all that. He'd already bought her that ring and was planning to propose.'

'Maybe Aunt Grace knew that things were getting too serious and started to worry,' I say.

'Yes, but if Marek hadn't died, then I think he would have flown over and found her and not given up. I really believe that.'

'Well, maybe she wouldn't have even wanted that to happen. She was too loyal to Elsie.'

'We'll never know,' says Tomas.

I look down and see the next envelope is still waiting to be opened.

'There's another one here. Shall I open it?'

'Yes!' shout Albert and Tomas in unison.

I am intrigued as to why Aunt Grace would write again a year after she broke it off with Marek. When I see the date on the postmark, I think I begin to understand.

'13 August 1995

My dearest Marek,

I hope that hearing from me again doesn't come as a shock. I wanted to pick up the phone to you but thought it might be better to write down what I have to say.

Perhaps you have met someone else by now and want to throw this in the bin. I don't blame you and completely understand if you never want to hear from me after what I did to you. I know you were talking about us getting engaged, but I just panicked.'

'I thought as much,' I say.

'Why would she panic about something so wonderful though?' asks Tomas.

'She was worried about her commitments at home. About Elsie.'

'If I've learnt one thing from these letters, it's that finding a special love is more important than trying to keep other people happy. If Tomas here met someone from another country, I'd give him my blessing. Even if it meant he leaves me here alone,' says Albert.

Tomas clears his throat and gives out a funny little cough. 'Yes, so, what else does she say?' he asks.

I look back at the letter and am glad to change the topic of Tomas finding love as I continue reading.

> *'I knew that I had to be at home. Putting Elsie into a care home wasn't an option for me. I'd never do that to family. Her son might not have been the kindest, but Elsie was a good lady who deserved to live out her days at home. I don't think she had it easy with Harry's dad either.*
>
> *I don't regret what I did, but now that she has died, my circumstances have changed. Goodness, this is so hard to say without sounding like you're second best.*
>
> *I totally understand if you've moved on, but if there is the teeniest chance that you haven't and would like to pick things up where we left them now that I am free of family commitments, then please would you write back to me. I do hope I will hear from you.*
>
> *I wish you all the best, my darling Marek.*
> *Always yours,*
> *Gx'*

Albert shuffles around in his chair, obviously feeling uncomfortable as the man who could have told her that Marek had died. I try to remember that he thought he was doing the right thing at the time.

'How sad that she spent all this time thinking that he didn't want to give their love another chance,' says Tomas. He looks over to Albert, who turns away and stares into the distance.

'What's done is done,' I remind him.

Tomas looks at Albert and back to me, then shrugs his shoulders.

'I think Albert already knows he should have told her, Tomas.'

What happened to Marek is so awfully sad. But maybe it was for the best that Aunt Grace didn't know the truth about how he died. She may have blamed herself for him trying to make extra money to get back to her, and I couldn't bear the thought of that. Perhaps it is better to have an unrequited love after all. It seems she always carried that shred of hope that they might get reunited one day, and that is what kept her positive.

I turn back to some of the letters that Marek had opened, which mostly talk about the family again. They are all jumbled in dates and show the depth of the love they had for each other as their relationship grew. It is also clear to see they have been spending a lot of time on the phone when Aunt Grace apologises for the huge telephone bill Marek has received.

'Oh look, here's a letter that mentions you, Tomas,' I say.

'Really?' Tomas shuffles closer to me on the sofa that we are sharing and leans in.

'Wow, what does it say?'

'Maybe you should read it?'

Tomas looks over the letter and smiles.

'It says how lovely it was to speak to Marek on the phone, usual sort of things, and then she says: *"How wonderful that your nephew, Tomas, is starting university in the UK. What an opportunity for him. He sounds like he has a very good head on him. What a sensible, hard-working boy."'*

'I was a little older than some of the other students, but I took the chance as soon as I could. Maybe that's why I was more sensible,' laughs Tomas. Then he looks back at the letter and starts reading further.

> *'I'm thrilled you told Tomas and the rest of your family about me. That's so kind. I hope you understand that it is a bit different for me, having not lost Harry that long ago. People around here would think I was some kind of harlot and never forgive me for moving on so fast. I suppose it is easier for you, having never been married. It is so much simpler when there are no complications.'*

'I know what she means about *complications*,' says Tomas.

'You, boy, make things difficult for yourself. In your heart you have the answer and know what you need to do,' says Albert.

Albert gives Tomas a look as though he is warning a naughty child to behave. I can't help but smile at how he treats Tomas even though he is a grown-up. I adore the relationship these two have together.

'Stop it, Uncle,' says Tomas, rather sheepishly. 'Let me read the letter.' He continues, 'She then says that she would love to meet us and that I sound as enthusiastic about everything as Uncle Marek.'

'Aww, it's nice that Aunt Grace compares you with your uncle, Tomas,' I say.

I certainly see the enthusiasm in him when he talks about the city he lives in and the love he has for Albert, even if they do bicker like an old married couple sometimes.

'She's right. Marek was always enthusiastic about everything. It's what got him into trouble in the end. He never worried and always thought things would be okay,' says Albert, looking slightly tearful.

'Are you okay, Uncle?' asks Tomas.

'Yeah. I'm fine. You know, I'm tired. I think I'm going to have a lie-down.'

'Do you not want to go through more of the letters?'

'No, I need a rest. You two enjoy each other's company. Make the most of each other,' he says.

'Oh, no, please, it's only lunchtime. Won't you have some lunch with us?'

'I'm not as young as you two. I didn't sleep well last night. Enjoy yourselves without an old man like me in the background.'

That's the first time I've been called young in a long while.

'Oh, please don't say that. We love your company.'

Albert waves his hand as he makes his way to the bedroom, dismissing my comment.

'See you in a bit.'

'Maybe I should leave. I don't want to disturb Albert if he's trying to have a sleep.'

'No. He likes his afternoon nap. Please stay, I'm sure he'd be happy to see you still here when he gets up.'

'If you're sure?'

'I am. Now, how about a lunchtime glass of wine? It is still officially Christmas, after all.'

I feel reckless as I agree, thinking of all the alcohol I have already drunk this week, but, as Tomas insists, it is still officially Christmas. He pours us two large glasses of wine. I will definitely be detoxing when I get back home.

'I'm so glad you extended your stay,' says Tomas.

'Thanks. Me too. I should be just about walking back into my house now, had I flown today. I can't believe you managed to fix the hotel and flights up for me.'

'Anything for you,' smiles Tomas.

I don't know where to look as he gazes at me.

'You know, you have a very beautiful smile. I'm sure you've been told that many times.'

'Well, no, not really. I don't like the gap. You know, here.' I point to the gap that separates my two front teeth.

'I was so self-conscious of it when I was in school.' I don't know why I had to say that. Why could I not just say thank you instead of giving him too much information? 'But anyway, that's very kind of you to say. You have, umm, beautiful eyes... And hair.'

Now, it is Tomas' turn to look embarrassed.

'Well, thank you. I'm so glad we met. I can't imagine if we'd never bumped into each other outside like we did. That would be sad.'

'It would indeed, but I suppose we'd never have known what we were missing out on.'

'That's an awful thought,' says Tomas.

He hands me my glass of that lovely Moravian wine, and I take a sip. I am definitely glad I met him, but I don't let on quite how much.

Being so close, I can smell that musky scent he wears again. It reminds me of the day in the lift, and I am not complaining about being in such close proximity again today.

'I really enjoy your company,' he says.

I feel a flutter in my tummy. I wonder if I should hint that I find him utterly irresistible. Am I brave enough to let myself go that much?

There is no time to decide as Tomas gets closer and closer to me until, finally, our lips touch. His kiss is soft and tender. I hold my hand up to his cheek. His skin feels so smooth compared to Craig's rugged complexion. I sit back and look at him. He is so incredibly handsome. Until now, I have tried not to acknowledge the beautiful, kind face he has, or those eyes and long eyelashes. I tried not to look at those defined arms that make me want him to hold me and keep me safe.

But before I can think any further about what I have tried so hard not to notice, Tomas moves his head away from me, and all my thoughts instantly shatter like a glittery glass Christmas bauble falling off the tree.

'I'm so sorry. I shouldn't have done that. I have someone I need to speak to before I can do this; her name is Milena.'

I look at him, not knowing what to say. From the little titbits I have heard between Tomas and Albert, I assumed he wasn't seeing her, or anyone else, for that matter. I get up from the sofa, desperately trying to remember where I left my handbag. I need to leave and am furious with myself for letting my guard down like that.

I fling cushions around until I find my bag. I throw it over my shoulder as the strap slips down over and over again. I am so annoyed that I brought the posh Christmas bag out with me today. I should have used my sturdy handbag that I take everywhere. I am not the sparkly person who carries a fancy Christmas bag. Who did I think I was trying to be? Living this romantic, adventurous trip, pretending to be someone I'm not. I am no Cinderella.

'I'm so sorry. It's just something I need to clear up,' Tomas shouts after me.

I don't want to listen to his apology and walk out of the door, slamming it shut. I forget that Albert is sleeping and am sorry that I could have woken him up, but I had to get out of there quickly.

As I go out into a freezing cold Prague, I just want to get back to my hotel.

Luckily, I remember the sign for the metro close to the apartment and run towards it. I ask for information and jump on the first metro heading in the direction of the town and make my way back. It is amazing what I can do when I am desperate to get out of somewhere.

While I walk towards the hotel, my phone bleeps, and I see that it is a message from Tomas. I read what he has to say for himself.

> I like you so much, but I have to sort my life out first. I'm so, so sorry.

Well, I'm sorry too. I am sorry I changed my travel plans because I was growing far too attached to a man that I obviously knew nothing about. It feels like some kind of Groundhog Day as Christmas is ruined by another man I trusted.

Chapter Eighteen

The days between Christmas and New Year are always like no man's land, but this year is worse than ever. I have no itinerary, no plans, and I am stuck in Prague until I am due to fly home. I curse myself for getting so carried away. What a fool I am.

All I need now is for Dewi to ring. I couldn't cope with his cheeriness as I want to curl up and hide inside my hotel room for the next few days. I feel as though everyone downstairs will be laughing at me. Do they all know that I am the idiot who fell for the chef who used to work here with the volatile girlfriend? It sounds like something from a really clichéd holiday romance. Am I that lonely to almost fall for that old trap?

To make things worse, I suddenly remember that I have a touristy medieval dinner booked for tonight. It seemed like a good idea when I was happy and relishing being a tourist, and I had the extra time after extending my stay in Prague. Now, not so much.

I ask myself where it all went wrong. Tomas was the one who kissed me, but I should have asked him straight out if he had anyone in his life, rather than allowing myself to get swept away with the idea that Milena was a thing of the past. This has happened all because I didn't want to think about any emotional baggage he may have. I wanted to live for the moment for once – but look where it has got me.

Thankfully, I never made a move on him, despite wanting to in the horse-drawn carriage as we huddled under the blanket. I do my utmost to blame him for all of this. After all, he knew more about his situation than I did.

As I munch on my room service meal, I call the airline to change my flights. I am very happy to swap a flight home for the planned tourist excursion I have booked, so I wait patiently on hold for the airline to pick up the call. Of course, they finally answer just as I put the biggest crust of bread into my mouth. I swallow quickly and, with desperation, tell them that I want to be on the next flight out of here.

I feel sure there must be seats available as most people will have travelled by now for the Christmas break. I beg the agent for any seat she can give me.

'I'm afraid the first date available is the second of January and you're already booked on that one,' explains the reservation agent.

It seems I didn't plan for the fact that everyone is travelling back home after the holidays.

After pleading and telling her that I really must get home, I realise it is futile. Unless I am strapped on the wing, I am not going anywhere.

It is no use trying to get out of here; the truth is that I am well and truly stuck in Prague. I thought being spontaneous would be exciting and that I could be a new, less cautious version of myself. But now I realise why I always try to be so sensible. Things go wrong when you are not cautious. I am so angry with myself and wish I could get my axe right now and take all my frustrations out on the pile of logs that are waiting for me back home.

I can feel a tension headache throbbing at my temples and just want to be at home with some painkillers in my own bed. But that is impossible. The room is starting to feel suffocatingly hot, so I grab my woolly hat and prepare to go outside. I keep my head down all the way through reception, hoping that nobody I pass is any of Tomas' contacts from when he worked here. For all I know, he may even have laughed with them about what happened last night. Why did I have to stay in the hotel he used to work in, where he knows everyone?

I walk out towards the Christmas markets despite all my festive excitement having drained away. However, I soon realise that I should have stayed hidden in my room because as soon as I get outside, I spot Tomas. What are the chances of that? Surely, he should be with Milena somewhere.

I quickly try to duck into a shop doorway, hoping that it is open and I can hide and pretend that I want to buy some of the speciality cheeses that are on display. Unfortunately, the shops haven't yet opened, and so I stand in the doorway with nowhere to escape. I am cornered like a frightened rabbit. I try to turn my back to Tomas, but it is obvious that he has seen me.

'Olivia, hey.'

I turn around slowly, wishing I could pull my hat over my eyes and hide.

'Just wanted to buy some cheese.' My neck does that thing where it reddens and goes all mottled whenever I lie, and I am thankful for my stripy rainbow scarf that hides it.

'I'm so glad I caught you. I was coming to the hotel to speak to you. We need to sit down and talk about last night.'

'Do we?'

'Yes. Please come and have a coffee with me and listen to what I have to say.'

'It's best we don't.'

'I'll treat you to a hot chocolate instead… with cream? I know a great place.'

'I really don't think we should discuss anything. Hot chocolate or not. Your poor girlfriend!'

A couple walking past look at us and, rightly so, stare at Tomas.

'Please, I have to explain. Don't make me beg you out here in front of everyone.'

'What is there to say? I've been taken for a right fool.'

'Just one hot chocolate, and you don't ever have to speak to me again.'

Finally, I give in, despite knowing that there is nothing he can say that is going to make me feel better about last night. As we walk towards the cafe that Tomas suggests, we don't utter a word. It is awkward between us, to say the least, and it makes me wonder why Tomas has even bothered coming here to look for me.

After checking which toppings I want, Tomas orders our drinks at the cafe, which has cute little tables and gingerbread men on display. It is a cosy, warm place, and the horse from the carriage ride we took trots past the window. If I was in a better mood, I would be quite keen on this place. Right now, it annoys me how Tomas always chooses the places that are just up my street. He stirs his coffee over and over until the point comes where I want to grab the spoon from him, but then he finally speaks.

'It's going to sound terrible, however I say this,' he starts.

'It is,' I agree. I take my spoon and stuff a huge blob of cream into my mouth.

'So, the thing is…'

'Yes?'

'Sorry, you've got a big bit of cream stuck on your lip.'

Tomas points to my lip, leaving me embarrassed, and I quickly grab my napkin to wipe it away.

'So, I should explain. Milena and I had been dating for five years. We ran a cafe together, and it was so popular that sometimes we'd have a queue outside the door. Yet, suddenly, we were making a loss. I asked the staff why this could be. I felt terrible as I started to blame a new guy who had started. I became paranoid that he was saying things to put people off, or taking something from the till. I couldn't understand it. The staff told me things about Milena, but I didn't believe them. Milena can be bossy, so I thought they were just stirring up trouble. Am I making sense?'

'No, not really.'

'Sorry. So, they told me she'd treat the place like a hangout for her friends. She gave them drinks and food on the house. I still had to pay for all that stock. Milena likes to be the popular one, so you can imagine just how much free stuff she gave away.'

'Okay.' I'm not sure what he expects me to say, as I don't see how this affects what happened last night.

'I installed CCTV because I didn't believe Milena would treat the business like that. It turned out the staff were right. Milena wasn't bothering to help around the place, and her friends filled seats that paying customers could have taken up. We were full, yes. But most of them weren't paying. Milena was just sat on the side of their

167

tables, leaning over and laughing with her friends. It's like they were using me. I didn't realise. I trusted her to get everything sorted while I went to the wholesalers and promoted the business on social media and stuff. By the time I arrived, it always looked as though she'd been working hard. I guess it was partly my fault because I took her word over my loyal staff. Also, I should have been there myself. I got caught up in everything that goes with running a business.'

'Well, no. You're the boss. You should be able to leave people in charge when you're not there.'

'Yes, well, Milena insisted she was fine with running it. Then I could see why.'

Tomas takes his mug in his hands and then puts it back down. Clearly, he hasn't finished ranting about Milena.

'This might sound silly, but what hurt me more than anything was that Milena didn't care for the business like I did. That place was my dream. Do you know how hard I worked to set that up? All those late nights I worked at the hotel. I saved and put everything together so I could start my own business. The day I opened the cafe was the proudest moment of my life. It was everything I always wanted. She threw it away, all because I trusted her. She didn't care about my dream.'

'Well, for sure, sometimes we trust the wrong people and don't listen to the ones we can trust.'

'Exactly right. I told everyone the business closed because of the cost of food, but that is the truth about what happened. Milena didn't care for the business and ruined it. I heard she was also rude to customers. I know she can be a bit abrupt, but you have to get to know her. I had words with her, but whenever I said anything, she would accuse me of being mean.'

'Why do you make excuses for her being rude? She doesn't sound very nice, and she's obviously hurt you badly.'

'I know. Uncle Albert has no time for her. I decided that enough was enough. We split up. But she says she's sorry for what happened and wants to give it another go. No matter how many chances I give her, she always does something to spoil our relationship. I am done with her, but she won't take no for an answer. She keeps giving me time to change my mind and thinks we could get back together. It's over between us, but she refuses to listen. I hate being mean to people and don't want to be stern with her. We have a lot of what you could call "water under the bridge" but, until she accepts things, it's difficult to move forward.'

'Well, I can understand. It's not easy coming out of a relationship, and the last thing you want is to…' I stop before saying 'jump into another relationship', since this isn't something that is necessarily on the cards.

'I guess it's not as easy as it sounds. I suppose I should explain. Milena and I grew up together. Our parents knew each other. In fact, she was there for me when my parents died. She held my hand at my parents' funeral when they both died in a car accident. She made sure I ate and got out of bed for the days after. It was such a shock to lose them both at the same time. You see, Milena isn't all bad. She helped me get through that time. That's why I always feel indebted to her, despite everything. Then she did all of these things after we opened the cafe. I don't know. Despite all of that I feel like I owe her because she helped after my parents died. Albert gets mad with me sometimes, but he's a harder man than I am. He likes to say things as they are, while I perhaps, what do you say, "sugar coat" things not to upset people.'

Tomas reaches his hand across the table until he touches the tips of my fingers.

'I don't want to be someone who seems confused about my feelings. That would make me a terrible person. I wouldn't treat you like that. But I didn't expect to feel the way I do about you, When we went on the boat and the horse and carriage, I told myself I was being a good host, showing you the country I am proud of... I know that's not true anymore. So, that's why I have to tell you the truth. I need to sort things out with Milena properly first. That's why, as much as I wanted to kiss you so much last night, I had to stop myself. I need to have a clear conscience that I have done nothing wrong, and I'm not giving anyone the wrong impression. I guess it's time to stop sugar-coating things.'

I think of Craig and how he behaved. I suppose I am at least grateful for Tomas' honesty. I also realise that we have another thing in common when faced with something we don't want to deal with. It seems we both have a habit of trying to keep others happy at the expense of ourselves and making excuses instead of being firm.

'Well, thank you for the explanation.'

Tomas strokes my hand.

'Can we please be friends and stay in touch after you leave? It's so strange, but now that we have met, I can't imagine you not being in my life. Does that make me sound weird?'

If it does, then we are both weird because, as I accept his explanation, I realise that I feel the same, even if we only remain friends. There is definitely a connection between us, whatever it is.

'No, it's not weird. For sure, let's stay friends.'

'Definitely. We still have to get through the box of letters, and Albert isn't going to let you get out of it that easily.'

'It's hard to know if he wants to hear what the letters say sometimes. I don't know if he's getting upset by them, and I really don't want that, Tomas.'

'No, I know. It's emotional for him, of course. But, also, he kept this secret about knowing about the letters for years. I mean, he never told anyone, and deep down, he knew it was wrong and that he should have written to your aunt to tell her. He's carried a bit of guilt with him, and now I think he feels it is closure.'

'I'm glad of that.'

I finish off my hot chocolate and think about where I should go next. Now that I am no longer following an itinerary, I have no plans until I go to dinner this evening, but I don't tell Tomas that.

'By the way, I hope I didn't ruin today's plans for cheese shopping.'

'No, not at all.'

'I'm not doing anything now. Would you like me to take you to a place where I used to get the best cheeses for my business?'

'Oh no, it's okay. I don't need any. I was just looking, really.' I actually get migraines after eating cheese, so it was very unfortunate that he caught me in the doorway of a cheese shop of all places.

'Then, may I suggest something? If you don't think it's forward of me?'

'Sure.'

'How about I take you somewhere really fun? To make up for last night? There won't be alcohol involved, so I promise not to get carried away again.'

'What sort of fun?'

'Do you trust me?'

After last night, who can be sure, but being with Tomas always makes me feel adventurous and so I agree. On the condition that he doesn't try to kiss me again. Although, as I say it, I feel regret about how we have such a wonderful connection that seems so complicated right now. But, if Tomas can put the attraction we have to one side, then I am sure I can too.

Thirty minutes later, Tomas introduces me to a fat-wheeled electric scooter called a Scrooser. With my lack of balance, I protest that I won't be able to ride it but he assures me that it isn't difficult. I tie my helmet on extra tightly in case I immediately fly off it and flip over the handlebars. Tomas seems to have complete faith in me, though, and as I start to move off, I wobble about until I slowly get the hang of it. For the first few minutes, I am full of apprehension, but, as we ride side by side on a quiet road, it becomes so much fun. I never thought I would ever see myself on one of these! As I let myself go and zoom around the streets of Prague, I take in more new scenery. I pass little boutiques I never noticed before, and I am tempted to stop and look at their gorgeous window displays. A bright gold sparkly bomber jacket catches my eye, and I come to a halt so that I can get a closer view.

'It would suit you,' says Tomas.

I shrug off his comment. It would have suited the old me, but that was the sparkly sequin-loving Olivia.

'Go and try it on,' pleads Tomas.

'No. It's not my kind of thing.'

'Don't you at least want to take a look?'

I jump back onto my Scrooser before Tomas can insist any further.

'No, it's fine. It's very beautiful, but we'd better get back. We only rented these for an hour,' I say.

I glance back at the jacket one last time. It is rather lovely.

On the way back to the Scrooser rental, Tomas leads me uphill and then further along the streets that have views of the city. Whatever angle I look at this place from, it feels magical. Despite the cold wind hitting my cheeks, I laugh with joy as we whizz about, passing old brownstone buildings and then colourful stonework façades. As we cross a bridge, Tomas shouts at me to look at a hugely asymmetrical contemporary building. It is impossible to miss as it's so different to the usual baroque and Gothic architecture that I have got used to around here. Its windows appear uneven, and its modern glass façade is incongruous with the rest of Prague. It is certainly a statement piece, with a huge twisted metal structure on top, like some kind of crown. We stop for a moment to look at it.

'That's called the Dancing House,' says Tomas.

'Wow, it's fabulous. Is that because the sculpture looks like it's dancing? I suppose it does, really.'

'Yup. It's like Fred Astaire and Ginger Rogers dancing. Sometimes it's called "Ginger and Fred" too.'

I smile at Tomas.

'You know, maybe you should forget the bar. Be a tourist guide instead. Hey, I know what you should do. You should be one of those people who combine food and tourism. You know, like, ride around on a bike with tourists and do some kind of culinary bike tour. Oh my gosh, you must!'

Tomas smiles and grins.

'Look at you, caring about my career. I already signed the lease, but that's a brilliant idea. One day, maybe.'

'Oh, you have to. You'd be so perfect at it.'

'Come on. Time's running out. Let's get these back,' says Tomas, changing the subject.

Once we return the Scroosers, Tomas suggests we head over to Albert's to go through more of the letters. I agree that we should probably get through some before my dinner tonight.

When we arrive at Albert's he seems so happy to see me; he is almost relieved. I begin to wonder if he knows about our tiff yesterday. After all, I did slam the door. Despite having done that, Albert welcomes me and tells me how pleased he is that I have returned. Somehow, I get the feeling that Tomas and Albert chat about everything, including me.

Settled down with our usual coffees in front of us, I look at the next letter from Aunt Grace. This time, it's dated four months after they last saw each other.

But just as I am about to start on the letter, the intercom buzzes from downstairs. Tomas answers it, and I hear the voice of a woman. He immediately buzzes her in.

'It's Milena,' he says.

'This woman is no good for you. I've told you this so many times,' says Albert. Since he says this in English, I get the feeling that he is saying it for my sake rather than Tomas'.

Either way, Tomas ignores him as he goes to answer the door. I get up to leave. I don't want to be here when she walks in despite being unable to hide anywhere at this point. I begin to wonder how big Albert's wardrobe is.

'Please don't leave because of that woman,' says Albert.

'No, I must be going anyhow. I booked a medieval dinner for this evening. I don't know what I was thinking sitting here. I really should start getting ready or it'll be a bit of a rush.'

Milena walks in as if she has come off a catwalk. She wears skintight pleather leggings and has a fake fur coat wrapped around her. Even if I tried to imagine a beautiful woman as my love rival, I couldn't have imagined this. She is stunning. She has the darkest long hair, and as much as I search for split ends, there aren't any. Not even frizz from being out in the cold air. This woman looks as though she has some kind of superpower when it comes to her hair. Either that or Czech hairspray is unbeatable. But I remember what Albert and Tomas have said about her. Maybe she isn't as perfect inside as she looks on the outside. Still, I feel like shrinking into the wall as she sees me when I attempt to walk past her. It was obvious she couldn't exactly miss me.

'Hello.' I think she may have actually purred that out. Even her voice is as smooth as her locks.

'Hello, I'm just off.' I try to smile at her, but she eyes me suspiciously.

'You don't have to leave,' says Tomas.

'No, I do. I have a dinner and… Well, I'll let you two catch up.'

I close the door behind me and wonder exactly what they will be catching up on. Has Milena come dead set on mending the remnants of their relationship? This thought hits me right in the solar plexus.

Chapter Nineteen

Carol singers in the market croon like Christmas cherubs as I make my way to the medieval dinner. Now that Milena is with Tomas, perhaps my plans for this evening aren't as dreadful after all; at least it will take my mind off everything. Although I can't help but snigger to myself with a teeny bit of satisfaction as I imagine Albert sat on the sofa listening to every word and possibly causing mischief. I know I shouldn't be so wicked.

Meanwhile, at a candlelit tavern on the other side of town, I am welcomed with a five-course all-you-can-eat-and-drink menu. The way I am feeling this evening, as I think about Tomas and Milena together, I may drink as much as I can.

I order my first jug of wine, which tastes like something that is definitely reserved for tourists. I am not sure the higher echelons of society in Prague would enjoy this stuff, but I don't complain. Right now, I'll take anything to numb all the different emotions I am feeling.

As I tuck into my medieval banquet and bite down on a chicken drumstick, two pirates with swords fight in front of me. They whip them around, and I flinch as one of the swords gets a bit too close for comfort. I feel the air whoosh around my head as I duck down and the sword flies back up into the air. I wonder what the relevance of all this is. After all, it is hardly authentic when there can't have been many pirates swashbuckling around landlocked Prague.

Then, a belly dancer sways her hips in my face. I clap politely, but, really, I am desperate to pop the next chicken drumstick into my mouth.

Next, a magician comes out and asks for audience participation. I put my head down. *Not me, please. Don't pick on me.* Isn't it funny how, by looking down, you think you can hide from someone? When I look up, he is pointing right at me. He is like one of those annoying teachers I had at school who picked on me as I shrank down at the back of the classroom, not wanting to be seen.

'Madam, pick a card, please, and show everyone what it is,' he says.

Oh no. There is a restaurant full of people. Why me? I look around and see everyone watching me closely. I tell myself to choose a card and just get this over with. Of course, nothing is ever that simple, and I manage to pull the card out, lift it to show everyone and then drop it on the floor. As I go to pick it up, I bang my head on the table. And this is why I hate audience participation! I rub the right side of my head and see that everyone is still gawping at me. Finally, the magician takes the attention off me for a moment as he shows the audience the card I picked, and everyone gasps. I am sure I saw him pull it out from under his sleeve, but I don't want to make another scene.

With the trick finally over, I breathe the biggest sigh of relief and return to my jug of wine and the not-very-Czech chips that have arrived and are already cold. But, as I sit alone, the memory of Milena comes back to haunt me. I wonder if they are fully made up now. What if they are going to announce their engagement as they decide to never let each other go, after all? Why does there always have to be someone prettier, more talented, or more... whatever, out there? I remind myself that I must not think like that as Milena has known Tomas a lot longer than me, who has only just shown up in the country. She has known him most of her life; I have only known him for, what? A week? Plus, she was very kind to him after his parents' demise. They have a bond, and I need to accept that.

A juggler takes my mind off Milena as he comes out to entertain the crowd and juggles some fire clubs. With all the candles around here and the fire juggling, I do hope they have the fire brigade on standby. It does look impressive in the dark, though, with all these flames, so I pick up my phone to take a photo.

I see there is a message. It can only be from one person, as I'm sure even Dewi is off duty until the New Year. I hesitate before reading the message.

Hi, are you okay? You rushed off.

I'm fine. I didn't want to be in the way of you and Milena.

I take a sip of my wine and notice that Tomas is already typing. Milena didn't look like the type of person who would put up with someone beside her not giving her attention and being on the phone all night.

178

> You should have stayed.

> No, you two have a lot to sort out.

> Yeah, I guess we do. I'm finally going to get things sorted with her. Anyway, I just wanted to see if you were okay and wish you goodnight.

It's not even 9:30 p.m.; he must be exhausted if he is going to bed already. Or is he off out with Milena to "get things sorted" and is saying goodnight now so that I don't think of disturbing him? What am I thinking, trying to work out what is going on over there? It's none of my business what he is doing.

I message back.

> Goodnight

I put my phone back into my bag and tell myself that I won't think any further about the messages. He has things to sort out with Milena, and quite rightly so. Still, the fact that he has checked if I am okay has lifted my spirits somewhat, and I find myself starting to enjoy the show a little more. One jug of wine later and I am even up dancing with the belly dancer.

When I sit down because my hips aren't trained to do such boisterous movements and I worry I may need a hip replacement if I carry on, I see a light flashing in my bag.

My phone seems to be ringing. I can't answer it with the noise of the music and people talking so I ignore it, even though I can see that it is Tomas who is trying to get hold of me. What on earth can he want now? I hope Albert hasn't had one of his falls or anything.

I message him back, explaining that I can't talk as I'm in a rowdy place, but he can text me. Immediately he starts typing again.

> Sorry, I didn't realise you were out. I forgot you said you were going for dinner. It's okay. It can wait until tomorrow.

Oh, how I hate that! He might be able to, but I can't wait until tomorrow. I am not that type of person. If someone starts something, I need them to finish it, or I will overthink all evening.

> Is it Albert? Is he okay?

> Yes, he was snoring on the sofa when I left him and came home.

> What is it then?

> It's silly. It's nothing. Honestly, I just couldn't sleep and wanted a chat.

180

Well, I'm not surprised at this time. It's too early for bed.

Yup, you're right. It's just one of those days when I need an early night. A lot on my mind. Can I pick you up in the morning to finish the letters? Around 10?

Yeah, sure.

Perfect. See you then, Olivia.

I return to watching the belly dancer, who is now in a different costume, and finish off my wine. I wish I knew what was going on in Tomas' mind. Maybe I should call that magician back and ask him if he can mind-read in return for my participation.

By the time I get back to the hotel, all I can think about is Tomas. I was never looking for love or any relationship with anyone and had isolated myself to make sure I would never get hurt again. Yet, he has managed to work his way into a part of my brain – or maybe my heart – and he stays there no matter how hard I try to blank him out. Maybe it is because he is unattainable in a way. If you can't have someone, then nothing can happen, and they can't hurt you. Although something tells me that isn't true. Whatever is between him and Milena needs to be sorted out. I expect that if Albert got his way, he would make sure Milena never contacted Tomas again. Albert is a nice man;

he is not the type to detest someone unless he has good reason. But I guess managing to destroy your nephew's dream business counts as having good reason not to like someone.

As I lie down in bed, I struggle to sleep. I begin to wonder if Tomas has managed to sleep yet, or if he is tossing and turning in his bed too. But, if he is, it is probably his relationship with Milena that is troubling him and certainly has nothing to do with me. So why do I feel that the attraction between us is so strong?

We have something between us that I never thought I would feel again, and I sense it coming from him too. Aunt Grace and Marek had a similar connection after a short time, despite such different backgrounds, and now we do too. I rest my head on my pillow and fall asleep, wishing that things were different. If only Milena was not in the picture.

Chapter Twenty

I switched my phone off early so that I would resist the temptation of sending any drunken messages to Tomas. That certainly wouldn't look good, plus Milena would probably strangle me and sit on me with her strong muscular thighs. So, when I finally get around to looking at my phone, I find a message that Tomas had sent shortly after he said goodnight. Perhaps he didn't sleep well after all.

> Hope it's okay if I pick you up at nine-thirty instead? I have to visit the bar later, so will be busy in the afternoon.

It is already 9 a.m.! Yikes. I find myself panicking as I look around the room for something to wear. I am in such a rush to get ready that I throw on some jeans with my Christmas jumper. I would prefer to look my best for Tomas, but I don't have time to iron any of the stuff that got crumpled in the suitcase. Besides, my Christmas jumper might help cool down the passion between us.

I rush downstairs to meet him and only just catch my breath when I see him. I immediately see that look again. His eyes light up, the smile he gives me seems to radiate from the heart, and he greets me happily by kissing my left cheek. I kiss him back. Every time I see him, it gets harder to ignore all these signs.

'So, how was last night?' asks Tomas.

I could ask him the same, but I am not sure that I want to hear what he says. So, I tell him all about the dinner and the performers who kept me entertained whilst I sat there alone. Of course, I don't admit that I banged my head on the table and made a right fool of myself with the magician. I would prefer him to think I am a bit cooler than that.

Back at Albert's apartment, Tomas holds the entrance door open for me like the true gentleman he is. 'Lift or stairs?'

I hate that claustrophobic lift, but it is also my one chance of being close to Tomas. I tell myself to take the stairs, but it just doesn't come out like that.

'Lift,' I smile.

Since we can only just about stand side by side in it, our hands brush each other's as the lift jerks upwards. I wish my body would stop automatically wanting to press closer into him. The lift moves slowly, and my hand smacks Tomas on the bottom as he shuffles around. Oh my gosh. I swear that was not on purpose. I stand there sweating. What do I do? Do you ignore something like that or come clean and apologise? My mind is in overdrive as I think about what to do. It is not like I can blame someone else in here for the terrible mistake. Do I acknowledge it? Or is it better to hope he doesn't notice? Oh no. I am horrified. Of course, he noticed.

'Sorry,' I say.

'Sorry for what?' asks Tomas.

I knew I should have pretended nothing had happened. I can't say out loud that I have just touched him accidentally and inappropriately.

'Oh, just sorry I banged into you. It's a bit cramped in here, isn't it.'

Tomas smiles politely, and I begin to wonder if he has any feeling in his bum. Perhaps he didn't notice after all.

When I see Albert, all thoughts of Tomas and his numb bum are soon banished.

'Good to see you,' he says. Albert seems to be in a very good mood today, and I become curious about last night. What if Tomas had some kind of final row with Milena and she is never coming back and now it is all *sorted* as he says? I imagine that would certainly please Albert.

'I hope Tomas has told you about his New Year's Eve party. Please tell me that you'll still be here for it?' says Albert.

'Yes, I'll be coming. Maybe I won't be able to stay too late though. I'm normally in bed early on New Year's Eve.'

'Nonsense. You'll have to stay until the early hours with me in case nobody wants to talk to the old man.'

'Of course, they'll want to talk to you.'

Albert shrugs his shoulders and smiles.

'It will be great to have you there. It's the one night of the year that Albert dresses up in his black tie,' says Tomas.

'I like to make the most of it. You never know when it will be your last,' says Albert.

'What have we said before? You're as strong as an ox,' says Tomas.

'Well, I shall look forward to seeing you dressed up, Albert.'

'I'm so happy you stayed on for it. You'll have a chance to see my new bar before you fly home. I don't quite have everything I need, but I'll try and make it look okay for the party. That's where I'll be this afternoon. I have to start cleaning it out and getting it ready.'

'Oh, if I can help, I'd be happy to.'

'No, you're my guest. That wouldn't be polite of me.'

'I don't mind. It's not like I'm doing anything.'

Then I think what if Milena is there? What if things were sorted with Tomas to her favour? Three's a crowd and all that. For all I know she could be trying to make amends for the last business she ruined and doing her utmost to help him.

'I want you to enjoy the sights of Prague. You're our guest here. You shouldn't be working and helping me.'

I would very much like to be working beside him, but I try to bury any salacious thoughts.

'Well, I'd love to see your new venture. After my last tourist excursion, I had considered doing a ghost walk this evening; but I don't think I'll bother now.'

'A ghost walk! You don't believe in all of that, do you?' says Albert.

'Well, I don't know. Some things can't be explained.'

'Like what?'

'Like the fact that we're all sitting here now, brought together by death,' I say.

'That's not a ghost, is it? Your aunt sent you here,' says Albert.

I want to tell him about the robin who appears from nowhere. It is comforting to believe we are sent messages, especially at Christmastime, when we miss those who have passed on more than ever. Albert seems as though he is the type to put it all down to nonsense, though, and I certainly don't want to fall out with him over our different views. So, I don't mention anything further and turn my attention to searching in the box for the next letter and open up a random envelope. I notice that this letter is six months after they first met.

'2 January 1994

My dearest Marek,

It was wonderful to celebrate Czech New Year with you, even if it was from what feels like the other side of the world. I am sorry I had to rush off the phone, but Elsie was shouting and kept asking who I was on the phone to. You'd never think I was a woman in her fifties, would you!

After I put the phone down, Elsie and I had a game of dominoes together. I'm quite sure she cheated. Sometimes, I do wonder if she is quite as ill as she claims to be, but I know she loves living with me since Harry died. Do you know dominoes? If not, I'll show you when we finally meet up. Although, somehow, I don't think we will be playing dominoes together.

Did you mean what you said on the phone? That this will be our year? Wouldn't that be a lovely thought. It would be wonderful to see you again.

Your mention of an engagement so soon was a beautiful thought, but it took me by surprise. A lovely surprise, and something I would very much love. How about we wait until it's been a year together and then commit to each other? Please understand that I need a little more time because of all the family commitments. I know you said that life is short, and I can't argue with that, but

what if we spoil the magical thing that we have? I
couldn't imagine how awful that would be.

> *We were so busy talking about us that I forgot*
> *to ask how your family are? How is young Tomas*
> *getting on at uni? I do hope he's enjoying some*
> *Welsh hospitality in Cardiff…'*

As I see what comes next, I stop reading the letter. 'That's
it, then, it just says the usual, "*With all my love, forever*",' I
say.

I keep the letter in my hand, making sure nobody reads
the rest of it. I quickly glance down once more, checking
that I really did read that correctly. I look over the words
that shock me to the core as I read it the second time
around.

> *I have to confess, I wish Tomas could have bumped*
> *into Olivia. From what you tell me about him,*
> *they'd be perfect for each other.*

Trying to compose myself, I think how I can hide this
letter. I don't want Tomas to see it. Things are complicated
enough between us as it is.

'Did you want another coffee before the next letter?'
asks Tomas, getting up and heading towards the kitchen.

'Oh, yes, please. My mouth has suddenly gone very
dry.'

Chapter Twenty-One

The moment Tomas reaches the kitchen, I ask Albert an innocuous question about an ornament on the Christmas tree to make him look the other way. Then, I crush the letter into a ball and sneak it into my pocket.

'Which decoration?' asks Albert as he turns back to look at me.

'Oh, that one,' I point. 'I thought it was a snowball, but now I can see that it's a swan. Sorry. You know, we saw some swans on the canal.'

'Yes, Tomas told me what a nice time you two had on the boat. But, you may need to get your eyes checked if you think that's a snowball,' laughs Albert.

Tomas told him how nice it was? What else did he say?

Although, more importantly, I breathe a sigh of relief about the letter being safe. I am sure Aunt Grace wouldn't want to embarrass me like that in front of Tomas.

The good thing is that at least I have some forewarning that she is discussing the two of us, and now I can screen the letters before I read them.

I lift out a letter that was lying underneath the one that is now safely in my pocket. I almost start shaking when I read the words. I look at Albert and Tomas, who are staring at me intently, waiting for me to speak.

'Sorry, I need some coffee.'

I feel my hand shake as I put the mug back down. I am only grateful that it is not a fragile cup and saucer, or I would probably have smashed it into smithereens. I have to press the letter down on my lap to read it out loud, as I am shaking far too much to hold it in my hands.

'15 October 1993

My dearest Marek,

How many months will it be until we will see each other? Perhaps I should start marking off the days on the calendar. I can't wait to see you again. We'll book somewhere special to stay in London. I know you're saving to come over, but I am saving from here too. I want to make sure that we can have the most special time. I think we both deserve it after being apart.

Oh, Marek, can I tell you again how much I love you? I never thought I could feel like this about anyone, let alone after just a few months of knowing you. I don't know why, but I thought love was just being with someone and knowing them inside out. What we have is nothing like that. I can't stop thinking of you every moment of every single day. What we have is something that doesn't come along often. This is once in a lifetime. I realise now what I have missed out on all those years I was married to Harry. I am scared of what the future will hold with our different lives, but if it is meant to be, then we will find a way.'

At this point, I stop reading aloud. I look up at Tomas, who is clearly thinking about something and smiles at me.

Then, I silently go back to the words that jumped out at me when I picked up the letter. I read over the paragraph, taking each word in like a stab in the chest.

> *I'll have to tell you about my dear niece's boyfriend one day. She's so young, and so I pray it's not serious with this Craig chap. I'll tell you more soon, but she's in for trouble if she stays with him. I do hope Tomas is more sensible when it comes to love! They are a worry, these youngsters. You just want to protect them, don't you?*

'All this reading is making me exhausted. I think we need a break. Do you agree?' I say.

I must stop here. I have no idea what else she will say in her letters about Craig or me. I need to read the letters alone.

'You know, a lot of these letters are the same, really. Don't you think? I mean… All they do is tell Marek how much she loves him. Do we need to open the rest of them? I could dispose of them all if you like. Perhaps the hotel has a shredder.'

Even as I say this, I know I am being so terribly dishonest. But these letters involve my private life now. This is different, and ultimately, they are my property.

'You can't shred those letters. They meant so much.' Albert looks appalled at the suggestion, and I wonder if I should have worded it differently.

'No, of course.'

I stare at the box and wish I had X-ray vision and could see what was in those remaining letters.

'Okay, I've an idea. How about I take some of the letters back to the hotel with me? It's just that it makes me feel so close to her reading these, and there are so many memories here. I can open them and tell you what they're about?' I feel a tinge of guilt as I say it.

Tomas looks at Albert and then at the box. 'Hmm, there are a lot left to read.'

'Sure, but if there's anything important that we should know, you'll tell us, right?' says Albert.

'Of course I will.'

Before Tomas takes me back into town for a quick look inside his new bar, I rummage through the box full of envelopes. I am desperate to find the letter that could perhaps tell me what Aunt Grace really thought about Craig, and I shove my hand around as if I am trying to find the best prize in a tombola.

I scoop up a pile of letters and stuff them safely inside my bag.

'Okay. Are you ready to leave now?' asks Tomas.

'I am indeed.'

Tomas gives me one of his breathtaking smiles, and I melt. I am spending far too much time with him, and as much as I try to ignore any feelings, it is becoming harder and harder. Especially now that I have learnt Aunt Grace would have been a matchmaker between us if she could have.

When I look at Tomas with that smile of his, I wonder if that is how Aunt Grace felt when she looked at Marek. This family certainly has an irresistible genetic makeup.

We eventually say our goodbyes to Albert and head to the bar. When we get to the front door, Tomas is like a child opening a Christmas present. He seems to finally be getting over the fact that his last business failed, and I am pleased to see him so excited about the new venture. In fact, he fumbles with the keys and drops them as he is so eager to open the door for the first time. He only got them this morning from the landlord, and I can see that he can't wait to get inside now that it is officially his.

As we stand looking around the bar, Tomas takes me by surprise by putting his arm around me. A shiver runs right through me at his touch.

Aside from how I feel about him, I'm glad of his reassuring touch as the bar looks like something from a haunted house. I wouldn't want to be on my own in the dark in here. It's full of dust and cobwebs. It's as though it was forgotten in time with its old-fashioned ceiling corniches and dark wooden bar area. I'm glad I didn't bother with the ghost walk. Who needs one of those when you can come in here?

'So, this is my new bar. Do you like it?' He is grinning like a Cheshire cat now.

'It's fabulous. I definitely see its… potential.' His enthusiasm is infectious, and I can't help but feel excited for his new venture, despite it clearly being a work in progress. If enthusiasm makes a business work, then he will certainly make this a success. Even though the place is covered in dust now, a little imagination is all it will take. Although I can see that it is going to take some work to get this place sorted to have a party here in two nights' time. I don't know how he plans on getting it ready by then, but I can't let him do it all by himself while there is no sign of Milena or anyone else helping him.

I point over at the dilapidated bar area.

'Please, Tomas, will you let me help you get this place sorted? I know you said you wanted me to enjoy the sights of Prague, but I'm happy to help clean up the bar for you. A bit of elbow grease, and we'll have this place ready before you know it.'

'No, I would feel terrible letting you help me.'

'Not at all. Anyway, it can be a thank you for showing me around Prague and for all those coffees and the fabulous food you made for me.'

'Hmm.' Tomas looks over at a corner of the bar that seems like it hasn't seen a mop for years. 'I have to admit, there is a bit more work than I thought there would be.'

'That's settled then. I've not got anything planned for tomorrow. We can work on it all day. I'll stop by the supermarket near the hotel and pick up some cleaning products.'

Tomas peers at me from over his glasses. It is the first time I have seen him wear them, and he really suits them. Can this man please be less perfect? It is becoming infuriating.

'If you're sure it's not a problem.'

'Not at all. I've had a wonderful holiday, and you have taken me on so many lovely trips around the city. The least I can do is to help you out and get the place ready for your party.'

'Well, I appreciate that. Thank you.'

I leave Tomas to look around for a while. It's important I return to the hotel to open the letters. I can hardly wait, and the moment I get back to my room, I throw them onto the bed and start reading.

As I guessed, many of them are in a similar vein, telling Marek all about Wales and Grace's daily life. In one of the letters, I am shocked to learn that she had always dreamt of joining a local rock band as a backing singer, but Uncle Harry wouldn't dream of allowing her. I knew she had a beautiful voice and belonged to a local choir up until she was almost eighty. I wonder what other dreams Uncle Harry held her back from.

21 November 1993

Dearest Marek,

I hope all the family are well there?

How's Tomas getting on? Will he be back with you for the Christmas holiday?

After we spoke, I took your advice and told my sister Julie how worried I was about Olivia. She didn't seem to have the same concerns as me though. She always has been wrapped up in her own world. She said it was up to Olivia what she does with her life. But I'm so worried she will end up in a marriage like I did. I don't know why, but she seems besotted with this Craig. Something about him reminds me of Harry at that age, and that's what scares me. I suppose that Julie is her mam, and if she isn't worried, then perhaps I am being a bit over-protective. I can't help it, though, when Olivia has always been like the daughter I wished I had. I just want her to have the best life and not follow in my footsteps.

Oh, Aunt Grace. You were the best aunt anyone could ever have wished for. You always cared for me so much. I think back to the beloved hobby horse she surprised me with when I had my tonsils removed. My mother wasn't as happy as I was, though, and told her off for being irresponsible as it would mean that I would want to jump on it and hop about after just having an operation. They compromised, and Aunt Grace kept it at her place until I was fully recovered and ready to use it. If I am honest, a lot of the time I got on better with my aunt than my mother. I suppose being an aunt is easier than being a parent though.

I fold the letter up and put it in my suitcase to take home with me. There is no need for Tomas and Albert to know about this.

I am apprehensive as I pull out a letter from an opened envelope in case it contains anything else unexpected. What if there is some kind of devastating secret about my own family? But as I open the envelope, I see it is a Valentine's letter.

12 February 1994

Dearest Marek,

Happy Valentine's my love. I wish we were together to celebrate, like I always do when it's any occasion. I hope it's not long until we see each other. It's strange, but over the past week, I've been having the same dream over and over again. I see your face when we said goodbye as you had to travel back home. Isn't it weird that I keep seeing the same thing over and over? Your face is crystal clear, and you look sad. In my dream, we both hold our hands out to reach each other, but somehow, no matter how far we try to stretch, our hands just won't touch. What do you think it means? Perhaps it is just my subconscious reminding me that you're over there and I am here.

Or perhaps it is because I am a bit worried at the moment. Elsie is in hospital, having had a stroke. The doctors think she may need full-time care now. She won't be able to be left alone, which means I don't know how I can escape to London if you come over. They will provide us with carers to help, but I will have to see what happens. I am

trying not to worry too much. It's all very early
days.

Oh, my dear Marek. It's as if the universe has
other plans for us sometimes. Anyway, I want you
to know that I love you more than life itself. Why
does life have to be complicated?

Her words remind me of how I feel about Tomas. Yes,
Aunt Grace, I agree. Why does life have to be so complic-
ated? I open up the next letter that I have and look down
in shock.

16 May 1994

Dearest Marek,

I hope all the family are well.

I had to write to you as I feel you're the only
one I can confide in, and I'm in a bit of a panic.
You remember how I told you that I don't like that
Craig, who Olivia is seeing?

My stomach starts churning immediately. I can already tell
that I am about to learn something I might not want to
know.

Well, I saw him coming out of a house not far
from mine. A young woman in a Chinese-style
silk dressing gown was kissing him as he left! I
knew I had to tell Olivia. So, I planned on telling
her when we were due to meet up the following
day. She rang me and said she had important
news, and I was relieved. I thought perhaps she
had found out for herself what a little toad he was
and wanted to tell me that she had broken up with

him. What could I say when, instead, she turned up, the happiest I have ever seen her, flashing a silver engagement ring!

Oh, Marek, how my heart sank. I was torn between wanting to protect her and not wanting to spoil her wonderful news. So, I kept quiet, and I know I am so wrong. I only hope that time will show her what he really is like. What would you do?

I throw the letter down on the bed in shock. Why didn't Aunt Grace tell me? She always wanted to protect me yet let me carry on. Of course, she dropped hints, and I always knew she was no big fan of Craig, but I just didn't pick up on it. To think Craig was already cheating when we got engaged! Would she have told me had I not broken the news of our engagement that day? I feel sick that she never told me. Why would she not protect me from making such a big mistake? Maybe my life would have been completely different had she told me the truth. But I do understand why she didn't want to be the one to break my heart. We were always so close, and Aunt Grace only gave me happy memories, never sad ones. She always made my dreams come true, not shattered them. I thought I had already had my fair share of surprises when I received the letter from Dewi informing me of the will. This is a completely earth-shattering one that now involves me. Although, it also makes me come to terms with the fact that Craig was always a snake and so I mustn't waste a moment of my time on my past and must only move forward from here. I could resent Aunt Grace for not telling me, but I don't. In a really foolish way, she was trying to stop me from getting hurt, yet it was the opposite in the long term.

That's enough for one day. I put the letters back on the dressing table and feel a mixture of emotions. On the one hand, I am happy that Aunt Grace had such a wonderful love in her life after what she must have endured with my uncle, but the feeling is mixed with sadness because I have learnt something about my love too.

Chapter Twenty-Two

The following morning, I resolve that this is a completely new start. The past is behind me, and I must take steps to live my life to the fullest.

As Christmas music blares out from the speakers at the supermarket, I sing along. It takes me by surprise how much I am starting to feel the love for Christmas tunes once again instead of desperately blocking the sound out when I hear anything remotely jolly. I have never felt more positive despite the earth-shattering revelation in the letter. I try not to think that maybe this could be because I am excited by the fact that I am about to spend the day with Tomas in his delightful company.

I pop the cleaning products I expect we will need into my basket and then drop in a chocolate snowman that has been reduced now that Christmas has passed.

I am in such positive spirits that by the time I arrive at the bar to help with the cleaning, even the thought of scrubbing the floors and dusting down the walls doesn't faze me. Anyhow, I could probably do with having a bit of physical activity before I chomp on the snowman.

When I see Tomas, he is dressed more casually than usual and looks ready for the task at hand. As always, he gets away with whatever he wears, and his scruffy torn jeans and blue jumper look good on him. I glance at the glimpse of skin that flashes through the worn jeans and notice that he doesn't even have knobbly knees. Oh, come on, universe! Please give me something that makes him not so blinking perfect.

Tomas puts on an Eighties Christmas CD and my heart skips a beat. Surely, he doesn't like Eighties Christmas music too.

Even though I have a mop in my hand, I wiggle about and dance to the sound of Wham! I feel like the lady in that old Shake and Vac advert. Before long, the floor is sparkling, and it doesn't feel as though I have been grafting for a couple of hours as I have enjoyed listening to the music so much – and sneaking a look at Tomas from time to time.

I lean against a table that is now gleaming and unrecognisable and admire how well we have transformed the bar from a few hours earlier. It could be a different place, and Tomas agrees.

'It looks like new. What a great job we did,' he says, looking around.

'I know. I hope you took photos of how it looked earlier so you can look back at all you've achieved.'

'Ah, I forgot as I had so much on my mind. No worries. But, you know… Now it's done, after all that hard work, we must have some fun. How about we christen the bar?'

'Christen the bar?'

'Yes, with a drink.'

I look around, bewildered. He doesn't even have any stock here yet.

Tomas searches in a bag he brought with him and pulls out a bottle of what he calls *Slivovice*. It looks quite potent, and I don't even want to check the alcohol content. He pours it into two glasses that have been left behind by the previous tenant of the bar.

When I taste the *Slivovice*, its potency is the last thing on my mind. It is gorgeous and tastes of plum brandy.

'Ah, I needed that,' says Thomas as he drinks it down in one. Then he pours another immediately. Yikes, I won't be able to keep up with this pace.

I sip at my drink as we relax. It feels like I am seeing Tomas in a completely new light in this environment. It is just the two of us in this bar all alone in a private space, and there is no Albert, Milena, or even Zuzana from next door popping in. Tomas is more relaxed than I have ever seen him.

'Oh, before I forget, I have to ask you something,' says Tomas.

'Sure, what is it?' Tomas could ask me practically anything, and I would probably say yes.

'Albert called before you showed up and asked if you wanted to go for a meal with us as a family. Tomorrow. Zuzana would like to come too. They said it would be nice for us to all go out.'

'Oh really? Yes. I'd love that.'

'Cool, I'll make the arrangements.'

'That's so sweet of Zuzana to want to come too. Have Albert and Zuzana known each other for a long time?'

'Yeah, since they were kids, really.'

Tomas tilts his head to one side and looks at me with a curious smile.

'Why are you so interested in Zuzana?'

'Oh, I just want to learn more about all of you. It's just that with the language barrier, I didn't really get to speak with her. I was intrigued.'

'I don't think there's much to say. Albert and her sister Vania dated, and then they split up. He always said that he got on better with Zuzana than her sister. It's good that she lives next door to him. Everyone needs someone they can count on.'

As he says this, he focuses his eyes on me and leans forward. His voice softens. 'I'm so glad we met.'

'Me too.'

Following a moment of silence, I can't stop myself from asking him more questions. I feel I want to know all about him, and it seems like the perfect opportunity to quiz him about his past as we sit here alone. I just keep the subject of Milena out of it.

'Have you ever been married?' I ask.

'Wow. I wasn't expecting that.'

'Oh, sorry, it was just in my head, and I was curious. I shouldn't have asked.'

'No, it's fine. I was, but that was a very long time ago. It was a mistake for both of us. We were too young and didn't have the same goals in life. We were too different.'

I think of Aunt Grace saying I was too young to settle down with Craig. Maybe Tomas and I both made the same mistake.

'We should never have settled down. It was a young and foolish love. It's so different now. I mean, now, I'm looking for someone with the same interests to grow old with, you know?'

Tomas stares at me again, and I have to avert my eyes before I blush. *Someone to grow old with* suddenly sounds very appealing.

'Sounds good.'

I lift my drink up, which I vow will be my last, and clink against his glass.

'To next year, new beginnings and someone to grow old with.'

'What could be better?'

Tomas drinks up and pours himself another. 'Do you think we need some food?' he says.

'I've got just the thing.' I search in the bag for the chocolate snowman and push it towards Tomas.

'It's all yours,' I say.

'No, we have to share,' he insists.

He breaks off a chocolate arm and stuffs it into his mouth. It is so nice to see a man appreciate chocolate as much as I do. This was well worth the thirty koruna.

'Good choice,' says Tomas, waving the half-eaten snowman around.

'I love the chocolate here. Well, I love everything here.' Thankfully, I stop myself from adding, 'including you'.

Looking around this little bar, I can see its full potential and how wonderful it is going to be. I feel sorry that I won't be able to enjoy it as I head back home.

'I'm really going to miss Prague.'

'And Prague will miss you.'

For a moment, our eyes do that thing again where we look at each other and it is as though we are the only people in the whole world. The vintage espresso machine in the corner could blow up, and I don't think either of us would notice.

Chapter Twenty-Three

All through the next day, I can't stop thinking about the way Tomas looked at me as we sat alone in the bar. Perhaps it is just as well that tonight we won't be left alone at dinner. The presence of Albert and Zuzana should help stave off any romantic feelings.

Tomas arranged to pick me up to go to the restaurant, but as I hang around outside the hotel in the cold there is no sign of him. I begin to wonder if there has been a change of plan when I finally spot Tomas sprinting along from wherever he has managed to find parking.

'Olivia! I'm so sorry I'm late. The traffic was terrible. Everyone's leaving work to get home before the expected snow comes in.'

'That's okay. Don't worry. You look as though you've been rushing. We can take our time, it's fine.'

'Thanks. I really didn't want to leave you freezing out here waiting for me, so I'm going to have to quickly pop back to mine to pick something up. Do you mind if we swing by my house on the way to the restaurant?'

Tomas' face is getting pinker, and I don't know if it is because he has been rushing so fast or due to the cold, but he certainly looks flustered.

'That's no problem at all.'

I know I don't want to be left alone with Tomas for fear of falling for him further, but I am quite interested to see where he lives. So, secretly, I am glad that he is running late and we have to stop at his home.

As we drive out of the city, the magnificent views of the castle and all the sights come into view as the snow starts to sprinkle down like a fairy tale. Luckily, the traffic that Tomas talked of is all going in the opposite direction, and we soon reach the warmth of his home without a hitch.

I wasn't sure what his house would be like, but I can see right away that it has almost as much character as the mill and I am glad that we had to swing by. I always think seeing where someone lives gives you such an insight into their character.

It is painted a light yellow and has little wooden windows peeping out of the roof tiles where there is an attic room. The garden, just like at my mill, is full of apple and pear trees, although they are quickly being covered in snow.

'I hope you like it. It's an old house that I renovated,' says Tomas.

As we walk into the hallway, I first notice the low wooden beams, followed by a varnished staircase and shelves with antique ornaments that would look quite at home back at the mill.

'It's absolutely gorgeous. I love that people renovate old places and give them a new lease of life. It's a passion I have.'

'Me too,' smiles Tomas.

Why is it that every time I find out something new about him, it makes my feelings deepen?

'Don't tell me you watch DIY programmes on TV too. You know, those programmes where they renovate properties?' I ask.

Tomas raises his eyebrows and gives me a wide grin. 'I absolutely love them.'

'How did I know you were going to say that? They're my favourite. I have to stop what I'm doing every day at five o'clock to watch my favourite chateau DIY programme.'

'Oh, I'd love to renovate a chateau. Now that would be a goal in life.'

I shake my head in disbelief. Why do we have to have so much in common?

'Do you want to see my cellar?' asks Tomas.

If anyone else asked me that, I might well have a panic attack and think they wanted to lock me up, but seeing Tomas' cellar is an invitation I can't miss. I have never been in one before, and I am in awe as Tomas takes me on a tour around. One dark corner of the cellar is full of red and white wines, and I realise that Tomas must be quite the wine connoisseur, something I didn't know until now. Then again, in his line of work, I suppose that shouldn't be such a surprise.

'It's amazing. It's like a secret wine grotto down here.'

Tomas takes out one of the vintage bottles and tells me how he has been saving it for a special occasion and this is what he needed to pick up.

'I think tonight is special enough to open this. Luckily, you're allowed to take your own wine to the restaurant we're going to.'

I have never tasted a proper vintage wine before and worry it might be full of cobwebs. But I am sure Tomas knows what he is doing.

'Do you know what year it's from?' asks Tomas.

'Oh, I wouldn't have a clue. You're the wine specialist. I'm ashamed to admit this, but I just choose the cheapest at the supermarket.'

Finally, I have found something that we don't have in common, but I'm sure I could be persuaded to convert my ways.

'Well, it's from 1993. The year my uncle met your aunt. I thought it would be appropriate.'

'Tomas, that's so thoughtful. What a great idea. Goodness though, does 1993 qualify as vintage nowadays?'

'You'd be surprised,' laughs Tomas.

When Tomas goes to the bathroom before we leave, I take a closer look at my surroundings. Of course, I don't peek into drawers and things, but I look around the living room at the photos I didn't have the nerve to pick up when he was standing beside me. I pick up a silver frame.

Tomas looks so happy in every photograph as his smile radiates out. Even in the photos of him as a child in the Seventies, that big cheesy grin is unmistakable. He seems to have this positive outlook on life that shows on his face, and it is one of the things I adore most about him.

I look at the abstract paintings he has hanging on the walls. They are all bright and sunny and, I expect, reflect his disposition. Even his house is yellow like the sun. Everything here is so colourful, including the sofa and the bright blue throw that lies across it. It is such a happy home. It reminds me of the colour scheme back at the mill. It's almost a home from home. I peek through an open door to another room and see that it is his study. I look up on the wall to where his university degree certificate hangs. The university that brought him to Wales, where we sadly never met. We were so near, yet so far.

I wonder how different things would have been had we met there.

'Are we ready?' says Tomas, catching me with a photo of him in my hand with two people who are presumably his parents.

'Yes, of course. Sorry, I was just looking at this. Mam and Dad?'

'Yeah, it wasn't long before their accident.'

'I can see the resemblance. They look lovely.'

I could stay at Tomas' home all evening, but we are already running late for dinner.

We leave the house and drive through the lovely suburb he lives in, with its hip art galleries and cafes. It is quite a trendy area, which surprises me given that Tomas' house is tucked away and more traditional. Street art on the side of buildings blends in with the shop fronts, and I spot a painting of Charles Bridge in a shop window. It is the type of place I could definitely enjoy walking around, window-shopping.

When we reach the restaurant, Tomas holds the door open for me. I can't help but enjoy a bit of chivalry, even if that does make me old-fashioned to some.

I don't know if Albert chose the restaurant or Tomas, but I am delighted by its charm. A waiter leads us to a quieter table in the corner with dim mood lighting that reflects against the burgundy and gold damask flock wallpaper. The pristine white pressed tablecloths make me think how I wouldn't dare have something like tomato soup in here. The restaurant is packed with locals, and I can imagine Aunt Grace coming here with Marek, had they made it. I think how this might have been their favourite place, and they may have even come with Albert and Zuzana who are both already seated at the table. They get up to give me a hug as we greet each other. We chat about the snow, and Tomas tells Albert that he managed to pick up the vintage wine when Albert proposes we make a toast.

'I think we should celebrate Marek and Grace bringing us all together, don't you?' says Albert.

'I agree. If it wasn't for them, we would never have met Olivia,' says Tomas.

'Very true,' I say.

'Let's not waste time. Let's open the wine and make a toast,' says Tomas.

The waiter brings us wine glasses, and Tomas tells me about the corkage fee they have. It seems other tables around us have also brought their own wine. I love the idea of bringing your own drink.

I read the label on the wine one more time. '1993. A good year.'

'Indeed,' agrees Tomas.

'To Aunt Grace and Marek,' I say, holding my wine glass up.

'To Grace and Marek,' say the others.

We take a sip of our drinks and have a moment to remember them.

'What was your favourite memory of your aunt?' asks Tomas.

'Ooh, there are so many. That's a difficult one. I loved how she treated me like a daughter, especially after my mam had died. Even though she was grieving her sister, she was there for me. I loved the way she bought me the best Christmas presents. She always knew what I'd want. Like the time she bought me the hobby horse and a Tiny Tears doll that cried. Now I look back, I'm not sure why I ever wanted a doll that cried.'

I smile as I remember the doll that I used to push around everywhere, as if it were my own baby.

'What about you, Albert? What's your fondest memory of Marek?'

'Like your aunt, he was very generous. The way he bought those snow globes for us on his school trip. Of course, I didn't realise he took one back though. He could be naughty when he wanted to,' Albert smiles.

At this, we all raise a giggle around the table, even though Zuzana doesn't quite understand us.

'But, I'll never forget his face when he told me about Grace. He looked more alive than I'd ever seen him. He'd never found the one for him, and then, finally, when he didn't expect it, he did, and look what happened.'

I stretch my hand out to touch Albert's. 'I'm so sorry for what happened,' I say.

'It's nobody's fault. I realise that now. For many years I felt bitter. It was the rock and the river that took him from us. Nobody was to blame. You see, I told you, he could be naughty sometimes. He had a mind of his own. He was determined to sell anything to get back to Grace, even the trout from the river.'

'He sounds like a character, and we all know he was much loved,' I say.

'Yes, he was,' says Albert.

'And look what he did. Strangers from far away meeting because of Marek, all these years later,' says Tomas.

'It's lovely, isn't it,' I say.

'For sure. We're all here together, and I wish I could thank Marek for this,' says Tomas. He looks over at me and smiles as he says it. I smile back at him fondly. 'Learning so much about my uncle and meeting Olivia has meant a lot to me,' says Tomas to Albert and Zuzana.

'That's nice. You really mean that?' I ask.

'Of course. I mean, how else would I have got the bar ready for the party?' teases Tomas.

Albert and Zuzana are smiling as they watch us.

'I just can't believe I have to leave. I know I extended my stay before, but now I really have to go home.'

'What's stopping you from staying on?' asks Tomas.

'Yes, what's stopping you?' asks Albert.

I couldn't possibly stay here any longer. The idea is absurd.

'I have a home in the UK. The mill takes a lot of work to run. The pipes will be frozen. I mean, there are the gardens and badgers, the birds... Who would feed the birds?'

It takes a lot of work, especially since I have to do everything myself. In some ways, it would be nice not to have to chop wood and, instead, have a home with proper central heating. But it is home for me, and the thought of selling up because I am enjoying a holiday a little too much would never happen. Once it's gone, I can't get it back. I belong in Wales. I'll also have my inheritance when I return, and I need to decide what to do with the next chapter of my life. Sat here, I realise that I'm ready to start my life again, and this time around, I am not wasting a moment on worrying what people think of me.

'Besides, I'd have nothing to do here. I've done all the tourist stuff now,' I say.

'I need some help at the bar,' says Tomas.

'Yes, he does need help,' says Albert.

I look at the two of them, who have obviously been plotting together.

'I would certainly need more persuading than that.'

'Will this persuade you?' says Albert, pouring more wine.

'Hmm, you're heading the right way,' I joke.

Thankfully, everyone drops the subject when our meal arrives. We enjoy our Czech dinner with pork and potatoes, and it makes me think how much I will miss this glorious food. The more wine I drink, the more I want to stay in Prague. Do I really want to rattle around the mill on my own when I could be here with this lovely family? But, the truth is, Wales is home.

As I sip on the last of my wine, Tomas leans over to me.

'I meant it. I'm so glad we met. I was just teasing you about needing your help to get the bar ready.'

'I know.'

'I'm going to miss you when you've left,' says Tomas.

I don't tell him that I am going to miss being with him more than I have ever missed anything in my life. Instead, I smile and pretend that I am fine about going home.

'Let's try not to think about it. We have a New Year's Eve party to enjoy tomorrow first,' I say.

I lean over to him and give him a hug, which feels like the most natural thing in the world. If only I could stay holding him like this forever.

Chapter Twenty-Four

I sink into bed in a dreamy daze. You would think I'd be more sensible at this age, but Tomas makes me feel like a love-struck teenager every time I look at him. I tell myself I have to get a grip. I toss and turn and can't sleep as I think about my feelings for him. It annoys me that we have so much in common, that Aunt Grace thought he sounded perfect for me all those years ago and that I can't keep track of what is happening between Tomas and Milena. Exactly what has he sorted out between them? I have purposely avoided the subject because I am afraid of the answer. Everything about Tomas gives me conflicting feelings, from the biggest crush I have ever had on a man to frustration that it is all so complicated.

Eventually, I grab the remote and pop the television on to take my mind off things, but I can't find an English channel and soon turn it off.

I look across to the pile of letters on the dressing table that I still haven't read and consider doing some bedtime reading. But after having seen the letter about Craig, I feel hesitant to pick them up. It is all in the past.

Despite my reticence, I get out of bed and flick through them. Do I really need to know anything more? I come to the conclusion that I don't. Except, when I look at one envelope in particular, I feel compelled to read it. Perhaps it is the pretty bluebells embossed on the stationery that remind me of the bluebell woods near the mill, or the fact that the envelope looks slightly more padded out than the other letters. I can't help myself from taking out the letter from inside the opened envelope and promise myself that I will not read another after this. Then I see the photos inside. They are photos of Marek in London. In one of them he is standing in front of Big Ben with Aunt Grace. I expect Silvie must have taken these photos. He was every bit as distinguished as Aunt Grace described him. Some would say he was dapper-looking with his handkerchief in the pocket of his blazer and the cravat around his neck. I am not surprised Aunt Grace had never met anyone like that before. I read the letter that comes with the photos.

1 June 1994

Dearest Marek,

I have included some photos that Silvie took when you were in London. She finally went to get her camera film developed after all this time! I asked her what had happened to the photos, but she took forever to get the film developed. That's the problem when you buy a roll of thirty-six!

Anyway, I have copies from her negatives, so this is your set. I kissed the photo of us outside Big Ben before I posted it. It was so wonderful to see these photos. A marvellous memory. Oh, how I miss you. Some nights, when I wake up in the middle of the night and can't sleep, I wish you were next to me in bed. Those nights in London sleeping together meant the world to me. The memory of feeling our skin touch side by side all night has kept me company on these lonely nights.

I put the letter down. Perhaps I shouldn't have read that part. But then a name jumps out at me as I fold it back up.

> I meant to ask about your conversation with Zuzana. She sounds very lovely, and I'm glad you have someone so caring to confide in. Did Zuzana really think that we should...

Oh, my goodness, Zuzana is mentioned in the letters too. I wonder what Aunt Grace knew of her. But after that, there is a big watermark, and I can't read what it says.

Would it be incredibly nosy of me to corner Zuzana at the party tomorrow and tell her about the letter and ask her what she thought Aunt Grace and Marek should do? By the next morning, I can't stop wondering what Zuzana thought of Aunt Grace. I know we mostly just smile at each other because of the language difficulties, but I am sure I can ask her what she knew about her somehow. It would be nice to learn a bit more. Maybe she would like to see the photos too. I put them safely to one side.

—

In the morning, I decide to visit the Strahov Library, as Tomas has suggested, and see the Premonstratensian monastery with its collection of preserved books.

Like everything I have seen in Prague, there are beautiful views of the city around me, and the historic monastery is no different. The church brewery on the grounds comes as a pleasant surprise too. But, as I go inside the library, I am taken aback by its magnificence, and even better is the fact that there are apparently around 200,000 books here. I thought my to-be-read pile was big!

As I am taken on a tour around the baroque-designed Philosophical Hall, it seems that it isn't only families who have intriguing secrets, but buildings too. Amid walnut and gold-plated shelves, hidden behind fake books, is a spiral staircase that leads up to the second floor. No wonder Tomas calls it the most beautiful library in the world. My local community-run library is nothing like this. Well, they certainly don't have ornate scenes from Greek mythology and philosophy on the ceiling like this place does. In fact, their ceiling is about to collapse, and I will be putting some of the inheritance towards their fundraising.

After a full tour of the library, I have to tear myself away from all the books and head back into the centre of Prague. I take a walk along Charles Bridge before going to the hotel. The cold is making my nose go red, and I shield my cheeks with my mitten-covered hands to try and warm my face up. Then I pass the statue that Tomas showed me previously with the dog. I remove a mitten to touch the dog for a little extra luck for the forthcoming new year.

Once I have stroked him and walked a bit further, I accidentally head off in the wrong direction and find myself at Lovers Bridge. I remember from what Dewi told me that this was the place where couples sealed their love with padlocks. However, Tomas told me that it is frowned upon now as the locks rusted away, and it was terrible for pollution as people carelessly threw the keys into the Devil's Channel below. I had originally considered it to be a great way to somehow seal Aunt Grace and Marek's love together, but this is not a sensible option. I will think of something to do to tie them together one day though; I owe them both that much. They may not have stayed together in this world, but somehow, I want them to be connected again.

I stop for lunch at the Christmas market near the hotel since I can't resist the smell of onions being fried. This market does terrible things to my appetite, and I have my eyes on the doughnut stall next. I find a bench and watch people walk around the market as I eat the tasty Czech sausage with onions.

By the time I eventually reach the hotel, I am grateful for the fierce heat that greets me in the lobby. The temperature has definitely dropped further today, and not even my long red coat with its fur collar is keeping me warm. It is Baltic outside.

As I loosen my scarf from around my neck, my favourite bellboy rushes up to me.

'Madame, there is a package for you.'

'A package?'

'Yes, it came this afternoon.'

I take the package from him and squeeze at it. It is squidgy, almost like when I received the Christmas jumper from Dewi. Surely, he hasn't sent me another. But there are no postage stamps. This is a local delivery.

In the lift, I look at the parcel. What could it possibly be?

As soon as I reach my room, I tear open the paper. Inside, something is wrapped in lilac-coloured tissue paper with a heart-shaped sticker keeping it in place. Sequins reflect through the paper, and as I remove it, I can see that it is the sparkly gold sequin jacket that was in the fancy boutique Tomas and I stopped at. A card falls out that confirms my suspicions.

I know you loved this. Hope it fits. Thought it might be something for this evening, if you wanted to wear it, that is. Tomas X.

I throw off my coat and remove my thick, knitted jumper from underneath. I am so excited to try the jacket on that I can't wait. I pray it fits. I put one arm in and then the next. It fits like a glove. This will certainly brighten up the plain black dress I had planned for this evening. It is absolutely stunning. I twirl around in the mirror, watching the sequins as they catch the light and see the old me in my reflection. Can I possibly shine this bright again? I am hesitant about that as my confidence has been shattered so badly over the past few years. But wearing this lifts my spirits and makes me want to say goodbye to my self-inflicted lonely past.

This must be one of the most beautiful items of clothing I have ever owned. It seems all the best things come from Prague, and, just like my snow globe, I will treasure it forever.

Chapter Twenty-Five

I can see the effort that Tomas has made for this evening as soon as the taxi pulls up outside the bar. The chairs we left leaning against the tables are now decorated with pretty gold ribbons. The tables are covered in white tablecloths with centrepieces of gold candles. With the orange glow of the lights from outside, it is enough to draw anyone in.

Of course, tonight, it is closed to the public, which makes me feel like a VIP who has been invited to a private party. Particularly since I am wearing my special jacket. My look is a million miles away from my beloved onesie.

The invitations only went out to Tomas' friends and, when I enter the bar, I spot him talking to some people and wonder how close they are to him.

Tomas turns his head as soon as I walk in, and his eyes light up like they always do when he sees me. His smile tells me that he is pleased I have arrived. He waves and calls me over, which is a great relief as I don't know anyone else here.

He kisses me on both cheeks, and I get the intoxicating smell of his aftershave again.

'Hi, let me introduce you to my friends.'

Both men give me a friendly smile and shake my hand.

'I'm Eric,' says one of them.

'Vlad,' says the other.

They both look around Tomas' age. Perhaps these are friends from his school days.

'It's good to finally meet you. Tomas has told us soooo much about you,' says Vlad.

'Yes, sooooo much,' laughs Eric.

Tomas kicks Eric on the shin playfully.

'What's wrong? Come on, let's be honest here,' laughs Eric.

I wouldn't mind knowing what he told them, but now isn't the time to ask, as the three of them wave over to welcome a group of women who have walked in.

Tomas has hired some staff for the evening, and one of the waiters brings over a glass of prosecco. I swore I wouldn't drink too much as I want to remember everything that Zuzana says about Aunt Grace when I speak to her. I have scanned the room but there is no sign of her so far. I have to find out when she will be here.

'Is Zuzana here? And Albert?' I ask.

'They're coming together. In fact, they should be here by now. They can't be too far away.'

We both look towards the door as it opens with more guests, but it is another couple who walk in and then wave to Tomas.

'I wish Zuzana and I could understand each other better. I'm sure she has stories about Marek and Grace. It would be so good to talk to her if only we could chat properly instead of just smiling, but I know you're a bit busy to help with translating everything this evening.'

'I'm never too busy for you.' Tomas repeats his habit of putting his arm around my shoulders, and I feel joy in being so close to him again.

'Gosh, I forgot to thank you for this incredible jacket,' I say, as Tomas almost gets tangled on a sequin. 'What a wonderful surprise! It really is the most gorgeous thing I've ever seen. I can't believe you bought it for me.'

'Only the best for you. It's to thank you for coming into our lives. We've loved having you. You also worked your magic helping me here.' Tomas strokes the top of my shoulder, and I feel like grabbing hold of him but refrain from doing so. He needs more time to sort his life out.

The bar is almost full to capacity when I see Albert walk in with Zuzana. As soon as I finish the smoked salmon canapé I am nibbling, I plan on saying hello. However, for the next ten minutes, Vlad and Eric chat away telling me stories about the history of Prague and asking what I think of the city they are so proud of. They recount funny stories about their school days and include me in their conversations as though I know the people they talk of. Vlad and Eric are so warm and make sure to look at me as they chat away. Despite not knowing them, they make me feel as though I am one of the gang.

I laugh along with their jokes and tell them how fantastic I think Prague is and how it compares to Wales. They are so entertaining that I could spend the whole evening with them.

However, Vlad spots someone he knows, and so he and Eric both leave us alone for a moment. I'm about to tell Tomas what lovely friends he has when he spots one of his suppliers who has been invited. I decide that it is probably the time to excuse myself and head over to Albert and Zuzana.

They seem pleased to see me and hug me, just as they did at the restaurant.

Albert and I chat as Zuzana smiles. I wonder how I can find out what she felt Aunt Grace and Marek should do together. I think how Aunt Grace obviously respected her.

'Zuzana's so lovely, Albert. I can see why you're such good companions.'

I consider Tomas' friends too.

'Your family have so many lovely friends. You're all so close.'

I am embarrassed when I consider the friends that I have neglected. I feel nothing but shame and regret. They were there for me and offered me a hand when I was at my lowest, but I shunned them all.

Zuzana smiles at me. She is so glamorous, and just like Aunt Grace, her make-up is impeccable. Had they ever met, I know they would have been best friends if they could converse.

Albert speaks in Czech, and then Zuzana replies and nods her head at me.

Albert and Zuzana talk, and Albert translates for her.

'Zuzana is saying she wishes she'd met your aunt if she is as nice as you are.'

'Thank you. That's so sweet. I know, it's such a shame my aunt never came here. She'd have loved it.'

'I hope so,' says Albert.

'You know, I was thinking I want to do something to bring my aunt and Marek together so that their love can last forever.'

'Marek would have liked that,' says Albert.

'Right, well, I'm definitely going to try to think of something.'

Tomas comes over and joins us and tells me that it is time for me to make a wish for the new year.

'It's a tradition in our family,' he explains.

He leads me to a bronze bell in the corner of the bar. I thought it was a bell for telling the punters that it is time to go home when I first saw it, but Tomas assures me that it is a very important piece of equipment that can make dreams and wishes come true for the year ahead. Can a bell in the corner of a bar cause magic to happen? Probably not, but I am willing to join in on the tradition for a bit of fun.

I ring the bell and the crowd cheers.

'Now, you have to close your eyes and make your wish,' says Tomas.

I scrunch my eyes tightly and make my wish.

'Did you make it?'

'Yes.'

'Good, now you can't tell anyone until the wish comes true.'

'Ha, I doubt it will come true, but…'

'Don't doubt the wishing bell. You have to believe in its magic. It always makes wishes come true. Except when it comes to winning a lottery – it doesn't work for material things.'

'We'll have to wait and see, then,' I smile.

Albert and Zuzana ring the bell after me and make their wishes. I realise that Tomas hasn't rung the bell yet.

'How about you? You haven't made your wish.'

Tomas closes his eyes. I look at his perfect features and try not to think how cute he would look in my hotel bed, or how I would like it if we could spend the last of my time here together as lovers.

When he opens his eyes again, he is grinning. 'Let's hope it comes true.'

I would love to know what his wish was. What if it is something to do with Milena? There is no sign of her at the party. I did wonder if she would turn up. I bite the bullet and ask.

'I meant to ask, is Milena coming this evening?'

Tomas looks at his watch. I see that it is a few minutes before midnight.

'No, she's not. She wasn't invited.'

I feel a giant palpitation hit my chest like a wave that almost tips me over. Then I remind myself that even if their relationship is truly done and dusted, and he has stopped the contact between them, it doesn't mean he wants someone who is about to leave the country.

'I have to quickly change the music. Stay right there.'

A Czech song I have never heard before plays, and then we do the countdown.

Ten, nine, eight, seven, six, five, four, three, two, one! Happy New Year!

Balloons come down from a net that has been released above us, and golden confetti sprinkles upon us like magical gold dust. It is as though a spell has been cast, and a warm breeze seems to dance around the room as everyone huddles together to celebrate.

Tomas takes hold of my waist and kisses me on the lips. It is just a New Year's kiss, to begin with, but then it turns into something much more passionate. This man is utterly delicious. What is even more fantastic is that we definitely feel the same way, if that kiss is anything to go by. I pull my hair away from my face and move back. We smile at each other, and I wonder if the wishing bell is working its magic already. Perhaps the timing is finally right between us.

But then, I get this feeling that someone's eyes are boring into me. I lift my head away from Tomas' shoulder and look around.

Milena is staring right at us with a horrified look on her face.

Chapter Twenty-Six

Sometimes, it is easier not to understand a language. Milena is shouting at Tomas and giving me filthy looks. Why on earth did she turn up when she wasn't invited? Was Tomas lying about that? A moment later, and who knows what would have happened between us?

Albert wishes me a Happy New Year and takes me away from the scene.

'Don't let her upset you. She's a wicked woman. If she thinks she has competition, she'll make sure she destroys any chances, just for the fun of it.'

'I'm hardly competition.' Judging by the sleek silver dress that Milena has poured herself into, I don't think she has anything to worry about.

'Yes, you are very much her competition. Look at you. A kind, lovely lady. Someone who doesn't use people to get something from them.'

Looking over at Milena and Tomas, I see that they are having a heated debate. I suppose it isn't surprising after she saw him kissing another woman as the clock struck midnight. I feel like such a floozy and the biggest fool. I trusted Tomas that it was over and that she wasn't going to be here. I even wanted to believe that she had moved on. What was I thinking? I should have pushed him away. I begin to wish I hadn't come this evening and tell Albert that I am going to leave.

'Please don't go because of Milena. She doesn't care about him.'

'But now she's seen me kissing Tomas, and that's terrible. I thought they were over.'

'They are over. It's no relationship. Tomas isn't her boyfriend. It's just her making sure he can't have anyone else. That's what she does. As soon as she sees him happy, she tries to ruin it for him.'

Was he happy now? Once again, I wonder what Tomas has told Albert about me. I have no idea what everyone has been saying, but the fact is, just like Marek and Aunt Grace, we live in two different worlds. Milena, on the other hand, is here, and they have a history together. I begin to make myself believe that if I am not around, they might be able to make a go of it, even if Tomas doesn't realise.

I leave the party without saying goodbye to Tomas. As I close the door behind me, I look back and see him craning his neck to watch me. He looks as though he desperately wants to say goodbye and run after me, but ultimately, his feet stand rooted to the ground as Milena talks to him, or rather shouts in his face. It is best that I head home and cause no more trouble.

Back at the hotel, I burst into tears. For a moment, I thought my wish had come true, and I was living in some kind of beautiful fairy tale. What a foolish woman I am. I should have known that would never happen.

In between sobs, I realise that I still haven't spoken to Zuzana about what she knew of Aunt Grace and Marek's relationship, nor have I shown them the photos. I haven't even said a proper goodbye to them both after I rushed off like that. However, I don't think it is a good idea that I see Tomas again after this evening.

I will work out another way to go around there alone to chat with Zuzana and say my goodbyes. I am not going to message Tomas to ask if he can arrange a visit, so I decide that in the morning I will show up unannounced. I am sure Albert won't mind.

At least by leaving the party early, I don't suffer from a hangover the next morning. But I feel as though someone has well and truly taken the wind out of my sails as I head off to visit Albert and then Zuzana.

As I take a metro that is heading towards Albert's flat, I watch a British tourist talk into their phone, which translates something to a local passenger. Then the person answers them, and the phone speaks something back to them in English. Why didn't I think of this before? I can easily speak to Zuzana and tell her that she was mentioned in the letter without the need for an interpreter.

When I arrive at Albert's apartment block, I decide to make a detour next door first to speak to Zuzana about what I found in the letter. It is my lucky day when I arrive to find the downstairs door open, so I don't have to alert anyone of my presence and get buzzed into the building. I press for the lift with a tinge of sadness as it sinks in that I won't have Tomas close by my side this time.

I knock on Zuzana's door, hoping she is home so we can chat. I have decided to keep the photos as a surprise for her and Albert until later.

Thankfully, Zuzana answers after a few moments and looks at me quizzically when she sees who is behind the door.

I talk into my phone and ask Zuzana via the translation app if I can come in, which it then translates into Czech. Zuzana talks back to the phone, and it tells me to enter.

She leads me inside her flat, which is very different to Albert's. Zuzana has pot plants everywhere that hang from crochet potholders. I can't help but admire her skills in keeping all these houseplants alive. Zuzana leads me to her small kitchen and points to the kettle. I don't know what she is making, but I accept her offer of a drink.

She makes two coffees and gestures to me to sit down. It feels strange being sat facing the wall, knowing that Albert is probably on the other side of it.

'Can I ask you about my aunt, Zuzana?' I say into the phone. She nods her head in agreement.

'She mentioned you in a letter. She said you sounded "very lovely" and that Marek confided in you.'

I pause while the phone translates my words and watch for a reaction. Zuzana smiles, then she looks away from me and drinks some coffee. She talks in Czech for a while, fast and furious.

'Yes, I remember the time. Like everyone will tell you, it was so good to see Marek happy. He'd finally found the one true love. I told him he should run off with your aunt. That he should leave here and go back to the UK. I never told Albert, but sometimes I feel like maybe it was my fault he died. It was me who told him to get enough money together for his visa and to start a new life. Of course, he wanted to do this anyway, but what if I made him rush more? What if it is my fault he became desperate to find the money to go to the UK, and that is why he died?'

Zuzana dabs at her eyes with the corner of her cardigan. I dig in my bag to find her a tissue.

'Like I keep saying, it's nobody's fault he died. It was a pure accident. I guess that day, his time was up. There's nothing anyone could have done or can change what happened. Please don't ever think that.'

'Oh, I don't know... He was in such a hurry to get the money. He bought that engagement ring first. Then he saved everything so he could leave and show up in the UK with it. Why did it have to happen when he was at his happiest? It's unfair.'

She pauses again for the translation app to catch up with her.

I lean back on the sofa, taking it all in.

'I know. It's very unfair. They were obviously madly in love.'

'Yes, sometimes you just know it's right.'

'That's what all the romantic people keep telling me. I'm not such a romantic myself. I used to be, before I got divorced.'

'Well, maybe this is the year you get your romance back,' smiles Zuzana.

'I don't think so somehow. After what my ex-husband put me through and now Tomas...' His name slips out, and I hope somehow the translation app misses it and that Zuzana doesn't realise what I have just said.

'Tomas? Oh, Tomas never does bad things. He's such a good man.'

I think back to his face last night. He might be a good man, but he just kissed me in front of his on-off girlfriend, or whatever she is now, and I don't know what to think.

'You know, he's far too nice for Milena. If you don't mind, can I say something to you?'

My heart skips a beat as Zuzana stares at me intently.

'Sure.'

'You two suit each other so much better. I see the way he looks at you. I know enough about life to see that man is crazy about you.'

'No, our time has passed now. He chose Milena last night, and she chose him.'

'No, that's not true. I don't want to believe that,' says Zuzana. She shrugs her shoulders and looks back out of the window again. 'If a man really loves a woman, he'll do anything. He won't let you go.'

'That's a lovely thought, Zuzana, but I can promise you, after last night, I won't be seeing Tomas ever again.'

Chapter Twenty-Seven

I leave Zuzana in her flat and head to Albert's door. I hear the familiar shuffling of his feet as he gets closer.

'Olivia?' He looks almost as confused as Zuzana was.

'Hi.'

'Is Tomas coming?' he asks.

'No, he's not. I hope you don't mind me popping around on my own.'

'No. You're welcome anytime. It's just a shame that Tomas isn't here to see you also.'

I wish he would stop talking about Tomas.

'I'm here to see you, not Tomas. I thought I'd come and say thank you for everything. I leave early tomorrow, so I don't have much time left.'

'Ah, I see. Were you just talking to Zuzana also?'

'Yup. I was.'

'I thought so. You can hear every word through these walls.'

Oh no!

'Did you hear what we were talking about?'

Albert nods his head up and down. 'I did.'

'Every word?'

'Yes, and she was right about Tomas. He's crazy about you.'

I don't know where to look, so I pretend not to hear him.

'With your divorce, it sounds like it isn't only Tomas who has had relationship problems,' says Albert.

'Sometimes you have no control over love,' I say dismissively. 'Anyway, look, I was thinking. I'd like to pop in this evening with a little something for you to thank you properly. Will you be home?'

'Ah, I don't want you to feel you owe me anything. It's been enough having your company,' says Albert.

'No, you've been so nice to me.'

'Then will you please stay to have dinner with me?' asks Albert.

'No, thank you. I have a lot to do back at the hotel. As I said, I leave early, but I just want to give you a little something later.'

I would love to spend a last evening with Albert, but I don't know that I can face seeing Tomas walk in if he showed up. I would be a bag of nerves every time there is the slightest creak of a door within the building.

'Well, that's very nice of you. I told Tomas how you are very kind.'

'Thanks. Well, I'd better get going anyway. I'll be back around 7 p.m., okay?'

I rush out of the apartment and head back into the centre of Prague and out to the markets. On the way, I pick up a fancy-looking bottle of Czech wine at a nearby supermarket.

Since it is my last day, I search for some other bits for myself at the market. I also should look for something for Dewi.

The aroma of food being cooked on the stalls hits me as usual as I wander around the market. Oh, I could just fill my case with all the fantastic fresh food, but sadly, it would perish. However, a stall selling sweets attracts my attention. The stallholder hands me a sample, and so I suck on a fruity hard-boiled sweet and feel obliged to buy something. I look at the selection they have and see sweets that look surprisingly like Smarties, but I end up opting for two bags of *Haslerky* liquorice. One for me and one for Dewi.

Before I leave the market, I pass the stall where I bought Tomas' Christmas bauble. I can see they have some of the items reduced, and the little robin is one of them. I pick it up and look at it. Can I bear to put him back down? I decide he needs to come home with me. After all, I have decided that I will be putting up a Christmas tree next year. After this year, Christmas is no longer banned, even if it is just me celebrating alone. I could even invite Dewi and his family around for a mince pie.

The stallholder carefully wraps my Christmas robin up, and I pop it in my bag with the liquorice. I look forward to unwrapping both of these when I get home.

I carry on with my mission to find something for Albert. I know exactly what I am looking for and am delighted when I find an artisan stall selling silverware. I pick up a plain, classy-looking silver photo frame, perfect for the photo of Marek and Aunt Grace. I am smiling to myself when I head back to the hotel to pop the photo inside and then pack it up to surprise Albert.

I turn up at Albert's and find Zuzana is sat with him. I am relieved it is only her and that Tomas isn't here. I did think he might attempt to get in touch, but what is there to say? Perhaps he feels it is time to part ways in favour of Milena, after all.

Albert makes me a drink, and I tell Albert and Zuzana about the surprise I have. I pass the wrapped frame to Albert and tell him that I hope he will like it.

Albert and Zuzana smile at each other, unsure of what is inside.

'Oh, my dear. Thank you. Come here.' Albert is filled with emotion as he looks at the photo of Marek and Aunt Grace standing in front of Big Ben. He hugs me, and I feel his tears soak the collar of my shirt.

'I have more photos that you may never have seen. You can keep them. I took photos of them from my new phone so I can get copies made when I go back home.'

How did I manage for so long without a phone?

The three of us pass along the photographs, and Zuzana and Albert say some things in Czech to each other. Zuzana nods her head in approval.

'I'm so happy to see these. This is the best surprise I could ever have. To see Marek in London. I can't believe it.'

Zuzana nods her head again as if agreeing, even though I expect she isn't sure what Albert is saying.

'This is so nice for Tomas to see also. He'll be here very soon,' says Albert.

'Oh, but I have to go,' I say.

'I told him you were coming over. He'll be here soon.'

Oh no. Tonight is to surprise Albert and Zuzana and to thank them for their hospitality. Not for Tomas to turn up and tell me some story about Milena, or worse still, walk in with her.

A knock on the door startles me, and I am so nervous at the thought that it could be Tomas that I bite my lip, cutting it as I do so. Zuzana answers the door on behalf of Albert and, fortunately, appears to direct the person to another apartment in the building. As she closes the door again, I realise that I must get out of here quickly.

'I'm sorry, but I'll really have to leave. Anyway, I hope you can treasure the photos. Thanks again. For everything.'

Zuzana speaks to Albert, and he translates.

'Zuzana says it's been good meeting you and thank you for showing the photos. You'd make a good wife for someone she knows.'

Zuzana grins at me, and I blush.

'It's no problem. It's been so wonderful meeting you. You feel like family.'

'What about the rest of the letters? What do I do with the box?' says Albert.

'It's fine. You've had it all these years, you keep it here. I think we've read all the letters that we needed to.'

'If you ever come back to Prague, please will you visit us?' says Albert.

'I wouldn't dream of coming to Prague and not seeing you. Look, I'll write my address down for you. If you're ever in the UK, you're always welcome to visit me.' I give Albert the paper with my address on and bid them farewell.

'I'm too old for travelling now, but that's very kind,' he says.

'Now, I wish you two the best. Thank you for being such special people. I'll miss you both.'

They take turns to hug me, and I feel quite emotional leaving them behind.

Once outside, I start my walk to the metro station and breathe in the cold air. I turn around and peer up at the building for one last look.

As I look up, a snowflake lands on my cheek. It's snowing again. I hold my hand out to catch the snow as I walk away from here for the very last time.

Chapter Twenty-Eight

I don't know if Tomas asked about me when he turned up at Albert's, as by the time I leave for the airport, there are still no messages from him. I did consider messaging to say goodbye, but after that awkward moment on New Year's Eve, I decided better of it. There is no point. All the feelings I have tried to deny throughout the holiday have come crashing down around me as I stand here at the airport. For a while, I felt special and that someone cared about me. Tomas restored my confidence and even my faith in people, but maybe I was wrong.

As I see the aircraft on the tarmac waiting to take me back to the UK, it sinks in that I won't ever see him again. This is the end. Once again, I feel as though I have lost someone. I have lost my friendship with Tomas because we pushed things too far, and I am saying goodbye to a beautiful city that I have come to love. How could I attach myself to someone and to a place so quickly? It was as though I was part of that family forever, and now it's all taken away from me again. I am sad as I realise that although I said I'd come back, I most probably won't ever see Albert and Zuzana again. It is just one of those things you say that makes saying goodbye easier.

When they announce my flight departure, I join the queue to board the plane. Of course, in the movies, this is the point where Tomas would come running towards the boarding gate shouting my name. If this were a movie, I wouldn't hear him at first, and all the passengers would be willing for me to turn around. Then, eventually, he would catch up with me. I would see him and fall into his arms, and I wouldn't be going on any flight home.

However, this is the life of good old Olivia Edwards, divorced, originally from Llandysul, and nothing has ever happened to me that is remotely like the stuff you see in the movies. Still, I look over my shoulder and double-check that my name isn't being called by a surprise passenger behind me, and I somehow can't hear it because of the baby screaming in front of me.

Foolishly, I look at every face down the passenger line to double-check as they stare at me, wondering why I am looking at them. But there is no Tomas and there is nothing except a long queue of passengers and the squealing baby. Nope, Tomas definitely hasn't surprised me by secretly running after me. The truth is, Tomas hasn't even said goodbye.

By the time I land back in the UK, I have accepted that I won't be seeing him again, and I can hardly blame him when he has the beautiful Milena.

When the taxi arrives back at the mill, it is as though I dreamed my whole trip. It is raining, sludge is pouring out of the drain beside the front door, and there is no sign of my friendly little robin. Perhaps he got bored waiting for me to come back. With no sign of the robin, I find myself bursting into tears as I walk inside the empty mill. I am annoyed at feeling sorry for myself, but now, not even my favourite bird is at home waiting for me. I am alone, and whilst I was happy enough before, I had started to enjoy a taste of having friends again, and, quite frankly, I miss it already. The old stone walls of the mill feel cold and damp, something I never noticed before.

I drop my suitcase by the door as I am not in the mood to unpack right away. I manage to trample upon a red bill from the energy company lying on the top of the mail that arrived while I was away. With the inheritance money, at least I will be able to pay the bills without any worry from now on.

There is gurgling from the tap as I run the water to make tea. Then brown water eventually gushes out, and I realise the pipes have probably clogged up with the frosty weather while I was away. I am used to the dodgy pipework here, but I don't want to deal with it today. I find myself wishing I was back in the luxury of the five-star hotel.

The snow globe is right where I left it on the table, and I go over and give it a shake. As the snow comes down around the castle, it brings back fresh memories of Tomas and me being there. I can't remember enjoying myself as much in a long while, and I doubt I will again. I pick my phone up and check it one last time. Just in case. There is nothing from him. I look at his number saved on my phone and press delete along with every message. I don't need any reminder of Tomas. Like my trip to Prague, it is all in the past.

The mill doesn't seem to want to warm up, and there isn't enough firewood left, so I put my coat back on to get some more firewood from outside. It feels colder than Prague in here.

As I get to the shed where I have stored the logs for moments like this, I have to look twice. The little robin is hopping about outside the door.

'You're still here.' I smile.

My favourite robin is a sign that I must have hope for the future. I was fine before I went to Prague, and I will manage once more. Just like the robin, I have spread my wings, and I can do it again. I will not let my experience with Tomas rob me of my new-found confidence.

I get the robin some food and head back indoors to get the fire going. Finally, it starts roaring and all that is needed are the comforting sweets I have in my suitcase. Calories don't count at times like this.

I go into my suitcase to search for the bags of liquorice. Right on top is the gold jacket, which I certainly no longer need. I may as well give it to the church jumble sale. It is not like I can wear it to feed the birds! I throw it over to one side on the floor, step over it and head back to the sofa to toast my feet in front of the fire. Then I eat my bag of liquorice until my tummy hurts and send myself off to bed before I end up greedily searching for any more snacks. Besides, I have an early start tomorrow as my homecoming coincides with Dewi's return to the office. He needs me to sign the paperwork that will see my inheritance transferred to me.

–

The one good thing about my trip to Prague is that I am no longer afraid of going into town. For the first time in two years, I drive confidently. After travelling to Prague alone, this is a doddle. I realise that I can conquer more than I thought and will no longer doubt my capabilities.

By the time I walk into the solicitors' office, clutching the bag of liquorice, I am quite excited to meet Dewi for the first time. We have spoken so many times before, and although we still haven't met face to face, I immediately recognise him from the newspaper article.

'Well, hello, Ms Edwards. So good to put a face to the name,' says Dewi.

'You too. It's great to meet you, finally.'

I hand him the bag of liquorice, and he looks thrilled.

'Well, how lovely, thank you. So, sit down. Tell me all about Prague then.'

I tell him how wonderful it was and what the letters were mostly about.

'Well, well. That was some love story between the two of them, wasn't it?'

'Yes, it's all very sad, really. If only he hadn't had that accident in the river, then they'd have been together.'

'I know. What a terrible pity.'

'You know, I wanted to do something to honour them. I thought about a padlock on a bridge in Prague with their names on, but that wasn't a good idea.'

'No, that could even be considered criminal damage doing something like that to those lovely historic bridges.'

'Yes, exactly. But anyway, I'll think of something for them. Maybe I'll get a rose bush named after them or something. Can you do that? Or a bench somewhere? That would be nice.'

'Was Marek buried, do you know?'

'No, he was cremated. Albert, his brother, still has his ashes at home with him.'

'Well, that's interesting. Grace was cremated too, wasn't she?'

'Umm, yeah.'

'You know. I have an idea. Why don't you put their ashes together? Take Grace's ashes to Prague. Albert would have to agree to let go of Marek's ashes first, of course. That might be possible. I suppose you'd need to speak to him and his family about it...'

'No, I don't want to go back again. I've left now, and…
well, Tomas, Marek's nephew, well, he…'

'Great, you can ask this Tomas if he can arrange it then.'

'No, I don't have his number.'

'I'm sure you could find it out.'

'No, I don't think that's a good idea. I'll think of something
else.'

'Like what?'

'I don't know.'

'Oh, come on, you have to at least ask. The two of
them could be together for eternity then. Imagine!'

For a solicitor, he certainly has a lot of meddling time
on his hands.

'I don't know. I can't exactly ask Albert or Tomas such
a question.'

'Can't you?'

'No! Now, what was it you wanted me to sign?'

Dewi looks through his file and gives me a form to
sign saying that I have been told about the will and the
estate I will inherit. I sign it whilst he goes through the
paperwork.

'Drat. There's a form missing. You'll have to come back
again. I am so sorry. I've got a new secretary, and she gets
a bit confused with things. That's the problem when you
hire a family member.'

'No problem. Just let me know when it's ready.'

'Okay. But in the meantime, will you please have a
think about asking the family about the ashes? You never
know. I mean, Albert must be in his seventies or eighties.
They can't keep passing them down through generations.'

I remember that there are no generations after Tomas.
Still, it is not my problem. I am not getting in touch with

the family again, and I am not going back to Prague. Besides, I have deleted Tomas' number for a reason.

I get up to leave and ignore his plea. Unfortunately, this is something that I simply can't be a part of.

'Oh, Olivia. Before you go… So sorry. What am I thinking? This file's got into a right mess. There's a letter I must give you. Your aunt instructed me to give this to you once you had completed the trip. She said it was very important.'

I look at the letter with my name on. I flip over the envelope and see that Aunt Grace has marked a kiss where she sealed it.

'Oh no. What's this about?'

'I've no idea.'

I look at Dewi, and I'm sure he must know more than he is letting on.

'I swear, now. She didn't tell me anything. She just told me to make sure you received it after you'd been to Prague and, if you didn't go, you were never to receive it. That's all I know.'

'Right. Okay.'

Back in the car park, I gently place the letter on the passenger seat of the car. It sits there like an unexploded bomb. I dread to think what revelations could be in there.

I take a deep breath, look at it again and decide to get it over with. If I have learned anything these past few weeks, it is to face things head-on.

I tear at the envelope and open up the letter, resting it on the steering wheel of the car.

> *My darling Olivia,*
>   *Well done. You did it. I hoped you would go to Prague, and I am so proud of you for doing it.*

It's been horrible watching my bubbly niece turn into a shell of herself. I hope that travelling alone has given you the confidence to believe in yourself and know that you don't need Craig in your life to do things. I know that can seem hard when you've been married to someone for so long and you have to start over. But he was always a snake, and you were far too good for him. I should have warned you about him, but I didn't want to hurt you. I regretted it every day, and I fear I made things worse by not telling you what I really thought of him. He did not deserve you and your beautiful, kind heart.

So, now that he is gone, it is time for you to start the second chapter of your life, and there's no reason for it not to be the best.

I hope you managed to meet Marek. You will understand by now that he was the love of my life, and if things had been different with my family commitments, then I am sure we would have been so happy. Please don't make the same mistakes I made in life. If you ever find a love like I had during that short time, you must never let it go, because it might never come back again.

Tears run down my face. I wipe my eyes with the sleeve of my jumper. Oh, Aunt Grace. I understand why she didn't tell me about Craig, but her words make me think of Tomas and how beautiful he is. Well, Aunt Grace, sometimes a love like that lets *us* go. Then we have no choice in the matter.

Anyway, I hope that the rest of your life is happy and all your dreams come true because you truly

deserve the best. Don't let anyone ever tell you
otherwise, my darling girl.

Until we meet again,
Aunt Grace x

I take the letter and place it back on the passenger seat,
trying not to look at it again as I drive home an emotional,
snivelling wreck.

Chapter Twenty-Nine

The weather forecast had warned that snow was on its way, so I didn't make any firm plans about signing the rest of the papers for Dewi. Sure enough, by the next morning, there is a blanket of snow settled on the ground and the branches of the trees are weighed down by the snowfall. We haven't had heavy snow around here since the Eighties when my mother and I were completely snowed in and had to walk to the nearest farm to get eggs and milk. Somehow, the sky looks as though it could be a repeat of the infamous blizzard of 1982 when it snowed for thirty-six hours straight.

Just in case my feeling is correct, I make sure the bird feeders are topped up as there is not much chance of the poor birds finding food in this weather.

As I open the back door to feed them, I am happy to be greeted by my favourite robin.

'Ah, there you are,' I tell him. The robin chirps noisily and then rushes off, eventually settling down on his favourite rock, which is now laden with snow.

With the birds catered for, I get some logs from the shed to stack up ready in the porch. I have been in this shed many times since Craig left, but until now, I didn't realise that some of Craig's tools were still in here. It just shows what a daze I must have been walking around in. I brush against cobwebs as I near the tools that are laid together in a pile. I wonder if he wants them back. We haven't spoken for a long time, but I will keep them safe in case he suddenly wants them returned. I have never been a vengeful person who would keep someone's belongings, although the fancy wrench laid next to the tools would certainly come in handy for DIY at the mill.

There are all sorts of things in the shed that I haven't taken any notice of when I have come in here before. Now I see it all with new eyes since returning from Prague. It is funny what you notice when you go away and come back home.

Craig put a lot of this stuff here when we first moved in. The tied-up bin bags probably needed throwing out years ago, along with the pile of old newspapers. I can't resist peeking at them. One has an advert for a sale at Woolworths on the front, and I notice one of the papers is dated around the time we got married. I wonder if our wedding photo appeared in there. Even though it is getting colder in here, and I am eager to get into the warmth, I stop for a moment and search through the newspaper until I find the marriage, birth and death announcements. I gasp when I spot a photo of Craig and I looking out from the page.

Craig must have kept the paper in here for safekeeping, as he was always pottering about in this shed. I never realised he was so caring, and this shocks me. Maybe there was a kinder side to him that Aunt Grace never saw.

But then, as I turn over the page, there is a big red pen mark ringing an advert for a 1983 Ford Capri. Ah, now that is more like Craig. I should never doubt Aunt Grace's judgment, which makes me think of Tomas again and how different he is. This makes me miss him terribly. His face comes to the forefront of my mind, and I see his smile again. I picture us on the horse and carriage, how he laughed when he showed me the upside-down horse tail in the shopping centre and the feelings I had for him during the boat trip in the snow. I recall how he bought me ballet tickets and gave them to me at beautiful Prague Castle, how he was so knowledgeable about everything and how his friends and family were so welcoming. Then I make myself remember his face as I walked away and remind myself that he chose to stay there with Milena. I bring myself back down to earth with a bump and get on with collecting the logs to take indoors.

From the shed window, I can see the snow is coming down heavily now, and it is certainly not going to stop anytime soon. I rush back inside, where the weather forecast on the telly confirms that we are facing a further heavy snowfall. I turn it off, enough of that doom-mongering. Thank goodness I had a food shop delivery ordered for when I got home. The groceries won't last for too long, but they will keep me going for a bit. I am also thankful for the multipack of crisps I threw in impulsively.

By lunchtime, I am starting to feel quite isolated. It is just me, the birds, and thankfully, the log fire, which is burning brightly. I pop the television back on for company. Perhaps I should listen to the latest update about how bad the weather is going to get after all.

Indeed, the news headlines are all about the snowstorm, and they are now talking about closing the airports in the next forty-eight hours.

They expect train travel will be disrupted by tomorrow evening as more snow is on its way. I am so grateful for my lovely, cosy home and the fact that I don't need to go anywhere. I suppose I should be thankful that I arrived home when I did. It is far from the ideal time to travel. Luck was definitely on my side.

I sit and watch the snow falling outside from my living room window. It looks so beautiful from here. I almost wish there was someone I could make a snowman with, or throw snowballs at. Perhaps if Ken manages to get up the road, I'll throw a snowball at him for some fun.

I can feel the draught coming straight through the window from outside, and I am glad that I have already planned on spending some of the inheritance on making the mill a little more energy efficient. It shouldn't be long before I can get new windows fitted, and the draught will be a thing of the past, and this beautiful home can be restored for future generations.

I watch how the birds outside leave their imprints in the snow. I love how their little prints leave a trail behind them. But the snow is getting thicker now and the trails are being covered up almost as soon as they make them.

By the next morning, I am practically snowed in. My onesie, with a thick dressing gown thrown over, keeps me nice and cosy as I get the fire going again. I throw on an extra log to get it burning to the maximum and listen to the sound of it crackling. But then I hear a louder noise that I can't work out as I watch the embers fly through the fireplace. I hear the noise again and listen carefully. It sounds like a screech. I run outside to check where the noise is coming from in case an animal is in trouble in the snow. But it is like a mirage. I can't believe what I am seeing. Ken is driving the post van and trying to make his way up the track. The van is skidding everywhere. What on earth is he doing? My post is not that important. I know he is committed to the Post Office and takes his job seriously, but surely delivering post in this weather and up this lethal track is going above and beyond.

The van nearly lands in the hedge before I see it start sliding backwards. Poor Ken, I will walk and fetch the mail from him; there really is no need for this. I search for my wellies but can't find them. I realise I've left them out the back. The slippers in front of me that I throw on quickly get soaked through as I try to reach the van. I feel the cold of the snow biting at my toes as I trudge along and focus on walking without slipping. I don't want to break anything out here as I am not convinced an ambulance driver would even be willing to come up this far now. Then, as I get closer to the van, I see that Ken is not alone.

I squint my eyes to get a closer look at the passenger. Surely, I am seeing things.

'Tomas?' I say. This is impossible. How on earth could Tomas be in a post van with Ken?

I know people can hallucinate from heatstroke, but I am beginning to think there is such a thing as snowstroke – my eyes must be deceiving me.

The post van door opens, and Tomas climbs out wearing a pair of wellies and carrying a plain black overnight bag. I watch in disbelief as he says thank you to Ken and taps his shoulder, as though he is some long-lost buddy.

'What on earth…?'

'Aren't you going to say hello?' says Tomas.

My heart beats so fast that I begin to feel dizzy. I can feel it pounding through my chest. A grin is spreading all over my face, but I am also shaking at the same time. What a state I am in!

Every muscle in my body feels as though it is trembling. I can't quite believe this is happening. I am afraid to blink in case Tomas is gone when I open my eyes. How on earth did he find me in the middle of nowhere? Ken explains some of it.

'I found your friend at the bottom of the road. He was trying to walk 'cause a taxi refused to bring him up here. I said I'd try to get him as close as I could in my van.'

I am so grateful to Ken for delivering him safely. What a kind thing to do.

'Oh, my goodness, Ken. You're an absolute legend. You risked driving up here in this weather to help a stranger. I really must write to the Post Office about you.'

'Oh, it's nothing.'

'It is. You're amazing, Ken. A true superstar. Thank you.'

I look at Tomas again in disbelief. 'Well, this is more exciting than the usual post Ken brings me.'

I hold my hand up to my mouth and just stare at Tomas. 'I just… Well, I don't know what to say.'

Ken grins at me and gives me a wink, and then he turns the van around as the tyres desperately try to grip the road and he heads off back down the lane, leaving me standing there looking at Tomas with so many questions. Why did he not message me? Why did he not say goodbye before I left? Why is he even here? But, while I do have all these questions, as I stand there with soaking wet feet, freezing in the snow, I can't help but feel a warmth spreading all over me as I look at the beautiful, gentle face that I have been missing since I last saw it.

'I'm sorry, I'd have brought you flowers, but it's all been a bit of a rush. I saw this when I got dropped off by the cab. It's not quite the same thing, I know.'

I smile at the branch of mistletoe that Tomas hands me. He must have got it from the tree I always pick from down the road.

'Wow. Well, now that you've picked this, it would be a shame not to use it.'

For once, I make the first move and lean over to him, holding the mistletoe above us. I kiss him on the lips, and then we hold each other. The snow is seeping into my onesie now, so it's not long before I have to pull myself away.

'Come on, let's get inside,' I say.

'Thanks. It's a bit cold out here.'

Once my feet have dried off, I make Tomas a hot chocolate, searching for a Flake I know I have somewhere so that I can impress him with the extra sprinkling of chocolate. After all, I remember how he is a man after my own heart with his love of chocolate. I sit him down at my large oak kitchen table and look at him in disbelief. The sight of him sitting there seems so surreal.

'How was your journey?'

'You don't want to know.'

'That bad?'

'The captain tried to land three times, the trains were delayed and then finally someone said I could get as far as Cardiff. I waited there for ages. Then I managed to find a train going this way. Got to the train station where there were no taxis, then I had to walk into a shop and ask if they knew of any. It's been a long day.'

'I can imagine. There's only one taxi in the area, and he doesn't work evenings. You're lucky you got here when you did.'

'Yup. I found that out. Then he dropped me on the main road out there as he refused to come up this way in the snow. Luckily, I saw the postman as I walked, and he helped me. He said he knew you. How was that for luck?'

Do I tell him that it isn't necessarily luck but just how it is around here, as everyone knows everyone and their business? If they see a stranger, then chances are they will stop them to find out what they are up to. I am sure even my ex-colleagues in the bank will soon learn that a mysterious stranger from Prague has turned up in the snow to visit me. That will definitely give them something to talk about when they get back to work.

'Well, I'm impressed with your tenacity. That takes some effort. I'm delighted you made it.'

'Thanks. It was a bit of a journey, but I felt terrible about the last time I saw you, so I wanted to apologise.'

'I wasn't really sure what was happening, to be honest. I guess I never expected to see you again.'

He came all this way just to apologise to me and found me standing here in a onesie with my hair sticking up after tossing and turning in bed all night. I hope he isn't disappointed.

'Please don't say that. I can't ever imagine not seeing you again. That would be out of the question,' says Tomas.

'That's nice to hear. Thank you. So... wow, I can't believe you're here.'

'Neither can I,' laughs Tomas.

We stand looking at each other in silence. Then Tomas hugs me tightly. The hug feels full of relief and longing, as though he has just crawled out of a natural disaster and thought he'd never see anyone again.

I have so many things I want to say, so many questions; but now is not the moment for that. After all, with the snowfall getting heavier he won't be able to leave in a hurry. Even the windowsills are filling up with snow, and we can barely see out. It looks as though the blizzard is starting to seriously take hold.

Tomas looks absolutely shattered after a night of travelling, and I can't help feeling sorry for him as he tries to stifle a yawn once we have both got over the excitement of seeing each other again.

'I've so much to tell you, Olivia.'

I put my finger to his lips.

'Shush, we have time. Why don't you go and have a rest first. You look exhausted.'

'As much as I want to stay here with you right now, that sounds like a great idea. What a journey!'

'Of course. I'll make the spare room up for you now.'

'That would be really kind, thank you.'

'It's the least I can do after all the effort you've made. You sit by the fire, and I'll get your room ready for you.'

I run upstairs to search for the spare sheets in the airing cupboard. I am still buzzing with questions and rehearse in my head what I am going to say when we eventually sit down to talk. I mean, why is he here just to apologise? Surely, he could have done that by post. What does it mean that he's come all this way to see me? I have so much hope that I can guess the answers, but I don't dare believe it.

Once the bed is made and I have removed some storage boxes from the room, I make myself a bit more presentable. Then I rush back downstairs nonchalantly and tell him that his room is ready. Due to Tomas' height, he has to bend down to enter the room or risk hitting his head on one of the old oak beams, but he seems to like the character here.

'What a lovely room. I'm going to sleep well.'

'I hope so.'

I leave Tomas to rest and go downstairs, where I smile to myself. The lovely Tomas has come all this way to find me in the snow. Could this finally be my movie moment? I look over at Aunt Grace's snow globe in the living room for reassurance that this is not a dream of some kind. If it is, then I certainly do not want to wake up.

Even though Tomas is resting upstairs, it feels nice to have company here. By the time he gets up, right in time for the snack I have prepared, I am showered and, for once, not dressed in my onesie.

'That bed's so comfortable. I feel so much better,' says Tomas, walking into the living room dressed in jogging bottoms and a tight white T-shirt.

I can hardly take my eyes off him.

'It's the least I can do after your eventful journey. Now, are you ready for something to eat?'

I spoon out the leek and potato soup and serve it with a warm baguette. I do hope that it is as tasty as the food Tomas makes, although that would be hard to beat.

'Thank you. This is exactly what I need,' says Tomas, as he breaks off some bread.

And you are exactly what I need, I think, smiling to myself. I admire him as he tucks into the soup. Gosh, he really is so lovely.

'I have to confess, I didn't realise you lived so far away from the airport.'

'Well, I like being tucked away up here out of the way.'

'I can imagine. It's a beautiful place.'

'I'm glad you like it, and I'm sorry you had such an eventful journey to find me.'

'It's fine. What's life without adventure?' says Tomas.

Even after his trudge through a snowstorm, Tomas amazes me with his positivity.

When he has finished his lunch, and I put the bowls in the dishwasher by the kitchen window, I see something in my peripheral vision. Amid the snow and all the trees, something is running around. I strain my eyes to look closer and see that it is a badger. I call Tomas over quickly.

'Look, there's a badger in the snow!'

He rushes over and catches sight of the badger as it runs in and out of some bushes. We both marvel at the scene.

'You do like snow, don't you? I love the way you act when you see snow,' smiles Tomas.

I grin back at him, full of happiness. Then he pulls me towards him, tucks my hair behind my ears and cups my face in his hands. At the kitchen window, where I have stood alone so many times, we kiss, and I don't ever want it to stop. Sometimes you don't need the excuse of mistletoe.

Chapter Thirty

There is nothing quite like sharing a bottle of Baileys in front of an open fire, especially when Tomas is sitting right beside me, confessing how he feels. I lean deeper into a cushion as he tells me everything.

'So, I know New Year's Eve was a disaster, but I hope we can start over. As I said, I came here to apologise and tell you that I, well, I have such strong feelings for you. I can't ignore them any longer. I know we've only known each other a short space of time, and maybe that's too soon for you to rush into anything, but that's just the way I feel.'

This has certainly happened very fast, but I also realise that I have never felt such chemistry with anyone.

'I've very strong feelings for you too, Tomas. But, before we go on, there's one thing I need to know… What about Milena?'

Tomas lets out a sigh and shakes his head.

'I want to be clear, she's not on the scene.'

'Thank you. I appreciate that. Was everything okay after the party?'

'I had already told Milena that I'd met someone I cared for. You remember when I said I was sorting things out with her? It didn't take much for her to realise it was you. I told her how she and I were so different, and she'd easily find someone who was better suited for her. We've discussed our break-up so many times, but she can't accept it when she doesn't get her own way. So she still turned up when she heard from someone I was having the party in the bar. Then she went mad with me after you left and grabbed my phone and smashed it in a temper. So, I lost your number. I thought I'd see you at Albert's, but I missed you. Then I wanted to call the hotel, or maybe visit you there, to apologise for putting you in such an awkward situation at the party. That wasn't fair on you at all. I picked up the phone to the hotel so many times. But each time, I put it down. I figured you wouldn't want to hear from me as it didn't look too good with her showing up. I was worried you wouldn't believe me. By the time I plucked up the courage to speak to you, the hotel said you'd already checked out. Luckily, Albert had your address.'

'Ah, of course. I wondered how you found me.'

'He insisted I fly over. He told me not to lose you. He didn't want me to miss my chance at love like Marek did. He could see I thought you were someone special and said that I have to come and tell you how I feel. He was right, and now I have.'

'Well, you can't have two people not tell each other how they feel, can you?'

Tomas smiles at me, and I melt as fast as a snowman defrosting in the sunshine.

'So, all thanks to Albert, you tracked me down here.'

Right now, I could throw my arms around Tomas and tell him how much I adore him. But I still feel slightly guarded, so I refrain from telling him quite how much my feelings for him grew in Prague and how I felt it best I disguise them. I simply nod my head understandingly.

'When you left, I knew I had to find you. You're not on social media, by the way?'

'No, it doesn't interest me. I'd much rather live an isolated life. As you can probably see looking around here.'

'It sounds like the best way to live.'

'It is... Most of the time. It can get lonely though.'

'Well, you needn't ever feel lonely now,' says Tomas.

We both take a sip of Baileys simultaneously. I can't believe I have allowed him to see my more vulnerable side, so I quickly backtrack.

'Anyway, it's fine. It's really no big deal. I like my own company. But yeah... I'm not on social media. I didn't even have a mobile phone for the past two years. By the way, don't you have stuff to do for the bar? How come you managed to escape all that work?'

'Some of the paperwork isn't ready for us to open to the public. It was the perfect excuse to come and see you, and I can't tell you how lovely it is.'

Tomas stares at me, and I feel my cheeks burn.

'Don't you think that it pays to be clear about what you want? I think if anyone has taught us that, it is Uncle Marek and Grace,' says Tomas.

'Yeah. I agree.'

'Well, in that case. I want to be clear here.' Tomas takes another sip of the ice-cold Baileys. 'I really don't want to lose you. How about we become more than friends who were thrown together because of our family? I have stronger feelings for you than that. I tried at first to pretend it was just friendship, that I was just taking care of a friend of the family, but I always knew it was more than that. I feel we have a connection I can't explain. We were brought together by an old love story, and I wonder if – I hope – we might have a love story of our own. I needed to come and tell you how I feel. Do you think we might have a chance?'

Oh, my goodness! This is my movie moment, after all!

I need a big glug of Baileys before answering, or I might screech out my response in happiness. Thankfully, the fire crackles and a piece of ash flies out, giving me a moment to compose myself. If I didn't know better, I would think it were a ghost of Christmases past telling me to hurry up with my answer.

'I'd like that very much.'

'Oh, that's a relief. I was so worried about telling you how I truly felt.'

'It's better to be honest with each other, and sometimes you have to take that chance.'

I draw Tomas towards me, and then we kiss again. Not a polite, friendly kiss, not even one like our New Year's Eve kiss, but a real, deep kiss as though we have been lovers forever.

It feels amazing to have that closeness to another person again, and it hits me how much I have been missing all this time. The mixture of Baileys, an open fire and the handsome, kind Tomas feels like bliss. Before too long, we can't keep our hands off each other, and I decide that he may have to move his things out of the spare room and into mine since we are certainly no longer in the friendship zone.

Craig and I never managed to make love in front of an open fire. Maybe that is another reason our marriage didn't last, because I would certainly recommend it.

For the rest of the evening, we lie in each other's arms, eat what is available in the larder and watch a Christmas movie that I have seen at least ten times before. As the snow comes down all around us, we are warm, well fed and happy. I cannot think of anything more perfect.

When we wake up the next morning, tangled together, Tomas leans over and kisses me. We stare at each other from our pillows and smile.

'I'm so glad I followed you over here and found you.'

'That makes two of us.'

'So, what shall we do today?' asks Tomas.

'It depends on the snow. I was supposed to go to the solicitor's to sign some papers, but I'm not sure we'll get out.'

I leave the cosy duvet and the warmth of Tomas' body to take a look out the bedroom window.

'Hmm, definitely looks like a snow day to spend at home. Don't think we're going anywhere.'

'Oh really, that's disappointing,' laughs Tomas.

'Yeah?'

'I can't possibly imagine a better day than being stuck at home with you in the snow.'

We both smile, and then I get back into bed. We spend the morning snuggling under the duvet and only get up to grab a cup of tea to bring back to bed. This must be the most delightful morning ever.

'I don't know that I've ever had a more enjoyable day of doing nothing,' I say.

'This is certainly the best snowstorm I've ever had,' says Tomas.

I kiss along Tomas' chin, which is starting to get a five o'clock shadow. I stop to look at him for a moment.

'I don't know what's going on between us, but how can it be possible to feel this close to someone you haven't known for long?'

'You know, sometimes, people are made for each other. Even when they've lived different lives, like we have.'

'Why did I not meet you years ago?' I say, looking into Tomas' eyes.

'Because some things are worth waiting for, Olivia.'

Tomas throws the duvet over us, and we sink into its depths and the day goes by in a lazy love-making haze.

Chapter Thirty-One

When we get up the following morning, I can see that the time has come to think about returning to the outside world again. The sun is shining, and the snow has started melting. In some ways, I am disappointed. I could hold Tomas captive here for a while longer. I am tempted to keep the curtains closed and have Tomas blissfully unaware of the change in the weather, but I realise I need to visit Dewi to finish off the paperwork, especially now that I have put the order in for new windows for the mill, and they need the deposit. Why did I have to be so practical?

'I think it's starting to thaw. I might be able to introduce you to Dewi by the afternoon if it continues,' I say.

'I'd love to meet him, after all the things you've told me about him. He sounds like a very kind man, getting you that Christmas jumper and everything. Which, by the way, will always be my first impression of you.'

'Oh dear. That's terrible,' I laugh.

'No, it's not. You were so normal and natural. As soon as I saw you, I thought how lovely you were.'

'Lovely?'

'Yes, kind and not pretentious. You have this aura about you, so sweet and approachable. Like someone I could trust. What did you think of me when you first saw me?'

'I guess something similar. You look kind and approachable. I thought you were quite hot, though, actually.'

Tomas laughs. 'Well, I can tell you that I felt the same way about you too. I regret not sorting things out with Milena sooner and being much firmer with her. I should have been, and I'm sorry you were caught in that crossfire. I knew as soon as I saw you that you were someone very special, and I never wanted to lose you. Can I let you into a secret?'

'Of course. We're both being honest here.'

'When we first met, do you remember how I said that you reminded me of someone? It wasn't true. I just made an excuse to stop you and find out who you were. That sounds weird, doesn't it?'

'No. That's quite funny. I wasn't sure what you thought of me.'

'You see, that is why we needed to talk. Guys never pick up on these things. I'd no idea you felt the same,' says Tomas.

'Well, I'm glad we've got to the bottom of how we both feel in the end. That's all that's important.'

–

By afternoon, the snow has cleared enough for us to go into town. Whilst I am fiercely independent and enjoy doing things for myself, I must say that it is incredibly handy having Tomas here to help get the car out. He scrapes the snow off the windscreen like a pro, and with his help, we manage to get the car down the track and out onto the main roads without any issues.

There isn't anywhere near as much snow on the bigger roads. It makes me realise just how isolated the mill is when I see that the town looks as though there never was any blizzard, and the only tell-tale evidence are the patches of dirty slush that have washed up on the side of the pavements. But I am not complaining. Thanks to the blizzard, Tomas and I have had an incredible weekend and learned so much about each other.

Tomas takes my hand as we walk to Dewi's office, and I snuggle into his shoulder. Why does it feel as though we have been together forever?

'Well, hello,' says Dewi when he sees us. He looks Tomas up and down, and you can see that he wants an introduction.

'This is Tomas. Marek's nephew.'

'Ooh, right. Well, it looks like Santa has been good to you after all. Very, very good, I'd say,' he says, giggling. This man really does have too much time on his hands.

'Don't embarrass me, please.' I laugh.

'All right. Better get down to business then, is it?'

'Yes, please,' I say.

Dewi gives me the last form to sign and tells me that we have completed everything. The first of the money will be in my account before long. I thank him for organising everything, and for all his time and help. If solicitors could be nominated for some sort of friendly, caring award, he would certainly be top of the list. I am not surprised that I read somewhere that he is up for an OBE because of all his community work.

I thank him once again as we get up to leave.

'Did you read the letter I gave you last time, by the way?' asks Dewi.

'Yeah.'

'I know it's not my business, but, umm, I can't help myself... What was it all about? Sorry, I shouldn't ask, should I?'

I know how Dewi gets over-invested in everything, and although it was a private letter, he has done a lot for all of us, so I decide to tell him her last words.

'She said if I ever found a love like she had with Marek, I must never let it go, because it might never come back again.'

'Oh, now then. Your aunt was always wise.'

Dewi looks at me and then at Tomas and then gives me a not-so-discreet wink. I shake my head at him in frustration. 'What are you like?' I laugh. Between Dewi and Ken winking at me all the time, I'm beginning to wonder if a bout of conjunctivitis is in the air!

'Oh, and now Tomas is here too, do you mind if I ask you if you spoke to him about you-know-what?' says Dewi.

'About what?'

'You know, the, ahem, ashes.'

I feel awkward asking Tomas about it, but I suppose now might be the right time.

'Do you want to ask?' I say.

'Ask me what?' says Tomas.

'Well, I said to Olivia that I thought it might be an idea for Grace and Marek to finally be together. I know it's not my family, and I have no right to even say this, but knowing Grace like I did, and after everything she asked us to do to find Marek, I believe she'd want to be with him. I wondered if their ashes should be scattered somewhere together. It was only an idea, you understand.'

I look at Tomas, wondering what he will say. It is such a difficult question to ask.

'I think that would be a fantastic idea, and I'm sure Uncle Albert would agree. I'll ask him.'

Dewi looks pleased with himself, and he and I breathe a sigh of relief. I am excited about the thought of getting them back together, and we all agree that, with Albert's permission, when the time is right, I will take Aunt Grace's ashes to Prague to be with Marek. Dewi has even offered to write an official letter, at no cost, to ensure that I don't get into any difficulty at customs. For which I am very grateful.

As we leave the office, I feel incredibly happy that Grace and Marek will finally be reunited. Not even in my wildest dreams could I have predicted how a clause in a will could bring so much love together.

Chapter Thirty-Two

It has been over two years since I have woken up beside someone, and as each day passes, it is becoming more familiar. I might not be able to stretch my legs out to the other side of the bed when I wake up any longer, or even go back to bed with a piece of toast and not worry about the crumbs, but I wouldn't swap anything for the feeling of waking up with Tomas beside me.

Once we have had our morning coffees and porridge to warm us up, I decide to show Tomas some of my favourite parts of the countryside that I love so much, which is so opposite to the hustle and bustle of Prague. Thanks to the blizzard and the essential visit to Dewi, I haven't been able to show Tomas the beguiling area I live in yet. So, the first thing I want to do today is to take him on my favourite river walk.

I could walk along the river for miles when I am alone, but with Tomas holding my hand, I could lose track of time. As we head down towards the direction of the stream, the ground is crisp with ice and scrunches beneath our feet. Snow still lies scattered in parts where the sun hasn't quite reached, and delicate snowdrops somehow manage to break through. It won't be long before this patch will metamorphose into a bluebell wood, the magical blue flowers bringing with them the hopeful signs of warmer weather.

'Snowdrops are my favourite,' I say.

'They're beautiful. Just like you,' says Tomas.

I blush, and Tomas strokes my cheek, making me blush even further.

I shrug my shoulders. 'I don't know. I'm just ordinary me.'

'You're not ordinary. You're beautiful from the inside, and it shines through. When you smile and laugh, you light up a room.'

'I wouldn't go that far, but thank you.'

'You really don't see yourself like I see you, do you?'

'Can we change the subject? I'm getting embarrassed now.' I smile at Tomas as he looks at me. 'But, may I say, you're pretty fantastic too. I mean, look at you!' I pinch at the side of his waist, even though it is mostly padding from his jacket that I get hold of. 'Not at all bad for a fifty-one-year-old,' I tease. I finally found out his age when we were talking over the Baileys.

'Well, age isn't an obstacle to keeping in shape.'

'No, not at all. I suppose I'm lucky I have all these long walks to go on, which keep me fit. Although, I do have a weakness for a hearty meal after them. Which makes me think of food. Are you hungry again?'

'I wouldn't say no to lunch. That porridge has gone down quickly. Must be the cold air.'

'Perfect, I know just the place.'

We walk another half an hour through the woods and across streams where branches crunch and snap as we balance on top of them. Tomas politely holds back the bough of a large tree for me to pass through a narrow opening in the woods. As I squeeze by, I finally get a view of the nearby road.

'There's a pub not far now. Almost there.'

The pub I want Tomas to visit serves amazing steak pies with masses of puff pastry, and they do a gorgeous fresh local salmon, so I am confident that Tomas will find something he likes on the menu.

I haven't seen the landlord, Emrys, for a long time. I would have last been in here with Craig a few years ago, but he still recognises me when he sees me.

'Well, well, Olivia! Haven't seen you around here for some time.'

The heat of the pub hits me in the face, and I feel myself flush as I try to answer Emrys. I find it awkward that I am walking in with a man who is not my well-known husband.

'No, I've been... Busy.' I don't want to get into a conversation about Craig, although I would imagine he has been here with Josephine by now, so hopefully, Emrys knows what has happened and that I am not walking in with someone I am having an affair with. Thankfully, he seems more interested in what we want to drink, and I realise that maybe people aren't all gossiping about me. They actually have better things to do. All this time, I thought there was only room for one of us in the community, and that was Craig. I am starting to believe that there is room for both of us.

'What can I get you, then?'

We order two local ciders, and I notice that my favourite table by the fire is free.

'Let's sit here. Is there anything better than a country pub with a log fire?' I say.

'Not much. Snuggling up with you comes close though,' grins Tomas.

'Cheers to that,' I smile.

After a sip of the apple cider, Tomas inspects the horse brass medallions with dragons and fleur-de-lys that decorate the fireplace.

'They look old,' he says.

'Aye, from the seventeenth century, some of these are,' says Emrys, as he puts down a menu on our table.

'You see, we have history here, just like Prague,' I say.

'And good food too, by the looks of this menu,' says Tomas, as he scans through it.

'Exactly. The same as Prague.'

We both decide to order the pie and when the huge meal arrives, Tomas looks pleased with his choice.

'This looks amazing.'

'Just wait until you taste it.'

Emrys has always had a knack for making the most flavoursome gravy in his pies. In fact, he is famous for them.

Over lunch, we talk about Prague and the fact that Tomas has to get back to his fledgling business. I have got used to his company and will miss him. We agree that we'll keep in touch, though, and make the most of this long-distance relationship as much as we can. Still, I make the most of having someone to enjoy a pub lunch with, and by the time we have finished chatting, it is almost time for the kitchen to close for the lunchtime orders.

'Now, you two love birds, will you be having a dessert?'

'Oh, I couldn't possibly,' I say.

'Are you sure? Special today is sticky toffee pudding or jam roly poly and custard.'

'Jam roly poly? What's that?' asks Tomas. I suppose it does sound strange if you are not familiar with it, and he was probably too busy in the pubs of Cardiff to be thinking of traditional British dishes when he was at uni.

'Oh, I guess he's going to have to try the roly poly after all. Two spoons, though, please,' I tell Emrys.

'You haven't lived until you've eaten jam roly poly,' I tease Tomas.

Even though I am fit to burst, I can't stop myself from devouring the sticky strawberry jam that is lavishly spread out between the layers of roly poly. Tomas enjoys it so much that when Emrys comes to collect our empty bowls, he asks him for the recipe.

Whatever I do with Tomas is always enjoyable, but a long and lazy pub lunch is another of the perfect ways to spend the day with him. By the time we eventually leave, the sun is going down over the trees.

'We'd better walk fast, we don't want to get stuck out in the woods in the dark,' I warn Tomas.

'Maybe if we get lost in the woods, I'll miss my flight tomorrow and have to stay a while,' he says.

'As much as I'd love that, you'd probably have hypothermia by the time we were found out here,' I say.

The temperature is dropping fast, and we need to keep walking to maintain our body heat.

'I know. I do wish I didn't have to leave though.'

'Yeah, me too. But you have a new business to launch, and it's an exciting time for you.'

'I don't know if it will be so exciting without you there.'

'Well, I'll come over as soon as I can. I promise.'

'I hope so.'

Tomas puts his arm around my waist and holds me tight as we walk back to the mill. As I think about how close we have become, I realise that I don't care where we are; being together is what matters. It amazes me that I have been guarded for so long, yet now I have fallen for someone so fast.

'When you leave, you'd better write to me. Just like Aunt Grace and Marek did,' I tell Tomas.

He smiles. 'I promise. I will phone you, write to you and video call you.'

'What if it ends the same way as Aunt Grace and Marek?'

'It won't. We must have faith and believe that.'

Tomas takes me in his arms and looks me straight in the eye. 'I promise, I'll never ever let you down.'

'Good. Then I trust you.'

Tomas kisses me, and I pray that our relationship will last the test of time.

For Tomas' last evening, we cuddle up on the sofa listening to Christmas music with an Irish coffee. It might be the beginning of January, but I am not letting Christmas go just yet. I want to make the most of it now I have rediscovered my festive spirit. After all, I have two years' worth to catch up on.

As I lean my head into Tomas' shoulder, he turns to look at me.

'I need to ask you something.'

'You look serious.'

'It's not that serious. Just something I wanted to know about you.'

'Sure, go ahead.'

I fumble with my earring, as I always do when I'm apprehensive and unsure of what is about to come.

'Did your wish come true?'

'What wish?'

'The one you made on the bell on New Year's Eve.'

'Oh, that wish.'

'Yes, because mine did,' says Tomas.

'Oh, really? What was it?'

'To be with you,' says Tomas.

'You wished for that?'

'Yes, I did. So, are you going to tell me what you wished for?'

'Well, I suppose there's no harm since it didn't come true.'

'Your wish didn't come true?'

'Nope. I wished that Milena would be in your past and definitely not show up at the party.'

'Oh, and she did.'

'Exactly.'

'But, we got there in the end, though, right?'

'We did,' I smile.

'Can I tell you a secret?' says Tomas.

'Oh, I love secrets. Go on then.'

'It's that I have one last wish. Not all my wishes have come true yet.'

'What is it?'

'That you'll come and stay with me in Prague. Otherwise, I may have to leave the business and follow you to Wales.'

'You'd do that for me? Give up your dream for someone you've just met?'

'As your aunt said, sometimes you don't need to spend a long time with someone to know they are the one. I know that you're the one for me, and I won't let the distance get in our way.'

I move over to kiss Tomas. I don't think I have ever met anyone in my life who would give up their dreams to be with me. It is the evidence I need to see that Tomas is nothing like Craig. I can trust him.

'Oh, but we can't have you give up your dream for me, now, can we?' I say.

'No?'

'Nope. You know, the mill would make the perfect holiday home. Admittedly, it's a bit isolated, but I'm sure people would love to stay in this lovely setting to escape the rat race. I can't promise, but I'll make some enquiries about letting it out for holiday rentals. That way, I could maybe spend more time in Prague with you, and we can make sure we're doing the right thing.'

'You'd do that for me?'

I realise that I would definitely do that for Tomas.

'Yes, I would. I think that's fair enough. We both get to keep our dreams but can also be together.'

'Now that sounds like the best compromise I've ever heard,' grins Tomas, and then we make love as I try to commit every precious moment to memory, knowing he is leaving tomorrow.

Chapter Thirty-Three

When I wake up the next morning, there is no sign of Tomas in bed. I feel a rush of panic. What if he has gone to the airport without saying goodbye? Did he mean all the things he said last night, or was it really too good to be true? I tell myself that Tomas is a man of his word, and I must have faith in him. If he said all those things then he must have meant them.

I turn over and face the bedroom door, which has been left open. He must be around here somewhere. I listen carefully to see if he is banging around in the kitchen, but I don't hear anything. Then, suddenly, I hear the latch on the front door. Is he sneaking out or in? I can't be sure. I sit upright to listen, and then I hear the water running in the kitchen.

'Tomas,' I shout.

'Yeah, I'll be up in a minute.'

I feel relief that he hasn't run out of here, and I tell myself that I am right to trust him.

When he finally appears around the bedroom door, he's holding a mug of tea he has made for me.

'Thought you'd fancy tea in bed.'

'That's very kind of you. What a nice way to wake up.'

As he hands me the tea, I notice his hands are red and feel cold.

'You're icy cold. What have you been doing?'

'Oh, nothing. It's cold downstairs. I got the fire going ready for you before you get up.'

Leaning over to kiss him, I tell him how thoughtful he is.

'I'm so lucky to have met you.'

'I'm so lucky to have met you,' says Tomas.

'No, I'm lucky.'

'No, I'm luckier to have my beautiful Olivia,' laughs Tomas.

'Ha, well, let's not have our first argument about who is the luckiest here. We're both lucky. It must have been the lucky dog we stroked. Oh, I love you, Tomas.'

I didn't mean to say the 'L' word, but it felt like the most natural thing in the world. I never believed that I could fall in love with someone so fast, but sometimes, it feels just right.

'And I love you too, Olivia. You walking into Uncle Albert's apartment block that day was the best thing that ever happened to me.'

'Me too.'

'It's amazing, isn't it?' says Tomas, sitting on the edge of the bed. 'I wish we could show our gratitude to Uncle Marek and your aunt for bringing us together.'

'Well, I guess we are thanking them by taking Aunt Grace's ashes to be with Marek. We'll be doing something special by reuniting them. That's the biggest way we could ever thank them.'

'Yes, that's very true. So, can I get back into bed now? It's cold out here,' smiles Tomas.

I throw the duvet aside. 'Get in here and let me warm you up. Although I don't understand how you feel quite so cold.'

'You'll see. Now come here and warm me up,' laughs Tomas.

As we giggle under the duvet, I don't think I have ever felt such happiness in my life. Aunt Grace may have been right about the second chapter of someone's life being the best. By the looks of it, I think mine certainly will be.

Tomas holds me so tightly it feels as though he will never let me go. However, when we are disturbed by the doorbell, I feel compelled to get up.

'Ignore it,' says Tomas.

'It'll be Ken. Nobody else comes up this way. I feel bad leaving it.'

'In that case, we'd better get up. I want to see him anyhow to thank him again for helping me get here.'

I hand Tomas an old white dressing gown and quickly jump into a onesie. The dressing gown looks far too small for him, and his long legs look funny as we run downstairs, chasing each other to open the door first.

When Ken sees us both open the door together, his face is a picture.

'Oh, now that's a happy sight if ever I saw one.'

'Aww, thank you. We are happy, aren't we, Tomas?'

'I've never been so happy. And I have to thank you again, Ken. You were very kind helping me in the snow like that.'

'It's what anyone would have done. You've got to help a man in need.'

'Well, thank you from me too, Ken,' I say.

'It's nothing. But, hey, I'm not here to be thanked. There's a recorded letter you have to sign for.'

'Oh, what is it now?' I look at the envelope and it looks like a legal letter from Dewi's office. I hope nothing untoward has happened. I have already signed all the papers he needs. Concerned, I open the envelope on the doorstep as Tomas and Ken talk about the weather.

'Still got some snow in the garden up here then,' says Ken to Tomas.

'Yeah, I made the most of it before it melted,' says Tomas. I look up at him and catch him grinning at Ken. What is he on about?

The letter distracts me from their conversation. It says that everything has been completed. All the money from my aunt's estate has been transferred to my bank account. I look at the final numbers once again. Aunt Grace was always so generous with her time, love and now her money. I will carry her in my heart forever.

'By the way, I've decided that I'll be moving to Prague for a while, Ken.'

'Will you? How wonderful!'

'Yes, but only on the condition that you can help make sure the birds are okay around here.'

'You know I will. The robin's looking well over there, isn't he? We've done a good job taking care of him this winter.'

I had noticed that the little robin hadn't visited while Tomas was staying, and I was hoping I could point it out to him. Today, though, it seems he is back with us again.

'Where is he?'

'Over by there,' says Ken.

'Where?'

Ken points around to where my favourite rose bush stands, and I have to step away from the doorstep to have a look.

As I turn in its direction, I see the robin on a branch. But it is not any old branch. It is a branch that has been used as the arm of a snowman that touches across to a snowwoman.

'Where did those two come from?' I ask, bemused.

Tomas and Ken smile at each other. 'I came out and built it this morning as a surprise,' he says.

Ken must have noticed them as he arrived, which is why he was smiling at Tomas.

'Oh my gosh, that's just so cute. No wonder you were cold. So that's what you were up to early this morning. Good job we still have some snow up here.'

'It's supposed to resemble us. You see. Their branches are together. They're holding hands.'

'That's just too cute. Come here.'

I give Tomas a kiss and intertwine my fingers with his.

I watch how the robin is happily perched on the branch and then lets out a big chirp. If I didn't know better, I'd swear he was smiling!

Chapter Thirty-Four

Prague, eleven months later

Christmas Eve

I look across to the dressing table where I left Aunt Grace's ashes until the time came to reunite her with Marek.

Wearing the red dress that I bought for today, I take the ashes in my hands. Red was always Aunt Grace's favourite colour, and it was quite the search to find something that suited me for this occasion.

'You look lovely,' says Tomas.

'Thank you. I can't believe the time has finally come,' I say, fighting to overcome my emotions.

'Are you okay?' asks Tomas.

'Yeah, I'm fine.'

'You must remember that today's a happy day. We're reuniting them.'

'Yeah. I know.'

I place the ashes on my lap as Tomas drives towards a place that I haven't visited before. Just like everywhere else I have seen in Prague, it is in another beautiful setting. It even has three parks surrounding it, and the gardens are impressively well-maintained. As soon as I see its location set high above the city, I realise that Tomas was right to choose this place. It is the perfect spot to spread the ashes.

We meet Albert and Zuzana at the car park so that we can find the final resting place together. My eyes well up when I see them both walking towards us. Albert carries Marek's ashes, and I head towards them carrying Aunt Grace's. Finally, they meet again. We all pause for a moment of silence.

We begin to walk around the gardens until we find the right place. However, above us, some clouds are threatening to erupt. *Oh no, this is not what we had planned for today.* The sun had been shining earlier. It looks now as though it can't decide whether to rain or snow, and a plop of slushy rain lands on my coat. Tomas notices my concern as I try to protect Aunt Grace from the elements.

'It's just a shower. Don't worry. Let's go under that tree until it stops.'

The four of us take shelter under a huge old tree on which someone has carved a heart. All it needs are the initials G & M to be complete. But, of course, I would never graffiti a tree!

As we wait for the rain to stop, the four of us talk about how happy Aunt Grace and Marek would be if only they could have known that one day they would be together again. Then, just as quickly as the shower started, it stops, and the sun pops out from behind a cloud. It looks like the right moment to spread their ashes has arrived.

We walk a little further and discover the most beautiful resting place in a patch of greenery overlooking the city and the Vltava River.

'This is it,' I say.

'Definitely,' says Albert.

Zuzana smiles and nods as she holds on tightly to Albert's arm.

'Perfect,' says Tomas.

'You ready?' I say to Albert.

'Yes.'

We unscrew the lids of our respective urns and scatter the contents together. The ashes fly about and dance together before merging into one another and forming a single cloud.

We all hug each other. Albert pats me on the back. 'We did it! We reunited them, and it's all thanks to you.'

I look up to the sky and see that a bright rainbow has appeared above us. It frames the four of us, the ashes, and the view of the Vltava River.

Aunt Grace always told me that after a storm comes a rainbow, and it is as if she is reminding me that after hard times, there is always hope. I look at Tomas, his eyes shining with emotion, his hair swept by the wind, and realise that I am grateful for those dark days after Craig left me, as I can truly appreciate the happier moments and will never take anything for granted.

'So, we'll see you both later for dinner, hey?' says Tomas, reminding Albert and Zuzana about the Christmas Eve meal we have planned for tonight back at our home.

'Looking forward to it,' says Albert.

'Sorry we have to rush off, but there's somewhere I must take Olivia now,' says Tomas.

'We understand,' smiles Albert.

Tomas won't tell me where he is taking me, but he told me yesterday that he had a surprise planned for today after we had reunited Aunt Grace and Marek. So, as Tomas drives us away from the park, I sit quietly, trying to work out where we are going until I realise we are heading towards Prague Castle.

It is almost a year since I first came to this enchanted castle that stands out amongst the views of Prague. The soggy sleet has turned into snow by the time we arrive, and it is falling fast. It is getting slippery underfoot, and I try to steady myself as I walk along the white ground beneath me, heading towards the castle. I am glad of the strength of Tomas' arm, which I grip onto tightly to make sure I don't fall head first.

We walk towards the castle that I saw last year when I was a tourist. Now, I am more of a resident, and I look around, remembering the stories Tomas told me about Franz Kafka and the bookshop here, the Gunpower Bridge and the tales from within these castle walls that have been told over centuries.

I take my time looking at the building, but Tomas seems to be in a rush to get around the sights of the castle today. Perhaps he wants to catch the changing of the guards, like the last time we were here. Although, I am also aware that we have a busy day and a lot to do before tonight.

He seems a little stressed, even though I have promised to help with the cooking for Albert and Zuzana. Fortunately, Tomas managed to find someone to hold the reins at the bar tonight. The culinary tours he now runs around the city have also been cancelled for the day. I am so glad he liked my idea, and they have become the success I knew they would.

'Let's head to the gardens. We don't have much time,' says Tomas as I stop to explore a colourful building on the Golden Lane. I am not sure why he wanted to come here today if he is going to be so worried about getting back home.

We rush along to the next part of the castle and make our way to the Royal Gardens, which is slowly becoming a blanket of brilliant white snow.

'Gosh, this is so beautiful, Tomas.'

I look around to see that we are the only two people about. Perhaps the inclement weather has kept people away.

'I thought it would be perfect here. Come closer,' says Tomas.

He takes one hand and then the other and pulls me close.

'Olivia, I have something to ask you.'

Suddenly, I feel nervous. I hope it isn't that he wants us to leave Prague. Surely not, as we love running the businesses. I also enjoy living here near Albert and Zuzana. I love that Zuzana's English classes with me mean that we can now communicate more. Although I am also trying my best to learn Czech, and fortunately, Tomas is a wonderful teacher.

The mill is so popular as a holiday rental that the regular visitors would be disappointed if I took it off the market if we were to ever think about going back to Wales. Everyone loves it, and it even has four and a half stars on Trip Advisor. Of course, there is always the meanie who has to complain about something, and someone knocked off three stars because they were woken up by the sound of foxes procreating in the bushes outside the back bedroom. Like it was my fault!

Looking at Tomas' serious face, I begin to worry. I enjoy my life here, and it has all worked out so perfectly. I have everything I never knew I wanted and so much to lose if Tomas doesn't feel the same way.

'Is everything okay?' I ask.

Tomas reaches into his coat pocket and fumbles about. Is my nose running in the cold and he wants to give me a handkerchief? How utterly mortifying!

Thankfully, it isn't a handkerchief but a little purple box. I immediately recognise that special box.

'Olivia, it's been a year since we first met, and I've never been happier. I want to make sure we never lose each other. I'm a bit nervous, to be honest. But...'

Tomas opens up the purple box, leaving what is inside in full view.

'Would you do me the honour of being my wife?'

Snow falls down right in the centre of the ring, and the diamond shines under the glistening snowflake. Tomas removes the solitaire from the box, wipes it over and holds it in his hand.

'What do you think?'

With the snow gently falling, the castle turrets watching over us, and Tomas looking at me in anticipation, there could only be one answer.

'Oh, Tomas! Yes, yes, yes!'

I almost rip my mitten from my hand, and Tomas puts the ring on my finger. It is the perfect fit. Tomas must have remembered that the ring was too small for me and had it re-sized. I hold out my hand and stare at my ring finger. Marek had such good taste. It is the most perfect engagement ring I have ever seen.

I stand for a moment, trying to take it all in. A castle, a handsome man in the snow and the engagement ring of my dreams almost make me want to pinch myself. Tomas has given me my fairy-tale movie moment once again.

'You'd better put your mittens back on. It's cold,' says Tomas, as I stand staring at my hand.

Tomas brings me back down to earth, and as I feel the cold at my fingers, I am grateful that my fairy-tale prince is not only gorgeous but caring and practical too.

'Is that why you were rushing me along?' I ask.

'Yes, you wouldn't believe how nervous I was.'

'Oh, silly, there's nothing ever to be nervous about with me.'

'What if you'd said no?'

'Well, there wasn't much chance of that. You and I are perfect together. Just like Aunt Grace and Marek. They'd be so proud if they saw us now, wouldn't they?'

As we turn to walk towards where Tomas has parked, a little robin suddenly appears. I am not sure if it is the chilly temperature or something more, but I shiver and get goosebumps all over me.

'Are you cold?' asks Tomas.

'Yeah, I guess so.'

'Come on, let's get home and get everything ready for tonight.'

I turn back to look at the robin one last time, but just as quickly as it appeared, there is no sign of it.

A Letter from Helga

The biggest of thank yous for choosing to read *A Christmas in Prague*. This book is dedicated to my wonderful loyal readers. I get so many lovely messages from readers who have enjoyed my books, which is why I wanted to give a little something back by dedicating my first Christmas book to those readers who are so supportive and just lovely! It is also partly dedicated to Tracey, my Gulf Air friend who starts celebrating Christmas before anyone I have ever known. Her husband, who is like some kind of magical elf, is given the task of helping decorate their lovely home every year. He has the patience of a saintly elf, and they spread Christmas cheer to all who know them.

I do hope you enjoy *A Christmas in Prague*, a story of a love that lasts over generations. It is a story of how sometimes you have to hold on to someone and make sure you don't let them go, because you may not have a second chance.

I am always very responsive on social media, so please feel free to contact me if you enjoy the story. You can contact me via:

www.twitter.com/HelgaJensenF
www.facebook.com/helgajensenfordeauthor
www.instagram.com/helgajensenauthor

Acknowledgements

As ever, I must start with the biggest of thank yous to Keshini Naidoo at Hera Books, who gave me my first book contract a few years ago. I will always be grateful to her for changing my life with that email I had always dreamt of. She is also one of the loveliest people to work with. On the subject of lovely people, where would I be without the gorgeous, amazing and truly wonderful editor, Jennie Ayres? She stays calm in a crisis and is the voice of reason. Her ideas fall in line with mine and I trust her suggestions implicitly.

Another thank you must go to Lindsey Harrad for the copy edit and Lynne Walker for the proofread. As always, Diane of D Meacham Design, thank you for this stunning cover. I think everyone will agree that this one is just magical!

It takes a team to get a book published and out into the world. So, I want to thank everyone involved in getting *A Christmas in Prague* out into the stores. Thanhmai Bui-Van, thank you for getting my books into so many wonderful bookshops. On that note, a big cheer for all the book shops that stock my books and for all the support. Two other names that deserve a mention are Victoria Books in Haverfordwest and Griffin Books in Penarth. Your support means the world to me.

Thank you to JK for putting up with me being locked in the study for hours on end, and Mr B for his cheerful tail wagging to keep the stress levels down!

To my wonderful friends, special people, and writing buddies, thank you. To writing best buddy Jenny, you're the best.

Of course, the most enormous thank you to every one of my readers. I am delighted that you pick up my books and can't thank you enough for choosing to read them.

Happy reading X